T0149212

8 Crazy Moments in Time

8 Crazy Moments in Time

Douglas J. McGregor

iUniverse®

8 CRAZY MOMENTS IN TIME

iUniverse books may be ordered through booksellers or by contacting:

iUniverse
1663 Liberty Drive
Bloomington, IN 47403
www.iuniverse.com
1-800-Authors (1-800-288-4677)

ISBN: 978-1-4917-9478-4 (sc)
ISBN: 978-1-4917-9479-1 (e)

Library of Congress Control Number: 2016906264

Print information available on the last page.

iUniverse rev. date: 04/18/2016

FOREWORD

The book you are holding is unique, unique because it not only entertains us by juxtaposing the moral world to that of the divine, but also because each short story allows us to remember important events and people in our history.

It is also special because it is written by my good friend Douglas McGregor whom I met in 1995. I knew my friend was an accomplished illustrator, (I love his cartoons) but when I read his first novel, I thought, 'Wow, he is so talented. How cool.'

Since that time he has written six novels. My favorites are the Jake McCluskie stories, three in all with a prequel entitled: **Limbo, Mississippi, A Ghost Story.** It's a poignant story of an orphaned boy searching for the soul of his father, and finding a whole lot more. I know Doug thought the novel deserved more attention, and I agree, because as a mother, I ached inside for his protagonist, the orphaned boy Curtis McGrath, wandering through the Mississippi woods looking for the soul of his father.

As much as I was captivated by that story, his novel, **Broken Time,** blew me away. Honestly, I never believed my friend could weave such a compelling tale.

Now I had Jacob McCluskie, now I had a character I cared about, a character I could sink my teeth into, a character like you and me, normal, ordinary, yet a character walking in a world with deities, a character associated with the Archangel

Lucifer (the Devil). How odd: McCluskie, a Catholic partnered with the Devil?

It is a beautiful mix of characters, yin and yang, good and evil, with the Angel of Death hanging around on stage just to make things interesting.

But there was more to come.

Doug's next Jacob McCluskie novel was entitled: **That Special Knack.** Every character you could image came out in that novel, and I must admit, I never expected any of this. My blood ran cold when McCluskie went into Oblivion (Hell) to rescue his friend, a trip that nearly killed him. Reading those pages before bed made for a restless sleep.

And then came Doug's next McCluskie tale: **Killing Time Till I Die.**

He may not admit it, but Doug wrote **Killing Time Till I Die** with a bitter edge, soured by the collapse of his a twenty-five year marriage. His character Jake McCluskie went on such a rampage, even the Devil questioned which of them was the evilest.

Many of the characters you'll read about in these short stories were along for the ride in that novel, a novel, I felt, highlighted by the section entitled: *Antietam.*

Doug included *Antietam* in this collection of stories because nearly everyone who has read his words agree—it is simply the best, a blood-soaked canvas of our history. If you read any of these stories, that one is a must. And so is the first story.

The Seven Day Date, has us meeting Jacob McCluskie's grandfather all the while witnessing a conversation worthy of a skit on Saturday Night Live. The story takes place in the home of one of the smartest men that has ever lived, and though the topic has us worrying about the impending rise of Hitler, I challenge you to keep a straight face while reading it.

Then in *Antietam,* we accompany Jake McCluskie aboard the Chinaman's train to his most horrific historical event to date. We sense his terror; mostly we sense his determination to save mankind by obtaining a very important piece of information. Luckily, he gets help from a famous general and the bravest Scotsman that has ever been written about.

H. G. Wells wrote the 'Time Machine' in the late 1800's; Doug's version has a lot more color and bite to it. *The Time Machine* introduces us to the Devil's Breath, a saxophone cursed to carry around the evils of the world. Through a mad scientist's time machine we are told of future events that will occur when it's played. Jake McCluskie's very existence is threatened, but a heroic dog with the help of a deity save the day.

In *Seven Mourners at Blackwells Corner* the story begins with us mourning Babe Ruth's death. From there we move to a special poker game at a gas station in California where the stakes are very high. As we all know, when playing poker, no one can be trusted. This is especially true when the Deity Fate is betting a certain saxophone…

And that saxophone takes center stage in Doug's next story: *The Devil's Breath*. One my think Craig is lucky for being the only man in his platoon to survive the Korean War. However, when you owe your life to the Angel of Death, you know you're in for a rough ride. Craig is doomed to play the saxophone, and wherever and whenever he does, you can be certain there will be casualties. It's not easy being Fate's pawn, and the story comes to a climax in a New York alley with a saxophone and a sledgehammer.

Hurricane Katrina hits hard in *The Out of Towners*. Kody, Jacob and Apollo are struggling against the storm, just to make things interesting there is a monster from outer space trying to kill them. It is going to take Charles, who can fix anything, Jackie, who can drive anything, and Mother, the omnipresent spaceship to rescue them in a race against time that made my heart beat faster.

In *The Last Cubicle,* memories of September 11th, 2001 come crashing through your mind and heart. It was a tragic event, a terrible moment in time, but some people were not meant to die that day, and Charles is one of them. Thanks to a bespectacled angel, he gets an opportunity to escape the devastation. How fast can he exit the building? And can he do it without changing the course of history.

The book ends with *Dead Flowers.* My favorite? Maybe. One thing is for sure, it finally put an end to the Third Reich. However, we are not in Germany and it is not 1945. Jake McCluskie needs to repay a debt to a fallen angel by boarding the Chinaman's train once again and bringing a bouquet of flowers to none other than the maniacal Hitler. Now we see Jake McCluskie, the most compassionate man in the world, seated across the table from the evilest man in the world in a paradoxical surreal scene.

These stories will make you laugh, cry, bite your fingernails and, perhaps like the author, make you drink more. However, no matter what behavior they elicit, I can assure you that you will enjoy them from the first word until the last. Happy reading!

Fondly
Kim Gromko

GLOSSARY OF CHARACTERS

Apollo.
The Out of Towners.
Rotund and gray, he is **Spaceman Kody's** wisecracking cat.

Bellick.
Dead Flowers.
A fallen angel, banished from Heaven for participating in the **Archangel Lucifer's** revolt. Now an enemy of **Lucifer** and **Jacob McCluskie.**

Belvedere.
Seven Mourners at Blackwells Corner.
A one-eyed British talking macaw with a passion for poker; owned by **the Gambler.**

Charles.
The Out of Towners and *The Last Cubicle.*
He is the saxophone playing mechanic from Redemption, Iowa.

The Chinaman.
Dead Flowers and the novel *Killing Time Till I Die(2015)*.
He is the chain-smoking deity who drives a time-traveling train.

Craig.
The Devil's Breath.
Korean War veteran, he is cursed by **Fate** to carry **the Devil's Breath.**

The Angel of Death.
The Devil's Breath, The Out of Towners, and the novels *That Special Knack(2014)* and *Killing Time Till I die(2015)*.
A Horseman; strongly associated with **Jacob McCluskie.**

The Devil's Breath.
The Time Machine, Seven Mourners at Blackwells Corner, The Out of Towners, The Last Cubicle, and *The Devil's Breath.*
Christened in Redemption Iowa in 1900, the saxophone carries within it the evil of mankind. Only in Redemption are its evil notes muted.

The Angel Envy.
Seven Mourners at Blackwells Corner and *The Last Cubicle.*
A compassionate, bespectacled angel; fond of poker; **Lucifer's** former girlfriend.

Fat Turk.
Seven Mourners at Blackwells Corner and the novels *That Special Knack (2014)* and *Killing Time Till I Die (2015)*.
A tender-hearted, low-level deity; a good friend of the Archangel Michael and **Jacob McCluskie.**

Fate.
The Time Machine(1900), Seven Mourners at Blackwells Corner, and *The Devil's Breath.*
A low-level deity; bitter enemies with the **Angel Envy.**

The Gambler.
Seven Mourners at Blackwells Corner.
A low-level deity; hosts lavish poker games with **Belvedere,** his macaw.

Giovanni.
Dead Flowers and the novels *That Special Knack(2014)* and *Killing Time Till I die(2015).*
Restaurateur; serves high-priced Cognac to **the Archangel Lucifer.**

Kelly.
The Seven Day Date.
School teacher from Redemption Iowa; in love with **David McCluskie. Jacob McCluskie's** grandmother.

Kody.
The Out of Towners and *The Last Cubicle.*
A gun-for-hire spaceman living in Redemption, Iowa.

Mr. Isaac.
Seven Mourners at Blackwells Corner.
A high-powered deity; doorman at **the Gambler's** poker games.

David McCluskie.
The Seven Day Date.
A handyman from Redemption, Iowa in love with **Kelly,** the school teacher. **Jacob McCluskie's** grandfather.

Jackie McCluskie.
The Out of Towners, The Last Cubicle, and *Dead Flowers.*
Works for **Kody;** drives **Mother** the interplanetary ship; **Jacob McCluskie's cousin.**

Jacob McCluskie.
Antietam, Dead Flowers, and the novels, *Broken Time(2012), That Special Knack(2014),* and *Killing Time Till I Die(2015).*
He is the leading protagonist in the Broken Time trilogy. Tethered to **the Archangel Lucifer.** He has the ability to see and hear souls, and has lightening fast reflexes.

Jacob Washington.
The Out of Towners.
A seven year old boy abandoned in Hurricane Katrina.

Jones.
Seven Mourners at Blackwells Corner.
A professional poker player.

The Archangel Lucifer.
Dead Flowers and the novels, *Broken Time(2012), That Special Knack(2014),* and *Killing Time Till I Die(2015).*
The Devil; **Jacob McCluskie's** archangel.

Mother.
The Out of Towners and *The Last Cubicle.*
An interplanetary spaceship.

Rex.
The Time Machine(1900)
A talking dog owned by **Rodger.**

Rodger.
The Time Machine(1900)
A mad scientist living in Redemption, Iowa; the inventor of the **Devil's Breath.**

The Texan.
Seven Mourners at Blackwells Corner and the novel *That Special Knack(2014)*
A low-level deity with a fondness for poker.

Smitty.
Dead Flowers and the novel *Killing Time Till I Die(2015).*
A high-powered deity; drives a black Chrysler 300 with a hemi; friends with **Jacob McCluskie.**

8 Crazy Moments in Time

The Seven Day Date

On July 23rd 1938, the smartest man in the world, at least according to my date, lived in a green bungalow on a quiet street in Franklin Lakes, New Jersey.

"According to the address on the letter, that's the place there," I said. "Egghead needs to cut his lawn."

"Will you stop calling him that?" she barked. "He's a pure genius. He thought up the Theory of Relativity."

"Who cares? What have you done for me lately?" Before she could respond—and yes, I knew a response was coming—I turned off the engine and climbed from the Buick, leaning in. "Are you coming, Kelly?"

She stared at me through thick dirty lenses, and I fell in love with her brown eyes again. "Do you think he's home?"

"It's Saturday morning. Where else is he gonna be?"

The storm from last night had moved out to sea and the sky was a cloudless shimmering blue. The air was cool, a welcomed break after the midsummer heat wave that had scorched the road from Iowa to New Jersey.

I scooted around the Buick and waited for her to climb from the car, taking her hand before walking up Einstein's bricked path. The slap of her bare feet stirred up a laugh in me I fought to stifle. I loved her too much to laugh, especially after everything she had been through; so instead, I stopped, gently took off her glasses, and cleaned them with my hanky.

"Why are you smirking?

I lightly placed her glasses on her nose, sliding the arms around her ears, my fingers touching the gold studs in her lobes. "Now you can see."

Her smile stung my heart (it always does), but it ran away like tears in the rain a moment later and her lips, red as roses, turned into a frown. "Not much to look at, Mr. McCluskie." Her eyes flashed behind the lenses of her black framed glasses. "I don't care for men with beards, and you need a haircut."

I flicked one of her black hairs off my finger. "Didn't stop you from kissing me last night."

"I was drunk," she shot back, "and I take the kiss back."

"Sorry, you can't take a kiss back. My mom told me that." I stuck out my tongue at her, turned and walked forward. "I'm having fun on our date."

"Date?" she questioned hotly. "It stopped being a date six days ago."

I turned back to her. "You wanted to come—not me. I was happy in Redemption." With no shoes on, she was six inches shorter than me, yet still tall for a woman, five foot nine anyway. She had meat on her bones, thick healthy shoulders, big bosoms, thin at the waist, and broad thighs that narrowed down into semi-plump calves.

"I have no shoes," she announced as though I might have been unaware. "I'm about to meet Professor Einstein, and I'm barefoot."

I smiled, and just to make her laugh, added, "I wished you had clipped your toenails."

"This isn't funny," she screeched in a whiny voice.

"What's the big deal? He's seen a woman's foot before. Oh, and if he asks—and he will—please don't tell him you lost your shoes running from a dinosaur."

Through clenched straight teeth, she hissed, "You know damn well it was a dinosaur."

"Could have been a bear."

Her eyes flashed outrage. "Then this bear looked reptilian and closely resembled a T-rex."

"It wasn't your average bear, I'll give you that. Still, I'm thinking bear. And who cares anyway? We got away." I chuckled a bit. "Okay sure, you ran out of your shoes, but at least you're still wearing your dress."

She quickly caught me up on current events. "I've been wearing it for seven days."

"The green and yellow floral pattern hides the dirt," I returned. "And you're not getting much sympathy from me. I've been wearing the same clothes for seven days too. I don't care for button up shirts with collars, and I'm wearing these black scratchy go-to-church pants cuz I wanted to impress you." I sighed with regret. "I wish I had my denim pants on." And then, just because I needed to share at the moment, I threw in, "It's the underwear thing that's really bothering me."

It must have been bothering Kelly too, because tears bubbled up in her eyes, dampening her eyelashes. Her tears broke my heart and I stepped over and hugged her tightly, racking my brain to say something profound; nothing came to mind (it had been a long week) so I kissed her cheek instead in hopes it would make her feel better.

"I like your hair now that you've got it tied up in an ant hive."

"It's a bee hive," she corrected me, brushing strands of hair from in front of her face, "and it's a mess."

I should have kept my mouth shut; of course, I didn't. "Okay, it's a little flat after the rain last night."

"Rain?" she cried out. "That wasn't rain, it was a hurricane of Biblical proportion. I'm surprised we didn't see the ark float by. However, we did see a dinosaur."

That got me chuckling, and we stepped up on the cracked cement stoop. I leaned over and rang the doorbell. A deep dampened gong sounded from within the house and I turned to her. "It was a bear."

You would figure she would let the issue drop, especially since she was the one without shoes, but no, not Kelly. She argued the point, in explicate detail might I add, and was making another point about the size of the dinosaur's jagged teeth when the door opened. And there—on the door's threshold dressed in a brown cardigan sweater and baggy gray pants—stood the smartest man in the world; well, at least according to Kelly.

I liked him right off. He had a pleasant face, a face that looked like it liked to laugh, and it looked like it had been laughing for a good sixty years. His salt and peppered colored hairdo was brushed up and wavy like the bristles of a well-used corn broom. His moustache was so thick he could use it as a 'hiding' place. His eyes were brown and bright and filled with a mystical knowledge I could never understand. Reading glasses hung off the end of his nose.

The shock of seeing us quickly wore off, and he looked at Kelly, blinking now in puzzlement. "Where did you see a dinosaur?"

"Oh my God, it's you," she managed, her chin quivering slightly. "I'm so honored to meet you Professor Einstein." She took his hand, and shaking it, introduced herself, adding, "I'm a school teacher from Redemption, Iowa."

He absently stroked the long white hairs poking out the top of his beige t-shirt and questioned, "A school teacher?"

"One room; all grades," she informed as though it was a big deal.

"Awe don't be patting yourself on the back in front of the genius," I said with a smile, moving closer to Kelly. "Hey Al, I'm David McCluskie. I'm a handyman from Redemption, nice to meet you." I reached out for a handshake. I got one—eventually. Not that I could blame the poor man, his odd, stunned expression concerned me. He looked like he was about to have a stroke.

"Why are you people here?"

"I saw it in the Virginia woods," Kelly blurted out. "I'm sure it was a T-rex."

"Trust me on this Al, it was a bear."

He cleared his throat. "Though I am mildly interested in the dinosaur story, I want the two of you leave now."

Seven days on the road had worn me down, and after everything we went through to get here, my anger boiled up real quick, and the smartest man in the world heard what I had to say. "Listen good egghead," and I stepped forward and dug the blood soaked letter from my white shirt pocket. "See this? Well, it's got your name on it. We brought it to you, all the way from Redemption, Iowa. So maybe you better give us a few minutes of your time."

His eyes grew wide, his bushy eyebrows looked like wiggling caterpillars, and he stared at the letter. "For me?"

"Your name is on it. We got it given to us in Redemption Iowa. Seven days ago. Kelly and I were on a date—."

"We're not calling it a date," she cut in abruptly.

"At the time we were," I told her, and turned to Einstein. "We were having drinks at the Redemption Inn, minding our own business when this young guy in a suit walked in. He was a messenger, and the messenger had more holes in him than Swiss cheese. He begged us to bring this letter to you—said it was important. So we did." He was short, coming in a few inches under Kelly's height, and I stared down into his troubled eyes. "Do you have time for us now?"

The genius didn't think about it for long. "Please come in," he said, and ushered us forward. We followed him down a dimly lit wooden hallway that creaked and groaned under our weight.

"Can you walk softer," I whispered in Kelly's ear. "You sound like a duck in bare feet."

"I should strangle you."

I chuckled. "In front of the genius?"

Einstein directed us to a small room at the back of his house. Bookshelves crammed with books lined the walls from ceiling to floor. The window behind his desk was opened. The screen was freckled with rust and the yellow curtains fluttered in the light breeze. Papers littered his desktop, a few held down by the candlestick phone. He directed me to a wooden chair in front of his desk, and then quickly retreated to the kitchen, returning with a chair for Kelly to sit on. The kitchen chair was upholstered in red shiny linoleum, and framed with chrome tubes. He set it down in front of his desk and guided Kelly onto the seat.

"You seem so unnerved dear child, please sit."

"Child?" I questioned, smiling. "As if."

He collected his papers together quickly as though we were spies and shoved them in a drawer. He sat behind his desk, his legs crossed, his fingers tented in front of his face in pensive thought. "Redemption Iowa?" He shook his head slowly. "I've never heard of that city."

"It's in the Northwest corner of the state, professor," Kelly informed with pride. "It's a beautiful part of the country."

"Trees and fields," I told Einstein, and turned to Kelly. "You figure a smart guy like him would know where Redemption is." I was back looking at Einstein, smiling. "We had a talking dog back in 1900."

"No we did not!" she barked.

"I wasn't born yet, but my parents talked to him all the time. He was a bulldog and his name was Rex."

She put her thumb to her lips, motioning like she was drinking from a liquor bottle. "He drinks," she confessed in a plaintive whisper.

I caught Einstein's attention with a raised brow. "No wonder. I've been hooked up with her for a week."

Einstein smiled, and then quickly caught himself, and turned serious. "How did the dog learn how to talk?"

"Glad you asked," I returned. "There was this crazy-nutty scientist living in Redemption named Rodger. You know, he was nutty smart like you. From what I understand, his next door neighbor Mabel drowned when her outhouse gave way."

I snickered. "How's that for a way to go, huh? Anyway, crazy Rodger digs her up after the funeral, takes out her vocal cords and puts them in his dog."

"That's an old wives tale," Kelly threw in with horrified embarrassment.

"It's true."

Einstein regarded me in bewildered amazement. "That's quite impossible."

"Don't listen to him professor, he drinks."

"You know it's true Kelly. My parents talked to Rex all the time. They told me he was very nice. The only thing that bothered my mom was that he licked his balls a lot."

Einstein's eyes bugged out a bit and he choked, his cheeks growing crimson. Kelly jumped out of her chair, went behind the desk and gently banged him on the back. "I'm sorry professor. I'm so sorry."

"It's true," I pleaded.

"You don't need to share those stories."

"It's a good story. I bet Al is gonna think about that all day."

Einstein caught his breath and took hold of Kelly's hands. "Thank you dear child. I'm fine now."

"Dear child," I scoffed. "She's older than she looks."

As Kelly retook her seat, shooting me a cold hostile frown in the process, Einstein turned to me. "It is remarkable story." As I went to respond, he continued with, "I must ask, what is your relationship?"

Tears built in Kelly's eyes. "It's our first date, professor," she choked up a bit and her voice cracked when she added, "our first."

"I don't know what you're crying about, I'm having fun."

She looked at Einstein, tears continuing to build in her eyes. "We've slept in the car for a week."

"Why are you complaining? The car has comfortable seats. I slept okay, well, except when you were snoring." I smiled at Einstein. "She nearly snored the doors off the Buick."

"At least I didn't 'break wind' all the time," she shouted back in defense.

"Guys fart Kelly, ask Al." I motioned at him. "Am I right?"

"Everyone's constitution is different," Einstein said tentatively.

"Awe, save us the mumbo jumbo. Men fart more than women, it's as simple as that." I turned to Kelly. "I bet Al is struggling to hold one back right now."

"Oh dear God," she whispered, shaking her head. "Please give him the letter."

I tossed the blood soaked letter on the desktop in front of him. "Maybe you better read this and we'll tell you what happened."

His reading glasses had come off during his choking attack, and he put them on, regarded the blood soaked envelope for a moment before tearing the seal. His fingers played with the letter inside, yet he failed to draw out the note. His eyes were on me. "What happened after the injured man gave you the note?"

"Injured man? He was Swiss cheese." I jerked my thumb at Kelly. "She wanted to call the sheriff. Good idea on that one school teacher."

"You have to call the authorities when someone is shot."

"It was past 8. Earl was drunk for sure. Mary-Lou agreed with me."

Einstein leaned over his desk a bit. "Who's Mary-Lou?"

"She was the bartender on duty at the Redemption Inn when Mr. All-Full-Of-Holes showed up. And I'll save you the question: Earl is Redemption's sheriff. And no sense lying, Earl's a boozer."

"I see." Einstein drew out the note and opened it, reading it silently for a moment before clearing his throat and revealing, "It's from my good friend Leo."

"Leo? Is he a Nazi, cuz he sounds like a Nazi, and about ten minutes after Mr. All-Full-Of-Holes showed up, the Nazis arrived."

Einstein forgot about the note, gasping as he looked at me. "Oh dear,"

"It was terrifying professor," Kelly yelped, leaning forward. "The Nazis were dressed in evil black suits, and they had Tommy guns."

I smiled at her. "Hey school teacher, how does a black suit become evil?"

She gripped one of Einstein's hands. "You know what I mean, professor. Not a nice church suit. And then the evil Nazis opened fire on us."

Einstein gasped. "Oh dear God. Are you okay?"

"Trust me on this Al, she was up and talking in no time."

He stared at me, and in a strangled tone managed, "They opened fire?"

"They were lousy shots," I told him, and shrugged with indifference. "It wasn't that bad."

"Wasn't that bad?" she repeated with a mocking laugh, and then gestured wildly with both hands, pretending to fire a machinegun. "Bullets were whistling by us!"

I smiled at Einstein. "You should have heard her squeal. My ears are still ringing."

"Oh dear God, what did you do?"

"We jumped over the bar," I said. "Good thing Mary-Lou is fat, cuz we landed on her. No bumps or bruises."

Kelly moaned. "The poor woman."

"She was fine, and she was happy about going home early. To be honest, you were the only stick in the mud. I wanted to drop the letter in the mailbox and go home." I looked at Einstein. "The barefooted school teacher said we had to take it to you in person."

"The dying man said it was urgent," she shot back. "He pleaded with us. He said the fate of Mankind hung in the balance, and that the letter had to reach Professor Einstein as fast as possible."

"Awe, don't take stock in that. The guy was rambling. He had about fifty holes in him." I looked at Einstein. "I know what that's like, cuz I got shot in France in 1918, and my buddies told me I rambled for days." My smile was back. "As you can see, I survived, though there have been times on our date when I wished I hadn't."

"Date! Date from hell, and it's still going on. Look at him professor, he's got a full beard."

"Sorry, I forgot to bring my razor on the date. If you want school teacher, I'll get a note from my elderly mom for you."

"I think you look elegant in a beard."

"Thanks Al, I like your 'stache' too."

He nodded a thank you, and asked, "What happened next?"

Kelly answered for me. "The Nazis chased us, professor." Her voice broke and she quietly added, "For days."

"It wasn't that bad. Oh, and the Germans are pussies. And they're lousy shots. Mind you, one of them got me in France. Had to be a lucky shot, don't you think?"

"We've all heard about your bullet wound," she said with hostile flare. "No one is interested."

"I'm just filling in detail." I leaned an elbow on the desk, grinning at Einstein. "I was only seventeen when I got shot, so it hurt more cuz I wasn't quite an adult."

"Oh my God," she said, shaking her head. "I'm so sorry professor."

He nodded quietly at her. "Please, tell me what happened."

"They chased us to the zoo," Kelly blurted out.

I banged the desktop with the flat of my hand. "There's another fun thing we did on our date. We went to the zoo."

She looked at me as though I'd lost my mind. "We were on the run."

"Who cares? It was still a visit to the zoo, and we got to see Susie."

"Susie?" Einstein questioned.

"The zoo has a baboon—"

"She is a gorilla," Kelly quickly corrected me.

"Whatever," I returned and was back looking at Einstein. "If you were a gorilla, you'd be Susie, that's how smart she is. She ate dinner—and I'm not making this up—with a knife and fork."

"She has better table manners than you," Kelly put in abruptly.

"Gorillas are an extremely high form of life," Einstein added.

"I agree Al. Sure, not as impressive as Rex, the talking, ball licking dog, but still, that's damn smart for a baboon."

"She is a gorilla," Kelly snapped, and turned to the professor. "Before the show was over the Nazis were shooting at us."

I thought about that moment in time, and laughed, looking at Einstein. "You should have seen everybody run—even Susie."

"This isn't funny!" she yelped at me.

"What's the big deal? We saw the best part of the show."

Einstein reached across the desktop and took hold of one of Kelly's hands. "What did you do?"

She jabbed her finger toward me. "He let the tigers out of their cages."

I shook my head. "It was the lions."

"Do you see what I've been through?"

"Why are you complaining Kelly? The lions ate the Nazis." I grinned at Einstein. "I guess they preferred a European cut of meat." After I laughed, (no one else did) I turned to Kelly and added, "After our visit to the zoo it was all smooth sailing."

"Smooth sailing!" she thundered, and turned to Einstein. "We were in a bank robbery professor."

"It wasn't a bad bank robbery."

"All bank robberies are bad!" she shrieked, and was back looking at Einstein. "And it was John Dillinger doing the bank robbing."

The news that Dillinger was still alive made Einstein pause. After he collected himself, he gently told Kelly, "I believe Dillinger is dead."

"I told her that," I said with an eye roll. "Dillinger got gunned down in '34."

Her eyes flashed angrily at me. "Well the people who gunned him down didn't do a good enough job."

I grinned at Einstein. "I believe Dillinger was on a date at the time. Even with the Feds shooting him I bet his date was smoother than mine."

"I should strangle you."

"I wish you had of seven days ago."

"I don't care what you say, it was Dillinger. I saw him plain as day."

"You need new glasses."

"And professor," she said, gripping Einstein's hands. "Ma Barker was driving the getaway car."

With two fingers I tapped the desktop. "Al, I heard about Ma Barker for days."

Einstein regarded Kelly with an odd bewildered look. "I believe Ma Barker is dead as well."

"Someone was driving that getaway car professor, and it looked an awful lot like Ma Barker."

I put my index finger up to my head and made a spinning motion. "What can you expect from a school teacher?"

Einstein turned to me. "How did you end up in a bank robbery?"

"We ran out of money, so I had my brother in California wire us some. We were at the bank picking it up when it happened." I looked at Kelly. "And no, it wasn't Dillinger. It was a guy with a gun. And what's the big deal anyway? I took you out for drinks after." I leaned over the desk, staring Einstein in the eye. "She ordered—and I'm not making this up Al—she ordered a Blue Lagoon. You should have seen the bartender's face."

"A blue what?"

"I needed something strong after the shoot out, professor," Kelly cried.

I laughed. "I needed something strong after I heard your drink order."

"What is in a –"

"Vodka is giving it the punch, but get this Al, it has lemonade in it."

He thought about it, nodding to himself, his eyes on Kelly. "It sounds appealing, most refreshing. I would love to try one of those, especially on a hot summer day."

"You know what's refreshing on a hot summer day—a cold beer."

Einstein smiled. "It sounds like you drink a lot."

I motioned at Kelly. "Can you blame me?"

"He does drink a lot," she threw in with a hint of desperation.

"Only beer," I said to her, and then to Einstein I added, "Mind you, after the week I've had, I would pretty much down a bottle of anything you got."

"You lush."

"I wouldn't talk, you like to throw them back too, Mrs. Blue Lagoon."

"Can you blame me?" she fired back.

Einstein laughed and came out of a chuckle with, "Teaching is a difficult profession. Many of my colleagues have turned to the bottle."

"Are they drinking Blue Lagoons?" I asked with a laugh, jerking my thumb at Kelly, "because this school teacher is."

"Being with you makes me drink," she returned with hot passion. "Not being with the children."

"I heard a different story on our long car ride."

"I should strangle you, right in front of Professor Einstein— and he wouldn't blame me."

Einstein motioned gently with his hands. "Please, let's talk this out."

"I noticed you didn't wanna strangle me last night." I shrugged a brow at Einstein. "After four Blue Lagoons she kissed me, right on the lips."

"I take the kiss back."

"You can't take a kiss back." I swung my attention to Einstein and leaned my elbow on the desktop. "Am I right on this one Al?"

The question threw him, and after a few seconds he looked at Kelly and shrugged helplessly. "I believe you can't take a kiss back."

"See, even the genius agrees with me," I said. "So what's the note say?"

"That's none of our business," she yelped.

"I think it is. It's been a long week, and I've been wearing the same underwear for seven days."

She scoffed at me. "Even if we hadn't left Redemption you'd probably still be wearing the same underwear."

"Three days at the most," I said, and turned to Einstein. "Underwear aside, people have died over that note. The school teacher and I deserve to know what's going on."

"I'm sorry professor. As you can see, I'm hooked up with a caveman."

"Caveman? Remember, I'm the one wearing shoes."

"I'm so sorry about that professor, I lost them running from the dinosaur."

"It was a bear."

"No sir, Mr. handyman," she bellowed at me. "It was a dinosaur."

He touched her hand. "Dinosaurs have been extinct for millions of years."

"That may well be professor," she said, tears building in her eyes. "But the dinosaur roaming around the Virginia woods didn't get the message."

"It was a bear, and why are you complaining to Al anyway? We got away."

"I lost my shoes. I'm in Professor Einstein's office in my bare feet."

"Don't keep bringing it up." I leaned over and gestured downward. "Try not to stare at her toenails Al. Remember, it has been seven days." I shrugged at her. "Don't worry. The egghead doesn't care if you're in bare feet."

"Stop calling him an egghead," she fired back, spittle flying from her lips. "Professor Einstein is the inventor of the Theory of Relativity. You probably don't even know what that is."

"Do I need to know? How does that play into my life? Hey, you wanna do something good Al? Invent a frozen dinner. You know, it comes in a tray, kind of like what you'd get in the cafeteria. And it's got everything, you know, meat, potatoes, maybe some peas and carrots, and a dessert. You buy it frozen, you pop it in the oven, and ten minutes later you're eating. You don't have to slave over a hot stove, and the clean up would be nothing."

"Are you that lazy?" she demanded, her brown eyes flashing angrily. "You can't make your own dinner?"

"I'm just saying, that would make my life easier. This 'relativity' stuff may look good on paper but it doesn't do me any good."

"I apologize for my friend."

"Well, at least you're calling me a friend."

She turned to me, pleading with her hands. "Don't you understand? You are in the office of the smartest man in the world."

"I don't believe I'm the smartest," Einstein put in quietly.

"He puts his pants on one leg at a time just like me Kelly." I looked at him. "Hey you got to admit, that frozen dinner idea is pretty good, no?"

He nodded. "It would make life easier."

"See, even Al agrees with me."

"I can't believe you."

I leaned an elbow on the desktop and added, "Hey Al, you know what would be another great idea?" I glanced at the candlestick telephone on the corner of his desk. "A telephone you could take outside. You know, an outdoor telephone."

Kelly sighed heavily. "You've lost your mind."

"I think it's a good idea. I'd like to take a call outside."

Einstein looked at me over the rims of his glasses. "What about the cord?"

"Well that would be your department Al. I can't think of everything."

"I can't believe you." She turned to Einstein. "I'm so sorry professor."

"Do you know what would be another good idea? Add a camera to the telephone."

She shook her head. "Oh dear God."

"This way, you could take a picture, and show it to the guy you're talking to."

"You've lost your mind," she told me. "Do you know that? You've completely lost your mind."

"I think it's a good idea Kelly. What do you think Al?"

"David, I believe our technology is not that advanced."

"Oh please, throw a few fancy math numbers on a piece of paper—you're good at that—the next thing you know General Electric will be mass producing them."

"I'm sorry for my friend. He must be traumatized after seeing the dinosaur—"

"Bear!" I put in quickly. "And please don't tell Al about the men from Mars."

"Mars," he managed, and began to choke. Kelly was back behind the desk gently banging on his back.

"Why do you bang him on his back? He's having a hard enough time as it is."

"We were taught to do this in teacher school."

"Is that where you learned to drink Blue Lagoons?"

Al choked harder, and his cheeks turned red.

"Kelly, we better leave soon or he might keel over. How's that to the end the perfect date? Killing the smartest man in the world."

"When are you going to get it into your thick head that the date ended a long time ago?"

"My lips tell me something else."

"I take back that kiss. I regret every going out with you."

Einstein recovered, and turned to Kelly, holding her hands. "I'm fine now sweet child. You don't have to keep banging me on the back."

"When you wake up tomorrow Al all bruised on your back, blame the school teacher."

Kelly retook her seat and smartly threw in, "I should strangle you, and I regret every going out with you."

"I'm having fun, and we got to meet Al."

"Yes, meeting you professor nearly makes up for all I've been through."

"All you've been through?" I rolled my eyes. "Oh please. This is summer vacation for you."

"Vacation!" She motioned at her clothing. "I've been wearing the same clothes for seven days."

"So what? It's summertime. Nobody cares."

"It's okay sweet child, I understand your hardship."

"Hardship?" I laughed. "Now she has a great story to tell the kids in September." I smiled at her. "I'm sure you'll have everyone's attention when you tell them about the men from Mars."

"You saw men from Mars?" Einstein asked her.

"We never saw the actual men, professor," she explained. "We saw their space plane."

"It was a cloud."

"A cloud with lights?" she question with a hint of bitter scorn. "I haven't seen many of those, have you?"

"Oddly enough I saw one on the way here."

Einstein laughed so hard I thought he was going to choke again.

"Oh, you're so funny. Are we going to hear the story about the talking, ball licking dog again?" She caught herself, and nearly jumped out of the chair. "I'm so sorry professor. You have to understand, it's all the pressure I'm under."

"Pressure? Oh please, I did all the driving." I turned to Einstein and smiled, "She did all the 'talking'. Bla bla bla. And then the cloud came by—"

She pointed her finger at me. "Men from Mars."

Einstein looked her in the eye. "I believe Mars in uninhabitable."

"Somebody ought to tell the guys flying around in the tea saucer that."

"See why I drink?"

Einstein laughed, and was still laughing when I asked a follow up question.

"So? What's in the letter?"

"Will you—"

"No, no, David is right," Einstein cut in. "You have been through a great deal." He paused, and after a good long thought, added, "If I wrote fiction, I could write an entire novel on your adventure."

I grinned at him. "Make sure you spell my name right."

"A horror story professor, a seven day journey through Hell," Kelly complained.

"I had fun," I told her, and to Einstein added, "And I got a kiss too."

Before she could respond—and oh yes, a response was coming—Einstein waved the letter to get our attention. "You both deserve the truth." He displayed the letter for us to see. "As you can see, it's written in German. The language of the pussies."

"Not you Al. I don't think you're a pussy."

"Will you shut up," she snapped, and then, in a softer tone said, "Please professor, continue."

"The letter was written by my good friend Leo. He is a physicist."

"I don't like the sound of that."

Kelly glared at me. "Do you know what a physicist is?"

"I don't need to know. I've got you to tell me." I turned to Al. "Is he a Nazi?"

He shook his head. "He is Hungarian, and I believe he is the smartest man in the world."

"Don't sell yourself short Al, you still have it going on upstairs."

"Thank you for the compliment David, I think you have it going on upstairs as well."

I stuck my tongue out at Kelly. "Al thinks I'm smart."

"Oh dear God," she muttered, shaking her head in mortified chagrin.

"Awe, don't be shaking your head at me. At least I haven't farted." She groaned with embarrassment, and I turned to Einstein. "Okay Al, what's going on with Leo the Hungarian physicist?"

Einstein's expression changed to a look of hurt and despair. "Leo is in grave danger. This letter was written and sent off only hours before the Nazis took him. He is being held in Germany."

I reached across the desktop and gripped Einstein's hands with force. "Your friend will be okay. Don't worry, Al."

He nodded a 'thank you'.

I pointed at the letter in his hand and pushed on with, "What's all the fancy looking math stuff?"

"It is the formula for an atomic bomb."

The words hung in the air like a bad joke, and Kelly gasped.

"Bomb, huh? That doesn't sound good."

"Do you know what an atomic bomb is?" she asked, her tone rising.

"Right now it's written down on a blood soaked piece of paper, but I gather it's not good."

"That would be an understatement, David," Einstein continued gravely. "Depending on the size of the device, it could wipe out an entire city."

It was my turn to say "Oh my God." I reached out and took Kelly's hands, feeling blessed I was with someone that mattered to me.

"Pandora is out of her box," Einstein said cryptically. "This formula can destroy the world." He looked sadly at me. "One day it will."

I stared back. "What the hell is wrong with people anyway? Why are people always looking for ways to kill each other?" I looked at Kelly and put my hand on her shoulder. "We should have stayed in Redemption."

She sniffled back tears and nodded.

"The Nazis that gunned down the messenger," Einstein went on, "the ones that chased you, desperately wanted the information in this letter so they could give it to their leader, Adolph Hitler."

Kelly looked at me. "Do you know who that is?"

"Yes I do school teacher. He's Time Magazine's man of the year."

Einstein cleared his throat. "The man of the year for 1938 is a dangerous man."

I thought about it, but not for long. "Dangerous or not Al, this Hitler is still a pussy, and he has no balls, well, maybe one. Not that it matters, if he picks a fight with us, he's gonna get his ass kicked all over Germany. Like the last time."

Einstein nodded somberly and continued with, "Because of you two, the formula for the atomic bomb is safe, for now, and I will write the President."

"Our President?" I looked at Kelly. "Roosevelt, right?"

"You don't even know who the President is?"

"I don't get out much," I said. "Look what happens to me when I do."

"Yes David, President Roosevelt. He needs to see what's written on this note. He needs to know what grave peril the world is in."

I climbed to my feet. "I have to tell you something Einstein, though since you're real smart I figure you already know: we are the worst species on the planet. Susie the baboon wouldn't do this to life, it's too damn disrespectful." I took hold of Kelly's hand and helped her up. "Thanks for being with me. You are a special person. And we should have stayed in Redemption. There's no evil there."

She hugged me and whispered in my ear, "I love you."

"I loved you before we left Redemption."

Einstein climbed to his feet, his knees cracking. "You two are heavenly disciples."

I smiled. "Thanks for making it sound romantic."

"Thanks to you and Kelly, Mankind is safe—for now."

"Thank the school teacher, she's Heaven sent. Not me. It's my grandson. A prophet told us he'll save Mankind."

"Don't listen to him professor, he's crazy."

"You know it's true Kelly. You were there." I grinned at Einstein. "It was after the bank robbery and she was three Blue Lagoons into the afternoon when we ran into the prophet so maybe her memory is a bit fuzzy."

"I should strangle you."

"In front of Al?"

She shook her head in disbelief, and stepped up to Einstein. "It's been an honor to have met you professor." And whether Al wanted one or not, he got a hug, a big one, and since Kelly towered over him, he disappeared during their hug.

"You're a creature of beauty my child."

"You're right about that Al, she sure is beautiful, and inside too. Then again, what would you expect from a teacher? And no lying, after a few Blue Lagoons, she's as funny as Gracie Allen. It's too bad you got the 'teacher' version."

"I was professional," she told me bluntly. "Not like you, telling Professor Einstein about a dog that licks his balls."

Einstein choked, but only a couple times, so Kelly, who was ready to pound on his back again, didn't need to. He came out of a choke with, "I must admit David, your story about the dog will stay with me."

"I know it will, Al."

Then, before I knew it, Einstein came over and wrapped his arms around my waist. His bushy hairdo came up to my chest, so I had to lean down to hug him, and as I did, I kissed him on the cheek.

"There you go, Al. Now you can't say we left here without giving you a smooch." I turned to Kelly. "It was okay for me to smooch his cheek, remember, he's European." I put my hands on her shoulders and smiled. "When I was hugging him, all his smarts soaked into me."

Kelly shook her head. "Oh dear God."

"I must say David," Einstein said, waiting for us to turn to him. "I have never met anyone like you. You are the most unique person I have ever met, and I mean this with all sincerity, you are much smarter than me. You outwitted the Nazis and…"

"For God's sake Al, don't bring up the dinosaur cuz I'll be hearing about it all afternoon."

"I should strangle you."

I gently squeezed Kelly's hand. "C'mon school teacher, we've taken up enough of Al's time. I'll buy you a Blue Lagoon. Give you a chance to kiss me again." I turned back to Einstein. "Oh Al, if you ever invent the outdoor telephone, make sure you include a button that turns the telephone off. Cuz if you don't, she'll be blabbing to me all day."

"Don't listen to him professor, he's crazy."

Einstein smiled. "I think you two are the perfect couple."

"Let's not get ahead of ourselves Al, we're still on our first date."

The End

...

The train grinded to a stop and sighed out puffed smoke.

The Chinaman turned in his chair and lit a cigarette. "We have arrived," he said, blowing smoke out his nostrils. "It's Wednesday September 17th, 1862." He motioned out the window. "Welcome to Sharpsburg, Maryland. Currently owned by General Robert E. Lee." He tilted his head to side, slightly puzzled, a grin working its way onto his face. "I wonder if that makes him the mayor."

"Lee won't own the place for long."

He paused for a moment, staring at me. "Are you okay McCluskie? Because you look whiter than you should."

"I'm just a bit scared," I replied, trying to control my breathing. I stepped over to the door, sliding it back. "I guess I'll go find a war."

"You're looking in the right place."

...

Antietam

The wild grass, long and green with yellow tips swayed around my knees and the heavy dew made wet patches on my black jeans. I worked my way up the hill, my steps wide to crush down the wet grass and came upon a dirt trail leading upwards. Last night's rain made the path muddy; but already the rising temperature was baking the earth hard.

The train chugged behind me, smoking white into the late summer air. On the horizon, a bright orange and yellow gloriously streaked the watery mixture of black and blue sky.

"It's too beautiful a day to die," I said to myself, and found the strength to sprint ahead, my mind racing.

I had an hour, only an hour to find the other half of the tablet and get back to the train. Was it enough time? I tried to convince myself it was, but I failed miserably. The Timekeeper once told me Time can be a bitch, and I had a sneaky feeling that 'bitch' part would come into play this time out. A few of Lucifer's well chosen words bounced about in my head as well. To quote the Master, "If you don't have an exit strategy, don't worry about it. Work it out as you go." Easy for him to say, huh?

Whether the train was there or not when I returned, I still had to face Antietam, I still had to get across the cornfield, and get to the church, and find Macpherson, and get the other half of the tablet. As for getting home? Well, why think that far ahead? Maybe I'll be dead and I won't have to worry about it.

The path ended at the woods, and I ran through a thick cluster of trees, the pine needles soft under foot. Keeping low to stay out of sight, I blinked into soul mode and detected vibrations ahead. There were too many to count. I had found the Union Army.

I ducked behind a huge tree, looking down the hill. The dark blue of their uniforms looked almost black in this light. They were scattered about in clusters of four or five men, hunkered down behind fallen trees and bushes and rocks. Some played with their rifles and polished their bayonets, a few smoked cigarettes, all of them looked nervous. Who could blame them?

I had read in Scoop's Civil War book that these men were from Wisconsin. I also read that most of them would be dead before breakfast.

I crept forward to another tree, and now I could see it in the distance—the cornfield.

The cornfield made everything real for me, and my stomach lurched so violently, for an instant, I thought I might puke. But the feeling passed. I took deep breaths. My heart thundered heavy in my chest and I stared ahead in hypnotic wonder.

I had read the cornstalks ranged between six and ten feet high; from my perspective, the stalks looked higher. The light wind eerily swayed the late summer corn, and the first slants of daylight hit the field. The glint of the sun bouncing off the bayonets chilled my blood, and with utter fascination, I watched the Confederates move about in the green and yellow of the corn like gray ants.

The fear cruising through me made it hard to breathe, and I turned away, panting like I'd run a marathon. I thought of everyone at home. And I thought of the Devil. "Work it out." Then the words of a good friend came to me, "Failure is not an option." Truer words had never been spoken.

Needing to get closer, needing to get right behind the Union forces, I ran in a crouch from behind the tree to another tree twenty yards ahead. The vibrations told me I was mere feet away from the Wisconsin unit.

Seconds passed…

And then all hell broke loose.

A muffled puff far off in the distance started it—and a blazing cannon ball trailing black smoke streaked across the sky from the Confederate side. That sure got everyone's attention, and an instant later the cannon ball struck home about hundred yards to my left and down the hill. The impact shook the ground. Earth and pieces of trees exploded upwards in a shower of violent red. Inside the red shower, two legs dressed in Union blue flew up, flying end over end before landing twenty yards away with a sizzling thud in a clump of bushes.

As I watched the legs smoke and twitch, screams came from every direction, and now everyone was shooting. Someone blew a horn, and the Union army raced from their positions, screaming at the top of their lungs. A kid wearing an oversized Union coat got so excited he shot the man in front of him in the back. The man went down with a yelp, losing his weapon, and landed face first on the trampled grass, his arms and legs thrashing. The kid who shot him, stopped and stared at what he had done. He didn't stare long, for a few seconds later, a Confederate round blew off most of his face and he spun to the ground spraying blood.

The cornfield lit up red: small pops of red light and then rising smoke. A maelstrom of bullets whizzed back and forth, lacing the air with white and gray smoke, and chewing up earth and trees and bushes and people.

Screams came from everywhere. The lucky ones died instantly—a head shot, or something to the heart. The unlucky ones survived, at least long enough to feel the agony of war.

A solider ran by me without an arm; another staggered up the hill, holding his head. Blood gushed between his fingers, which suddenly became the least of his troubles, for wandering upright in a firefight is never good, and a Rebel bullet nailed him in the back. He spun to the ground, twitched a few times, and then died.

More cannon balls sizzled across the sky. The ground shook, and the noise became too loud for my ears. I blinked out of soul mode, dampening the sound.

The carnage raged in bloody, explosive wonder before me. It was almost too much to bare. Union dead and wounded littered the hillside. The wounded screamed for help and water. Some sobbed. Some were missing limbs, an arm or a leg, or a foot or a hand, others were gut shot, or shot in the face, or shot in the shoulder or leg. Blood was all I could see.

I turned away for a moment, the sound of screams and whistling bullets in my ears, the heavy smell of smoke in my nose, stinging my eyes, and I tried to calm myself. I had to get to the cornfield, I had to get through the cornfield, that much I knew, but I couldn't move. Fear held me tight.

But I had to move.

I crept down the hill, and the first wave of Union forces began to fall back. They hunkered down behind fallen trees and rocks and shot wildly across the thirty yards of 'no man's land' separating the armies. Bullets flew back and forth. Cornstalks floated in the smoke laced air.

I heard soldiers behind me, and looked about to see a unit of Union medics racing toward the wounded. If they saw me, and I was easy to see, they ignored me, and did their job.

In the distance, cannon balls blazed across the sky in both directions. Thanks to Scoop's Civil War book, I knew General Sumner had started a frontal attack on Lee's troops, pushing toward Sharpsburg.

Gray smoke rose thick and heavy and drifted slowly in the light breeze and as I watched it, I failed to hear the man sneaking up beside me. His revolver clicked in my ear, and I turned and looked down the business end of a Colt.

My eyes zeroed in on him, and I recognized him, I knew this person, which struck me as odd because I never dreamt I'd come across anyone I'd recognize at this battle, not unless Abe dropped by, or Grant, and the only reason I'd recognize them is because I see their smiling faces on my money. But this guy I knew. I couldn't believe it, but I knew him, from somewhere.

He looked about twenty, thin like me, yet stronger and a bit taller. His hair was a dull yellow, and long to his shoulders, held down by his dark blue Calvary hat. His moustache hid a lot of his lips, and his face was narrow and dotted with strawberry patches from shaving too close.

His light blue eyes looked determined, and he calmly said, "You're not suppose to be here."

"Who is?" I returned.

The demon gun was tucked down the back of my pants, and he missed it, his left hand instead digging in my pant pockets. He pulled out my cell phone. That sure got his attention, and with his eyes glued to modern technology, I decided to take matters into my own hands. Michael gave me lightening fast reflexes, and before this man even realized it, I snatched his revolver from his hand.

I pointed the gun at his face, "If you don't mind" and I reached over and plucked the phone from his hand.

"What is that?"

"You don't need to know," I said, working the phone back into my pocket. I stepped back next to the tree. "What are you anyway? You've got bars on your sleeve so you're an officer. What are you? A lieutenant?"

"No…I'm a captain."

"I have to tell you Captain, you look damn familiar." Before I could continue, down the hill, the fighting commenced with a bit more intensity, and the Union peppered the cornfield. The Confederates responded. Bullets whizzed in our direction, so I grabbed the Captain by the front of his uniform and dragged him behind the tree with me. I put the revolver under his chin.

"What's your name?"

He hesitated. "Custer…George Custer."

A grin broke out across my face. "Well, I'll be damned. I do know who you are."

"You do?" he asked in awe.

"I had no idea you were at the battle of Antietam," I told him, shaking my head, thinking about what I learned in high school about the Battle of Little Big Horn, the Indian battle in Montana where George Armstrong Custer died. "Okay General, here's the thing…"

"I'm a captain."

"For now," I said. "I know of you as a general, so that's what I'm calling you."

His eyes widened, and he wanted to talk, but overwhelming confusion can be a bitch and nothing came out of his mouth but a breathless mumble.

"You're right about one thing, General, I'm not suppose to be here."

"A spy?"

"What's there to spy on? Both sides are killing each other. Everybody can see that." I glanced down at the fighting for an instant, then back at him. "I have to get to the church, which means I have to get across the cornfield."

"Who are you?" His mouth hung agape for a moment. "Where are you from?"

"New York City. Queens to be precise." I pulled the demon gun from my pants to let him see it because sometimes a picture is worth a thousand words. "I know you're full of denial, which is fine, but my New York, as I'm sure you've figured out, is not in the 19th century."

"A traveler in time? That's impossible."

"You saw my phone, and you're looking at my demon gun, so you might wanna reconsider the 'impossible' thing."

He chewed on the corner of his yellow moustache, his eyes narrowed. "What year are you from?"

"21st century."

"My God…"

"That's probably how I'd respond if I were in your shoes, General. Now, as I said before, I have to get across the cornfield to the church, and Stonewall Jackson and his boys are in the way."

"Jackson?" he shot back, his eyes wide. "He's at Harper's Ferry."

"Naw," I said, shaking my head. "He's in the cornfield. Well, at least his boys are."

"Intelligence reports said he and his army were south of here, protecting Harper's Ferry."

"Here's some advice for you General, don't always believe your intelligence reports. Cuz Stonewall and his boys are currently shooting it up with your Wisconsin units, and Stonewall still has both his arms."

His odd, strange puzzled look deepened. "Jackson loses an arm?"

I thought of the Timekeeper: if he knew what I had said, if he knew I revealed secrets of the future, he would have whacked me over the head with his cane so hard both it and my head would probably break. "Gee, I shouldn't be talking so much. It's cuz I'm scared."

"War will do that to a man. War is hell."

"I think some other famous person said that. And what's happening around you today General is not war, it's a damn slaughter. And as for it being Hell?" I shook my head. "I've been to Hell, twice"—I jerked my head in the direction of the shooting—"and what's going on in that cornfield is worse."

He started to speak, probably wanting to question me on the whole 'been to Hell twice' thing, but I shook my head.

"I'm talking too much. Listen General, as I was saying, I need to get across the cornfield."

He tilted his head to the side and looked at me through narrowed slits. "Why?"

"That's a question you shouldn't ask, but trust me, this has nothing to do with your war."

"If you're not from this time…" He paused, and thought about it for a moment, the shock of seeing me, a time traveler, beginning to wear off. "Do we win the battle?"

"Over twenty thousand casualties," I told him. "Who wins there?"

"My God."

"To date, my date in time in fact—the 21st century—today remains the bloodiest day in U. S. history. What do you think of that General?"

I thought he was going to say 'My God' again, but instead, he stared at me in total disbelief.

"Hey, how old are you anyway?"

"Twenty-three."

"No shit," I said, "and already a captain. Well good for you, sir."

He mumbled under his breath and managed, "Why are you here?"

"I need to go to church." I leaned in a bit. "I'm not a Christian this week. Go figure, huh? Still, I need a little church time. Need to say a prayer or two."

"You picked a bad church to say prayers in."

"Don't I know it."

I knew enough about him to know he had finished last in his class at WestPoint, which was a huge rub to his classmates because he ended up a General. So despite his grades, he was intelligent, intelligent enough to know I was going to church to say more than prayers. "What's in the church?"

I decided not to lie. "The most important thing in my time is in that church General. I won't be too specific, but if I don't get to that church, a whole lotta bad is gonna happen in the 21st century, and that bad is gonna end Mankind."

His eyes glinted with disquieted trouble, and he nodded once, his long blonde hair falling in his face. "I understand." Then he said, "You need to be better dressed." He put up his hands to show me he wasn't going to run off, and then slipped out of his coat. He handed it to me. "We're about the same size."

Stepping back a bit in the event he tried to get his gun, I shrugged into his coat. "Not a bad fit for off the rack," I said, plucking a long blonde strand of hair off the sleeve. "It's an honor to wear your coat General."

"A general," he said in awe, and then gestured at the revolver in my hand. "You'll want a rifle." And before I could talk, he hurried down the hill and picked up a rifle from out of the hands of a dead man. He scurried back, running low to avoid Confederate rounds. "Here." He held out the rifle to me.

I tucked the demon gun down the back of my pants, took the rifle from him, and then decided, 'what the hell' and I gave him back his revolver.

He holstered the weapon. "I have to ask you something."

"You don't have to worry today, General. You're not on the casualty list."

"I know that, because I'm still a captain, but…some day?"

"You're a solider, sir, what do you think?"

He nodded glumly, and sighed. "Okay, when the attack starts, follow the men, stay low." He had no further advice. Not even a 'good luck'. With a curt nod, he turned, walked down the hill to a solider crouched behind a mound of rocks. Custer spoke in the man's ear, and stepped aside. The solider stood, looked about at the men beside him and yelled, "Charge!"

True to his word, the man jumped over the small outcropping of rocks he hid behind and started running across no man's land toward the cornfield as if he was late for dinner. To his credit, he nearly made it. By the time he fell, he had to have been hit a half dozen times at least. The Union forces scrambled from behind their hiding spots and charged across the field. Custer walked over to me and, over the explosive sound of gunfire said, "History is about to get it's blood."

"Yeah," I said, trying to steady my nerves. I grabbed his arm at the bicep, and leaned in close to him. "One more word of advice General, stay outta Montana."

With that said, I raced down the hill and joined up with the last of the Union soldiers flooding across no man's land.

(2)

My thoughts slowed.

I jumped over and around bodies, staying low. The mob of soldiers in front of me opened up, exposing me, and bullets whistled by me. Suddenly, the rifle in my hand exploded. Wood chips splintered everywhere, spraying up in front of me, and I stared down at the rifle's smoking remains, unsure if I should pick it up or not.

In my peripheral vision, I noticed something, and reached over and pulled a shank of bayonet from the padded shoulder. The shank was eight inches long, pointed at the end, and jagged where it broke apart. I clutched it tightly and ran forward.

Men piled up inside the first few feet of the cornfield. The stalks were crushed flat, and I kept pushing on the back of the man in front of me. I tripped over a dead Confederate, and fell flat on my face. Maybe on the ground was a good place to be and I crawled forward through the maze of legs that seemed to move everywhere in a dance of death.

Screams filled my ears, warm blood splashed on me, and crushed cornstalks scratched my hands as I scurried forward. I came to a mound of Confederate dead, and as I crawled overtop of the fresh corpses, my life changed in a way that made the horror around me almost secondary.

A Confederate solider rolled over top of me. He was no more than eighteen, probably younger. His brown hair was long and dirty, his gray coat was splattered with blood. He landed on his back and quickly got to his knees. We faced each other, our noses inches apart, and he grabbed hold of my coat sleeves and struggled to push me over. I was stronger, and I slammed him back first onto the crushed cornstalks. His eyes filled with fear. And I saw the bayonet shank.

I had lost it in the brief scuffle, but saw it now, right beside us, and I dove for it, grabbing it with both hands. He was on top of me, struggling to get to the shank, but I was stronger, and I shrugged him off. Then, clutching the shank with both hands, I spun about and ran it into his chest.

He gasped, and his eyes turned up white.

Warm blood cascaded over my hands. The bayonet shank was lost inside him.

I sat up on my knees and stared at the blood on my hands. My bloody hands shook violently. Then a dead Confederate soldier fell on top of me, and instinct took over.

I hurried forward between legs and over and around bodies, and soon got to a section of the cornfield still untouched from the fighting. In a crouch, I ran down the rows of corn, unable to believe I was still alive. If only that thought stayed, but it didn't.

My mind blazed with agonizing remorse that grew and grew with each step, and then, nearly mad, straightjacket mad, I broke free of the cornfield and rolled out onto wild grass.

Tears blurred the blue sky, and I blinked them away and got to my knees. The sounds of war seemed far removed, and the air was clean and void of gun smoke. I looked at my bloody hands, stuck now with corn fibbers, and wanted to scream, but my mouth was too dry.

I had made it across the cornfield, but it had cost me dearly.

In the distance, I saw the church, and climbed to my feet. I had to keep going. I had a train to catch.

I peeled off Custer's blood-soaked coat, and looked it over quickly, amazed at how many bullet holes I found. I tossed it back in the cornfield and staggered toward the church.

(3)

The Confederates owned the church for the time being, and a unit of Confederate soldiers rushed by me. I got lots of looks, but no one challenged me, probably because I was unarmed and covered in blood. What did they care about a dazed man covered in blood anyway? They had other problems.

The wounded and dead lay along the path, and I tried not to pay attention to them, but found it impossible, and my eyes wandered, and I saw more blood and gore and human suffering. Tears came to my eyes, and I struggled to hold them back, but I kept thinking about the man I had killed, and I cried harder, and was still crying when I reached the church.

If the church ever had a door, it was gone now. The pews were gone too, stacked up outside. I stepped across the threshold inside the church. The air was hot and moist, and the wood plank floor was sticky with blood. The dead lay in piles in the corners, stacked up like wood. The wounded were strewn about, lying every which way.

At the pulpit, I saw a man dressed in a Union coat. He stood at the alter in front of a wooden table, his massive back was to me. He hunched over a Confederate wounded soldier. Blood dripped from the teeth of the saw in his hand, and he went to work on the soldier's leg, his hand a blur. The man screamed and thrashed about as two of his friends held him down, telling him everything was going to be okay. As if.

I walked slowly across the slippery wooden floor, picking my way around the moaning and sobbing Confederate wounded. As I approached, MacPherson stopped sawing, and glanced back at me. Blood dusted his round cheeks. "I'll be with ye soon, McCloud," he said, and went back to sawing.

McCloud? I thought, *close, but not quite.* His Scottish brogue was thick, and I noticed that he replaced the letter 'u' with the letter 'e' in his dialogue.

The lower half of the leg dropped onto the floor with a wet splat and blood sprayed from the man's thrashing leg. MacPherson wrapped the end of his leg tightly with a thick piece of cord. The blood slowed to a trickle.

He looked at the sweaty face of his patient. "You'll live." He waved his bloody hand at the patient's friends, and instructed them to take him outside.

"We're guarding you," one of them said.

"Where am I gonna run off too?"

The man thought about it for half a second, turned to his buddy and said, "We'll go for a smoke." And with that said, they picked up the patient and carried the half dazed man from the church.

MacPherson turned and tossed his bloody saw onto a table, and picked up a rag to wipe his meaty hands. He was short, only five foot five at best, with a barrel chest and a belly that ran into it. His legs were bowlegged and thin. The black hairs on his thick forearms were coated in blood. He was completely bald, and his cheeks were round and his eyes glinted cold blue ice.

"Are ye okay, McCloud, cuz ye don't look it."

The shock of what I had done was wearing off, but it was still there, clawing into my brain. My hands still shook, and I felt the need to confess. "I killed a man."

"Lots of killing here today, why should ye be any different?"

"He was innocent."

"We're all innocent when we're born. But it don't stay that way." He stepped up to me, and went to speak, but a cannon blast overhead stopped him. Dust rained down on us, and I coughed a bit. The dust clung to the tears rolling hot down my cheeks. He stared into my eyes. "Get a hold of ye self. Stop yer hands from shaking. Act like a man, McCloud."

He was right. What was done was done. I had to move on, conduct business and get back to the train. If it was still there, which got me thinking: how long had I been at Antietam? Twenty minutes? Thirty? I didn't know. But I did know one thing, I wanted him to call me by my right name. "My name is McCluskie."

He raised a brow. "Ye don't say. I heard different in my vision."

"Your vision is close."

"My hearing is a bit off because of the cannon fire." He smiled at me, his front teeth missing. "My name is Mac MacPherson."

"Not Ian?"

"I had it changed," he told me with a measure of delight. "I hate the name Ian, always have, always will, so I changed it." He winked at me. "Sure got my pink-haired demon off the track."

"She was an angel."

That made him pause. "Ye don't say. Angels can be evil?"

"This one was."

His smile was gone and his ice blue eyes narrowed. "Tell me something McCluskie, I've had no visions of the old witch lately, do I still have to worry about the pink-haired angel?"

I shook my head. "I have solved the problem." I pulled the demon gun from behind my back to show him.

He nodded with admiration. "So ye killed an angel, McCluskie. So ye do have something between yer legs after all."

"Sometimes."

"Ye must have a big pair between yer legs today," he said with certainty. "Ye made it here. Ye made it across the cornfield."

I nodded weakly and whispered, "I'll never eat corn again."

"I never cared much for it me self." He eyed me sharply. "I know a bit about ye."

"You didn't even know my name!"

He chuckled. "Do you have a bit of Scotchman in ye? Cuz ye have the wit of a Scotchman."

"No wit today," I managed. "I'm having a bad morning."

He grinned. "I thought you were gonna say bad life."

"...you didn't let me finish."

He leaned in closer, his eye almost asking the question, "Now tell me something, what it's like to be the Devil's dog?"

I motioned about the church at the dead and wounded, and at the pile of severed limbs oozing blood at the pulpit. "As you can see, it isn't much fun."

His grin was back, laced with a dusting of Confederate blood, and he chuckled a bit. "Oh, that's funny, I'd like to have a wee nip of the creature with ye."

"Creature?"

"Do you ever drink the hard stuff? I've only seen ye drinking beer in my visions."

"Right now I would down pretty much a bottle of anything you've got, and thanks for clearing up what 'creature' meant. If I make it home, I am gonna have to refer to the Devil's Cognac as that. That'll get a laugh out of him for sure."

"I'm glad you find me amusing McCluskie."

"I think the Devil will too."

He lifted his chin. "So, the tablet has come into play in yer time period, and ye has come for the other half of it"

"That's correct, sir."

He slipped off his coat and tossed it on the wooden table next to his saw. Wet patches stained the underarms of his white shirt and he lowered his suspenders, dropping his trousers to his knees, showing me his white boxer shorts stained with blood. "What do ye think of my tattoo, McCluskie?"

Tattooed on his hairy left thigh from the top of his groin down to his knee was the other half of the tablet.

"I like your tattoo. My compliments to the artist." I stepped closer to him and glared into his eyes. "Looks like your leg cutting days are over, cuz you're coming with me back to the 21st century."

"I saw it different in my vision," he said. "Don't ye have a funny looking camera?"

"I forgot about it. Good thing you're a prophet." With bloody, sticky fingers, I pulled the phone from my pocket, and discovered it had been struck dead center by a bullet. The face was shattered, and it wouldn't turn on. I held up the shattered phone. "Your vision is wrong."

He shook his head. "I saw ye take it out, and I knew it was a camera, and then ye put in yer pocket, like yer doing now. That's what I saw, and that's what happened."

I thought about it. "You got me there. But my fancy camera has been shot. No picture means you have to come with me."

"I saw it different in my vision."

"Oh yeah? What happens now?"

"It's time for ye to take out your angel killing gun."

(4)

I wrapped my sticky fingers around the handgrip of the gun, and as I did, I looked toward the door. A brief jolt of fear shot through me, but only brief, for I knew, knew what would be standing there.

The Hangman stepped into the church and smiled at me.

MacPherson's pants were still down around his knees, and he was too busy staring at the Hangman to notice it. I stepped in front of him, blocking the Hangman's view, all the while wondering—what kind of vision do these things have?

Before I could decide, I levelled the demon gun and fired off a round. The damn thing was fast, and saw the round coming, and vanished a scant instant before the round got there. With nothing to hit, the round went out the open door, and before it struck anything, MacPherson was beside me, talking in my ear. "The evil thing has seen me. It's seen the tattoo."

"Yeah, I know. Get your pants up. Cuz we are leaving." As MacPherson pulled up his suspenders, the demon round exploded. I couldn't say what it hit, but the explosion shook the church. It sure got the Confederates attention. Angry voices filled the air as the last of the explosion died out.

Green smoke poured from the gun, and MacPherson waved it away, complaining bitterly, and looked over his instrument table. He dug through the instruments, knocking a few onto the floor, and picked up a long, thin bladed knife.

"This will do perfect," he said, admiring the weapon. He motioned with his head toward the backdoor. "C'mon McCluskie, the good Lord wants us to run."

"I agree with the good Lord."

At the doorway, a Confederate officer lay close by, his eyes shut. Maybe he was dead, who knew? If he was, MacPherson had no trouble robbing from the dead, for he pulled away the revolver from the man's holster, and headed for the door.

We stepped out into the sunlight. A field of long, wild grass stretched out to a river; beyond that, I could see a few structures of Sharpsburg through the trees. MacPherson grabbed my arm and led me into the field.

"Your only chance is Sharpsburg," he said. "Get mixed up with the crowd."

"Mixed up in the crowd?" I motioned at myself. "That's gonna be hard to do covered in blood. Besides, I got a train to catch. And you're coming with me."

"I saw it different in my vision."

"You know something sir, I think your visions blow. Maybe you don't drink enough of the creature. No matter, I need that tattoo, and I'm not leaving without it."

"I'll get ye the tattoo, McCluskie, don't worry about that."

"Oh yeah? How?"

He stayed silent and ran ahead, and soon, we reached the river. The water level was low, and we could have easily crossed it in seconds, but he held up, and sat down on the bank, looking back at the church.

"They're rounding up some boys to come get me—come get us." He looked me in the eye. "So I'll have to make it quick."

He threw his suspenders off his shoulders and pulled down his pants. With his white legs exposed, he took out the knife, and made an incision at the top of the tattoo.

"Hope ye don't mind a bit of blood, McCluskie."

"Holy fuck," was about the only thing I could think of at the time to say, and I must of said it ten times in a row.

He cut away at the flesh, blood shot everywhere and dripped down his leg. I watched in horror as he carved a good quarter inch deep of flesh from his thigh.

"You are the toughest guy I have ever met," I whispered in awe.

"Keep an eye on things, will ye, McCluskie?"

I looked across the field. A group of soldiers, twenty or thirty anyway, stood by the backdoor of the church. Their gray uniforms were clean. They were fresh to the battle, and coming for us.

"Well, McCluskie?"

"We haven't got much time."

"Can ye be a bit more precise? I hit some bone, and I have to stop for a moment."

"They're gathering at the church and—holy fuck, are you okay?"

"I'm cutting off part of me leg McCluskie, do I really need to answer that."

"Yeah, I always ask stupid shit, ask the Devil, and uh…you might wanna pick up the pace a bit, because they are starting toward us."

He sighed wearily, and I looked away as he continued to cut into his flesh.

A few seconds later he breathlessly asked, "How are we doing?"

"I don't know how you're doing," I returned sharply, "but they are less than a hundred yards away."

"Okay, don't panic, I'm almost done."

He was right, too, for a moment later, he tugged away at the flesh on his knee, and the piece tore loose. It was at least a foot long, and rolling at the edges, the text of the tablet all crinkled and hard to read. It dripped blood. As for his thigh? It was hacked and bloody with raw white muscle exposed.

"My God…" was all I could say.

He rolled up his flesh, and handed it to me. "Put in ye pocket, and run."

I took the squishy rolled up flesh, my hands dripping now with more blood, and stuffed it down next to my shattered cell phone.

He jerked his head toward the town of Sharpsburg. "Only one way to run. Now go."

"You are the toughest man I have ever met—and the bravest."

"I feel the same way when I look at ye, McCluskie. Now run."

I took off running.

The Confederates charged across the field, and MacPherson levelled the stolen pistol and fired.

I heard him shoot off all six rounds, and as I crossed the stream, I looked back in time to see the Confederates run him through with bayonets. He rolled down the embankment, and the Confederates levelled their rifles at me.

I started running again, but I knew it was over. I waited for the impact of bullets, but I never felt a thing, and my world went black.

The Time Machine

The dream gripping his sleep exploded into blackness. His eyes flew open in time to watch a picture of Abe Lincoln fall off the wall. The frame splintered, the glass cracked and the picture of a very distinguished looking president ripped apart; not that Rex saw it, he was too busying watching the bookshelves fall over. Every tome the scientist owned spilled onto the floor with thunderous impact. It was a tidal wave of textbooks and novels. Dishes shattered in the kitchen, windows cracked, and the front door swung open, swaying in the mid-afternoon August breeze.

The house stopped shaking. Smoke poured up from the cellar. Rex sat up in the armchair, panting heavily from all the excitement, thinking, *Holy shit, what's going on?*

He blinked 'sleep' from his eyes, farted out loudly, and climbed off the armchair, careful of his 'manhood' on the decent. After navigating around and over the spilled books, he looked down the cellar stairs at the tendrils of gray smoke rising into the house. *Awe fuck, what has that crazy 'smart man' done now?*

He shook drool from his jowls and cried out, "Rodger! Are you okay?"

No response came, and after a few moments of indecision laden with grumbled swear words, Rex started down the stairs, cursing now at the distance between the risers. Why was he so short? Why couldn't he walk upright? Why was he trapped in a bulldog's body? He reached the bottom, finally. The jump off the last stair was short, and he was surprised to find the green linoleum coated floor warm. He suddenly needed to pee, but held it. "Rodger!"

Thanks to a wooden box covered with a shiny film in the yard harnessing the sun's energy, the house had 'current' and the cellar was well lit with glass tubes running across the ceiling vibrating light. Rex saw the scientist emerge from the smoke, waving his hand in front of his face. He coughed hard and wandered toward the stairs and Rex.

"What have you done now?"

The scientist took off his glasses. He was a tall man, six-foot-three, and thin, beanpole thin. His head, at least in Rex's opinion, seemed larger than most people's heads; and though only in his thirties, he looked to be seventy, his jowly face heavily lined. His white hair, yellowish at the ends, hung down past the shoulders of his white lab coat. He coughed, his blue eyes watering from the smoke. "Hi Rex."

The bulldog nodded politely, shook slaver from his jowls and, once again, repeated his question, this time throwing in an expletive, "What the fuck have you done?"

"I don't like it when you curse."

"I don't like it when you blow up the house."

"I had an accident."

"No kidding," the dog said bluntly and motioned up the stairs with his head. "Abe Lincoln doesn't look so good anymore, and you have five thousand books scattered over your living room." Then the dog noted, "I haven't been in the kitchen, but what happened in there didn't sound so good." He sat up and rested his front paws on his hunches. "So? What did you do?"

"I had a bit of a miscalculation."

"So it seems." The smoke had cleared enough for Rex to see what had been on fire. "It looks like your upright coffin with windows is smoking." He cocked his brow at the scientist. "What is that thing?"

Rodger cleared his throat. "It's a time machine." His words hung in the air like a bad joke, and he twitched a bit and asked, "Do you know what that is?"

"Yes I do, crazy 'smart man'," the dog said, his voice edging towards arrogance. "You taught me how to read, remember? So yes, I have read H. G. Wells' novel, so I do know what a time machine is and—are you out of what's left of you mind?"

Rodger twitched, his cheeks distraught. "You have a problem with this?"

The dog regarded him, dribble seeping off his jowls. "As a matter a fact, I do. See, when Wells is writing about the wild concept of time travel, it's fiction." The dog motioned with his head toward the upright coffin. "What's smoking in the corner over there isn't fiction."

"The fire is out now," Rodger said as though that explained everything. "Reentry from the Timeline produced incredible energy. I'll be ready for it next time."

Rex rolled his eyes and snorted out: "Next time." He scrutinized the scientist with growing trepidation. "Should you really be doing what you're doing? Should you really be messing with Time?"

"I'm not messing with Time, I'm only recording it." Rodger directed Rex toward the time machine, waving away the last of the smoke. "I installed my moving picture camera inside the machine." He gestured proudly at it. "What do you think?"

"Why did you build it like an upright coffin? That's not how Wells described the time machine."

"As you said, Wells' novel is fiction." Rodger pointed at his invention. "I don't need anything elaborate. So I improvised."

"Please tell me you didn't dig someone up to build this."

"Well…"

"Awe for the love of God." Rex blinked in astonishment. "What did you do with the body?"

"There was no body, only rocks." His shoulders and face twitched. "They never found poor Jeremiah."

"Poor Jeremiah?" The dog laughed. "Jeremiah ran off to Mexico with a stripper. Everyone knows that."

"Not his family," Rodger admitted, his grin rising up to expose his white dentures. "So I couldn't let the good wood go to waste."

"There's a joke in there somewhere," the dog muttered with a drool-laden grin, and gave his scrotum a quick lick.

Rodger looked away. "I wish you wouldn't do that."

"I wish you wouldn't build time machines."

"Trust me Rex, I'm doing nothing unethical here." He opened the door on the time machine, reached inside, and drew out a small rectangular box attached with a small glass funnel.

The dog stretched up to look inside the machine. "I see there're lots of blinking buttons and wires."

"That's what makes it 'go'."

"You don't need to talk down to me."

"I'm simply stating the obvious." He closed the door on the machine. "Even I'm not sure exactly how it works." He held up the camera. "Everything recorded on this might be blank."

"Somehow I doubt that. You're too crazy smart to fail." He shook spit from his jowls and waved his paw at the camera. "Why don't you patent the moving picture camera and make a million dollars?"

"It's already been done." He twitched and held up the device in his hand. "This camera is, well, not to brag—"

"Oh please," the dog interrupted. "You brag all the time. I invented this, and I invented that, and I invented—"

"Stating the obvious is not bragging," Rodger pointed out. "The camera in my hand is probably a hundred years more advanced then what is currently on the market." Before the dog could comment, he went on with, "Color hasn't been invented yet, but I have it."

"Everything looks black and white to me," the dog informed, before throwing in, "I do, however, dream in color."

"That's nice Rex."

"Don't blow this off like mere dust," he complained. "I need to talk to you about this, about my dreams."

Rodger leaned down, patted the dog on the head, and said, "We'll talk about it." The dog rolled his eyes. The scientist ignored the gesture and crossed the room to his work benches. He pushed aside jars of chemicals and a rack of laboratory glass tubes so he could get to a small wooden box nestled against the wall. With the lid raised, he placed the camera inside, carefully clicking it onto a metal stand. He looked at Rex. "It will take a few minutes to develop."

"That long?" Rex rolled out his watery lips. "You would figure a smart guy like you would make development of film instant."

'I'm not using film." He shook his head, strains of white hairs falling to the floor. "I've developed a sponge like substance that imprints images." He twitched. "It's very revolutionary."

"Stop patting yourself on the back," the dog said, "and again, why didn't you make your sponge like substance instant."

"Oh, don't be like that Rex. Anticipation is good for the soul."

"One year for you counts as seven years for me, so I have one seventh the time you do. So I don't like to wait too long."

"It won't take long. Besides, it'll be fun. Once the images are ready for playback, I'll project them on the wall." He cocked a wild, out-of-control white eyebrow at the dog. "Maybe we'll be able to figure out what year the machine traveled to."

"You don't know the year?"

The scientist pointed at the machine. "See the laundry cord? Well, I hooked it up to control the 'years' the machine will travel to."

"A cord makes it work?"

His shoulders and face twitched again. "It was all I had."

The dog shook his head with an exasperated huff. "You're too smart to understand. You're too smart to realize that even though you can do it, you shouldn't."

Rodger twitched. "Right now I regret putting vocal cords in my dog."

"Oh, here it is, right in front of your smoking time machine—going after your pet. And why do I sound like a woman?"

"Why do you think you sound like a woman?"

"Because I talk to our neighbors the McCluskies and I sound a whole lot more like her than him. And if you say anything about my hearing being off because I'm a dog, I'll bite your leg. Because you know my hearing is far more acute than any human's."

"I don't want to talk about it."

"You brought it up Mr. Crazy smart man. Or maybe I should call you Dr. Frankenstein. Yes, I read that one too. What the hell did you do to me anyway? I've read your books on biology. A dog isn't suppose to be this smart."

"I'm not sure why you're as smart as you are," he confessed, a finger to his chin in thought. "When I put the vocal cords in you, I hoped for parrot type responses. But you're right. You are as smart as anyone I've ever met."

"Your candor is most refreshing," the dog said with a smirk. "And I have to talk to you about my dreams."

"Can we do this some other time? I'm sure development will be completed soon." Rodger pointed at a small button on the top of the box. "It will flash green when it's ready."

"I don't see colors." Then he added, "Well, in my dreams."

The scientist ignored the comment and laid his hands atop a brass tube on his workbench. "Would you like me to play a song?"

The dog shook his head. "It hurts my ears. And what the hell is that thing called?"

"A saxophone."

The dog nodded shrewdly. "You have a book on the orchestra." He walked over, stretched up on his hindlegs, and sniffed the instrument. "So that's what it looks like."

"I made it myself," Rodger put in proudly. "And it plays beautifully."

"It hurts my ears," the dog complained curtly, and then pointed out, "It's a minor instrument in the orchestra. So why did you make it?"

"The entire universe is a vibration, and playing this instrument allows me to produce my own vibration." He twitched. "I love blowing into it, bending the notes out, draining them of their fullest, shaking them loose, and then producing fresh ones."

The dog chuckled and asked, "You're taking about the sax, right? Not a woman?" He laughed some more and added, "Most of the notes hurt my ears."

"I'm sorry it hurts your ears. I find the music most soothing."

"Soothing?" He gazed at the scientist in mock wonder. "You do realize you're crazy, right? Like you're not normal in the head."

"I'm completely sane, Rex."

"You built a time machine," he reminded him, "And you also made a second-tier instrument to play soothing music on, an instrument you christened—and I can't believe you did— *The Devil's Breath.*"

"That was odd," Rodger admitted with a touch of mysticism touching his thin lips. "It was the day the McCluskies moved in, and the words '*The Devil's Breath*' kept repeating in my head. So I christened and engraved those words on it."

"I don't like the damn thing, it gives me the creeps," Rex returned. "Just like your moving scarecrow."

"It's called a robot," Rodger informed. "At least that's what I'm calling it. I hope that one day it will do the jobs of men." He grinned proudly, and since the topic had been raised, he took the opportunity to brag about his latest invention, "I'm also working on something called artificial intelligence. I plan to install it in the robot's head. This way it will be smarter than most men."

His words 'smarter than men' scared the dog, and the implication of such a thing ground into his brain like the heel of a boot. Rex regarded his owner with aloof wonder. "Do you think that's a good idea? On your test run, your robot ran over my paw."

"I'm sorry about your paw. I'm still working out the bugs."

"While you're working out the bugs you're building time machines," the dog threw in with a laugh. "Where is your moving scarecrow anyway?"

"In the back yard hooked up to the sun generator."

"Why don't you make a sun generator for the McCluskies so they can have 'current' in their house too?"

"I'm too busy," he said briskly, and then with a slight scoff, he added, "This technology is so rudimentary the McCluskies will be able to buy one in a few years."

"You think?"

Rodger motioned upwards. "Everyone can see the sun." He shook his head in bewilderment. "I'm surprised I had to invent it."

Rex thought about it. "Yeah, you do make a point." He farted, excused himself, and threw in, "How much longer until we see history?"

"It will only be a minute, it will give us a chance to talk about the McCluskies."

"I'd rather talk about my dreams, but okay—what about them?"

Rodger twitched and asked, "Should you really be talking to them?"

"They're my friends."

"You're a dog," he pointed out. "I can't imagine what they thought when you started talking to them."

Rex thought about that moment, a smile growing on his drool-laden lips. "They were a bit taken back, especially the Mrs." He laughed. "Her mouth dropped open so wide her chin nearly touched her tits."

"Breasts," he put in. "They're called breasts."

"I don't care what you call them—I sure like them," the dog noted with pleasure and looked up at the scientist. "Why don't you have a Mrs.?"

"I don't need a Mrs.," he returned, and twitched strongly. "I have you."

"You know what I mean."

Rodger twitched again, and his cheeks tinted with a fine hue of red embarrassment. He looked away, and the dog felt bad inside for asking such a question. "You know Rex, strangely enough, I have never needed those pleasures." He looked down in shame. "I believe it's because of my superior intelligence."

Rex observed the scientist with a widening grin. "I'm not going to call you out on the bragging this time because I agree. You must be the smartest man in the world."

"Maybe not the world."

"Oh fuck please, no one is smarter than you—and what is wrong with the McCluskies? They're fine people."

He twitched, and looked away. "They're heavy drinkers."

"So? What do you expect? She's Irish and he's Scottish. I'm surprised they're not drunk around the clock."

The scientist nodded, and hand combed back his long white hair. "Did they enjoy the bottle of wine I sent over with you?"

"I don't know why you didn't come," Rex said with a hint of sorrow. "They acted disappointed."

He shook his head and sadly admitted, "I feel awkward around people."

The dog understood and leaned against the scientist's leg. "It's okay crazy 'smart man', I sure love you." He sat in front of Rodger and said, "Ian and I enjoyed the wine; the Mrs. wasn't drinking because she is with 'child'."

"Oh really," the scientist said, nodding with sudden inspiration. "I must make a baby crib for them."

"Build them a sun generator," the dog said, rolling his eyes, and then turned serious, staring into the scientist's eyes. "I have to talk to you about their baby."

"You've read my books on biology," he said whimsically, adding, "Do you need me to explain procreation?"

The dog frowned hard and grumbled, "I oughta bite you. Remember, I was the one that mentioned the 'waste of good wood' joke."

"You're very funny Rex," the scientist said with an eye roll. "Now, what's the problem with McCluskies' baby?"

"It's gonna be a boy," Rex said flatly. "A boy named David."

"How do you know that?"

"Because I dreamed of him," he said hauntingly. "Remember? I've been wanting to talk to you about it."

Rodger's cheeks paled and a "Dear God" seeped from his mouth. He knelt down, patting his dog's head. "You've dreamt about this unborn child?"

The dog nodded, spraying Rodger's hand with slaver. "David McCluskie is in his late thirties, and he's on the run with some school teacher named Kelly." He cocked a brow at the scientist. "Have you ever heard of the Nazis?"

He shook his head in puzzled wonder. "No. They sound evil."

"These guys are," he said. "The Nazis shot up the Redemption Inn trying to kill David McCluskie and his school teacher."

The scientist leaned forward. "You saw all this?"

"It was as though I was there in the room." He shook his head at the clarity of the images. "I'll say one thing for the McCluskies's unborn kid, he's damn smart. Not smart like you, he's smart in a different way, cunning, self assured, and full of common sense. He outwitted these gun-totting killing Nazis."

"This is remarkable," Rodger admitted, his eyes glinting utter disbelief. "What happened?"

"It was weird, McCluskie was operating a Buick."

The scientist blinked. "What's a Buick?"

"It's a carriage like you've got in the barn, but you don't need Annabelle to pull it. It goes on it's own, and you use a wheel to steer it."

"You're describing an automobile. I've seen them on display at the 1897 Expo in Copenhagen."

"Well McCluskie sure knows how to operate the Buick. Even with the Nazis shooting at him and Kelly yapping in his ear, he managed to get to the zoo." The dog paused, a quizzical brow rising. "By the way, where is Cincinnati?"

"Oh dear God," Rodger gasped. "It's in Ohio, and they have a zoo."

"In the 1930's they have a smart baboon, cuz McCluskie and Kelly watch the show, and then the Nazis arrived." The dog laughed. "It was an unhappy place for them cuz McCluskie"—and he chuckled—"with the school teacher screaming in his ear the whole time, let the lions out of their cages."

"Did they…"

"Eat the Nazis?" the dog finished for him, and shrugged. "As soon as McCluskie opened the cage, the dream fell away, and they were suddenly in this guy's office. He was weird looking, even weirder looking than you, and McCluskie kept calling him an 'egghead'. Whatever that means. Oh, and Kelly didn't have any shoes on." He thought about it. "She had nice feet."

"Remarkable."

He stepped forward a bit, his snout only six inches away from Rodger's noise. "You think that's remarkable, let me share another dream with you. I've dreamt about David McCluskie's grandson, Jacob."

"You've dreamt of an unborn child's grandson?" the scientist yelped, his cheeks growing crimson with alarm.

The dog smiled. "I bet you never thought you'd utter that sentence."

"This isn't funny."

"It is a little creepy I will say that."

"The grandson—"

"Yeah, Jacob McCluskie," the dog cut in. "I saw this McCluskie drinking beer with the Devil. And no, the Devil doesn't have horns and a pitch fork, he was well dressed, and a good looking man."

"It's only a dream," Rodger cautioned, thinking, *Please be a dream.*

"I don't think so," the dog returned with authority. "How many dreams do you have that come with dates?"

"Excuse me. You know the time this happened?"

"Will happen," the dog corrected. "Our neighbor's great grandson will be born July 7th, 1977." The dog smiled. "Less than 77 years from now. Lots of sevens don't you think? And get this, in the year 2015, he angers the Devil for letting some creature out of Hell."

"You're making this up."

"I wish," the dog said. "The Devil is so upset, he breaks McCluskie's table, and then, a second later, he flicks his hand, and it's brand new."

"Is this McCluskie evil?" Rodger asked, his eyes stained with nightmarish questions.

The dog shook his head. "That's the weird thing about it. McCluskie is tethered to the Devil, you know, Lucifer the archangel, but McCluskie is normal, a regular person."

"How can you be normal and friends with the Devil?"

"This guy is."

Rodger stood, shaking his head in disbelief. "He must be evil."

Rex cared little for the tone of Rodger's last sentence. "McCluskie is a Christian, and get this, he has no Cognac, and the Devil has to drink beer, and he bitches about it the whole time."

"You saw all this?"

"In color," the dog informed sharply. "And the next thing I know, they're at the South Pole."

"Antarctica? No one has reached the bottom of the world."

"McCluskie and the Devil are there. Though, to be honest, it didn't look like McCluskie was enjoying the visit. The Devil said he looked as cold as a popsicle. Do you know what that is?"

Rodger twitched. "No, but the word does sound cold." He leaned down. "What happened at the South Pole?"

"The Devil was playing chess with a Horseman named Pestilence," Rex said, "I can't say what happened after that because you blew up the house."

"Pestilence," Rodger breathed. "Revelation."

"Exactly," the dog said. "I have read your King James Bible. And let me tell you, the man at South Pole playing chess against the Devil didn't have a horse, and he sure didn't look too menacing. He looked as cold as McCluskie."

"Remarkable," he wheezed out, his eyes narrowed to menacing slits. "McCluskie must be evil," and he repeated the words to himself in a low cold whisper.

The dog's thoughts froze, and then a train of thought barreled out of the nothingness: *he can change Time and he knows it—he can kill Jacob McCluskie's grandfather before he's even born.*

"You know, this Jacob McCluskie is a lot like Ian, his great grandfather. He cares about people."

"He must be evil," the scientist breathed, and then the machine buzzed. Rodger brightened up. "Wonderful." The green light on the box flashed. "Let's see where the machine went."

*   *   *

Rodger attached the camera to the tripod with hurried enthusiasm. Once done, he flipped a switch on the side of the camera and a bight light shone against the wall. "Is the image big enough?" Before Rex could reply, Rodger moved the tripod back five steps, making the rectangular image about the size of a modern-day flat screen TV. With that done, Rodger walked across the cellar and pushed a button on the wall. The lights blinked out and a baneful darkness fell upon the cellar, the only light coming from the camera.

"Don't step on me."

"You can see better in the dark than I can," Rodger muttered, hovering above the camera. "Now according to the dial, we have three moving pictures, which makes sense because I pulled the cord three times."

"You also blew up the house," the dog noted with a laugh, adding, "Okay, a triple bill. Start the camera."

"Here goes," he said with a gleeful chuckle, his fingers moving across the camera's dial. He pushed a button, the white glow on the wall turned to black—and then to a city street coated in afternoon sun. The crystal clear image of thousands of pedestrians milling about the street in hurried panic reflected off Rodger's lenses, the colors as crisp as seeing it live.

"New York," Rodger whispered. "I've been on that street—Wall Street, but there are more buildings now."

"And the Buick McCluskie was operating looked a lot like those carriages," Rex threw in, his eyes glued to the screen. "More buildings and Buicks means your crazy upright coffin has gone into the future—30 years or more."

Rodger managed only a weak nod before the images of the pedestrian lined street turned—and sun glinted off brass. And then—an engraving, clear as day, shone on the wall: *Redemption Iowa, 1900, The Devil's Breath.*

"Holy fuck," the dog yelped. "That's your saxophone."

"It's in the future."

Fingers danced on the keys, and Rex asked, "Can't you make this thing do sound?"

"I never thought about it." And then he added, "It would be quite simple."

"Yeah, yeah crazy 'smart man' who cares? It's too late now, and who's playing? Those fingers belong to a lady."

"A woman has my saxophone," he breathed out in despair.

"I like her fingers," Rex remarked. "They're as nice as Kelly's feet."

Before Rodger could utter a sound, a boy appeared on the screen, and he carried newspapers. In his hand, he held out a paper for everyone to see. His mouth moved, but neither of them could read lips. And then the paper came into view.

"What's a stock market and why did it crash?"

"The date," Rodger said in a hush. "1929, October 29th. Can you see it?"

"Yeah I see it," the dog shot back. "29 years into the future, and what's a stock market?"

The screen turned to whiteness. The first pull on the cord was complete.

"This is remarkable," Rodger said, hovering over the camera. "The stock market crashes in 29 years."

"I'd be more shocked if I knew what the stock market was," the dog grumbled peevishly.

Rodger peered down, his white hair looking ghostly in the light thrown from the camera. "The stock market crashing would mean a hoarding of money." He thought about it for a moment. "Interest rates would spike wildly, and that alone would knock over enough dominos to throw our country into an economic depression."

"And while that's all going on, your horn over there was playing a merry tune we couldn't hear."

"I'll correct the sound thing soon," he said with confidence, shaking his head at his blunder. His eyes squinted as he gazed at the dog. "A woman? Who is she?"

The dog shrugged. "I like her fingers."

"Yes, you've mentioned it before."

"Don't get testy," the dog snapped, and leaned down to give his scrotum a quick lick. "Okay, so what's up next?"

The scientist frowned with disapproval. "Do you have to do that? Do you have to lick your private area? I find it most offensive."

"Offensive!" the dog said with a sharp bark. "If you could lick your balls, you'd be doing it all the time, and don't tell me you wouldn't be."

Rodger twitched. "Do you lick your balls in front of the McCluskies?"

"Sometimes, if the need arises, which it just did." He shook his head, the slaver spraying out at his paws. "I had a twinge that needed to be satisfied, so I satisfied it."

"I'm so embarrassed," he disclosed, adding, "What do the McCluskies say?"

"Ian isn't bothered by it in the least," he replied with contentment, thinking of his friend. "Mind you, the Mrs. looks away."

The scientist bowed his head in shame. "I can't imagine what she must think?"

"She doesn't care. I bet Ian scratches his balls all the time. She's more interested to know why I sound like a woman."

Rodger twitched. "I don't want to talk about it."

"I wanna talk about it Dr. Frankenstein."

A distraught look creased his cheeks. "Would you rather see what's on the second cord pull?"

"Whose vocal cords do I have?" the dog demanded.

Rodger twitched, looked away, and a word tumbled from his troubled lips, "Mabel."

"Who's Mabel?"

He looked down at his dog. "She lived across the street. A big, hearty woman with a dozen kids." He smiled at the memory. "She could holler so loud for her young'ins it would rattle the window panes."

"I can bark pretty loud," Rex conceded, and asked the brewing question, "What happened to her?"

"She went to the outhouse to handle her morning 'business', and, well, the outhouse needed fixing."

"For the love of God, please tell me no."

"It all fell in," he informed, thinking sadly of the event. "The entire structure. There was only a hole left, and deep, and filled with a hundred years of bodily waste. The smell made my eyes water."

The dog snorted. "I may puke."

"It took three days to find her," he went on. "I thought she looked quite good considering her 'ordeal'. And Rex"—he nodded shrewdly at the dog—"she still clung to the morning edition of **The Redemption Reader**."

"It is a fine read," the dog noted. "And in the winter when it's too cold to go outside, I love taking a shit on it." He snorted harshly and added, "I can't believe you used her vocal cords after such a horrific accident."

"Her vocal cords were pristine, and I washed them before I installed them in you."

"Is that the word you wanna use: 'installed'? According to your biology books you should have said 'implanted'."

"Pardon me," the scientist said with cynicism. "You're obviously far more intelligent than I am."

"Fuck off," the dog grumbled, and then, after snorting out drool, added, "Okay crazy smart man, let's see what's up next."

"If I recall, I pulled the cord not as hard, so if we jump ahead in Time, like I suspect, I estimate the images will be from 1937 or 38."

"I hope your saxophone isn't there."

Rodger pushed the button. The white glow turned to blackness—and then to broken clouds with the sun low in the sky.

"Seven o'clock at night I suspect."

"I won't call you out on it—and holy shit, what is that thing?"

A huge silver gray cucumber floated among the broken clouds and Rodger gasped. "It's a zeppelin," he said in awe. "It was just patented. A floating machine filled with hydrogen, used to transport people and cargo."

"Like a hot air balloon?"

"You've read Verne's novels," the scientist said quietly. "And yes, the technology is similar."

"It looks like a flying penis to me," the dog observed, adding, "What's it say on the side? I can't make it out…H..I.."

"Hindenburg, I think," Rodger replied, and then dooly noted, "German."

"German?" Rex frowned, slaver drooling over his jowls. "I think the Nazis that go after McCluskie and the school teacher with the nice feet are German." Rodger made no comment, his focus on the image of the Hindenburg, and Rex filled the silence with, "At least we haven't seen your…awe shit."

With the Hindenburg flying above, the late day sun shone on the tarnished brass rim of a saxophone.

"*The Devil's Breath*," Rodger gasped, as he watched female fingers dance on saxophone's keys. "The sax player is back, and she's on the Hindenburg's landing spot."

Her fingers moved with professional grace up and down the saxophone's body, massaging the keys, stroking them, playing a song neither of them could hear.

"We can't see her," Rodger complained.

Rex wanted to comment on her fingers again but, erring on the side of caution, he went with the next thought in line, a dark thought. "I'm worried about the Hindenburg."

"You don't have to be," he explained patiently. "A zeppelin is a safe mode of transportation."

"Safe or not, your horn is blowing evil."

"We don't know that," Rodger shot back with annoyance. "It's the woman I'm interested in."

"It's the first woman you've been interested in since I've known you," he said with a chuckle. "Awe, don't be like that, you know I love you." Rex rubbed up against Rodger's leg and sat next to him, watching the screen.

Her fingers stopped, and rested on the instrument, and now the Hindenburg filled the screen, descending toward the runway.

"See Rex, the zeppelin is fine." He quickly glanced down at the dog. "I suspect someone of great importance will step off the Hindenburg."

"Maybe it's you," the dog laughed.

"We're you this funny when you had dinner with the McCluskies?"

"Even funnier after Ian and I downed the bottle of wine," the dog confessed with a chuckle, his eyes to the screen. "By the way, wine makes me lick my balls more."

Rodger sighed darkly, his focus on the screen, and he told his dog what he thought, "By the position of the sun, I suspect it is late April or early May, and I still stand by my prediction. It is 1937."

"I stand by my prediction as well: the flying penis is in trouble."

"Look," the scientist flung back with a wave of his hand. "Does it look like it's in trouble?" As the question rolled off his tongue, a thin, evil mountain range of flames spread out across the Hindenburg's back—and suddenly a fireball filled the screen.

Rodger choked up, "Oh dear God", and watched in horror as orange and red fiery teeth chewed the Hindenburg into a crumpled skeleton. Black smoke stained the sky and the collapsed remains of the zeppelin fell like a wounded duck to the tarmac, shattering into an intense yellow inferno on impact.

The screen turned to white. The second pull on the cord was complete.

After a few moments of silence, Rodger sighed and looked down at his dog. "Do you have a comment?"

"What's there to comment on?" he returned with scorn, angry at what he had witnessed. "What I saw is gonna give me damn nightmares."

"It was disturbing," Rodger admitted quietly, and he twitched, and wanting to feel better said, "Some people got out. You saw that."

"If I were them, I'd ask for my money back," Rex replied smartly. "Oh, can you refresh my memory on what you said earlier about a zeppelin being a safe mode of transportation?"

"Hydrogen is highly inflammable."

"Can't you just say flammable? Do you have to throw in the 'in'?"

"Pardon me Rex," the scientist snidely shot back. "I thought I was engaged in a conversation with my dog, not a Rhodes Scholar."

Rex regarded the scientist with even temperance, and soon admitted, "I hate it when you're like this. I hate it when you're agitated."

"I'm not agitated. I'm upset about what I saw."

"What we saw," the dog corrected him, adding, "When do you wanna talk about your fucking saxophone?"

"I've been thinking about that."

"I've been thinking about it too, and I've also been thinking about how one of us should take an axe to it."

"It's not evil."

The dog scoffed. "Tell the people on the Hindenburg that."

"I have a theory," he began, crouching down to be closer to his dog. "I believe the saxophone is a catalyst for the time machine. Its proximity to the machine is why it is in the images. Next time I send out the machine, I will put *The Devil's Breath* in the barn."

"The bottom of the lake would be better."

He straightened up, his knees creaking, and closely examined the camera's dial. "Are you ready to see the third cord pull?"

"Yeah, sure, let's continue our macabre jaunt through Time."

"Let's think positively," the scientist said, looking down at the camera dial. "Perhaps this stop in Time will be better."

The dog cocked a brow at him. "Perhaps not."

Rodger pushed the button, and the screen turned to black, and then to an early morning gloom. A huge plane filled the screen, idling on the tarmac, spot lights gleaming off its silver hull, and all Rodger could say was, "A zeppelin with wings, a sky-craft."

"Okay, so it's a flying Buick. I get it. What I'm wondering is, do you get the part about how bad this is gonna end up?"

"You may be right Rex," the scientist admitted with mournful gloom.

"I hope the guy who owns the flying Buick is heavily insured."

"It looks like an army sky-craft. And look at the 82 on the tail. Do you think that's the year?"

"How hard did you pull the cord?"

Rodger thought about it. "Not that hard." He twitched with indecision. "If I had to predict, I would have said the images would be from 1945, maybe 46."

"Who knows? It's your laundry cord."

The plane taxied onto the runway, and took off in the direction of the rising sun, it banked and turned toward the darkness, the sun licking at its tail.

"Hey, do you see the words by the things' head?" the dog asked, continuing with, "Enola Gay. Is that what the flying Buick is called?"

Before Rodger could speak, the view faded, and changed to inside the craft. Men hurried about, and Rodger commented, "They're wearing uniforms. A military craft."

"It's headed for disaster," Rex snorted, and his next thought got washed away in what he saw. "Awe fuck—your horn is back."

In the belly of the craft, above a dark gray bomb with the words *little boy* scratched into its paint, *The Devil's Breath* played a song neither of them could hear. The woman's fingers danced slowly on the keys, and then the view faded, and changed to an exterior view of the Enola Gay now awash in bright early morning sunshine.

"What do you think?" Rex asked. "That bomb *little boy* is gonna blow up the flying Buick?"

"It would make sense," he said, and went to continue but the images on the wall stopped him.

Little boy dropped from the ship's belly and plunged downward through the broken clouds toward a city; and then, high above a bridge, the bomb detonated with flashbulb brightness, stinging their eyes. The dog cursed, Rodger gasped, and a huge mushroom cloud filled the wall…and then only whiteness.

The third pull on the cord was complete.

With a white image staining his eyesight, Rodger fumbled with the camera's dial. After an exasperated curse, he located the right button and turned off the camera. The cellar fell into darkness. "That was horrifying."

"Thanks for stating the obvious," the dog returned snidely. "What the fuck was that little boy? I can still see the blast in my eyes."

"It was a chemical reaction," the scientist noted. "Similar to what our sun does." He paused for a moment and added, "It would be like taking a piece of the sun and putting it down inside that city."

"So let me get this straight," the dog said, "your species can't invent the sun generator, but your kind can invent something from the sun that will kill people."

"It seems so Rex."

"What the fuck is wrong with people?" Then the dog asked another question, "Hey crazy smart man, what do you think of your time machine now?"

*   *   *

August turned into September; the leaves changed colors; and Rodger slowly turned mad.

Rex muttered, his eyelids flickering wildly as his dream of Jacob McCluskie and a tattooed woman rampaged through his head. Then, a heavy pressure on his leg made the dream dim. A hand shook him, and the remains of the dream evaporated. He opened his eyes with alarm. The scientist stood above him.

Rodger wore a tan coat and denim pants. The lenses of his glasses glistened in the early morning light slanting in through the window and his white hair, thinning and falling out in clumps at an alarming rate now, was neatly brushed back. A razor had recently crossed his deeply lined cheeks, and two nicks on his chin still dribbled blood. He nodded politely at his dog and adjusted his glasses. "You were muttering, Rex."

"I like to mutter in my sleep," the dog returned with angry scorn, pained with annoyance because his dream was interrupted. "I'm a bulldog. What did you expect?"

Rodger's eyes narrowed with sneaky suspicion. "We're you dreaming of Jacob McCluskie?"

At the time Rodger woke him, Rex's vivid dreams had been of McCluskie and a bald woman completely covered with tattoos. They held hands as they ran through a vast dark environment shrouded in swirling mist. The dog had read Rodger's beat-up copy of Dante's *Divine Comedy*, and knew they were in *inferno*—Hell. Something chased them. McCluskie kept firing at it, his pistol smoking green, and Rex kept muttering, yelling at him to run; and then the dream shattered and Rodger was shaking Rex awake.

"Well?" A malicious glint magnified behind his clean glasses. "We're you dreaming of that evil spawn?"

Rex sat up in the armchair, his mood angry over the hard questions, and he stared the scientist in the eye. He opened his mouth, yet his vast intelligence made him hesitate. *Would Rodger snap over what I say?* As the question lingered in place, the 'dog' in him, fueled by a male ego, nullified any potential peril—he didn't care.

"Was that evil spawn in your head?"

"Not that it's any of your business—you crazy fuck!—but no." He grinned with anger. "I was dreaming of Jeremiah and his stripper."

Rodger twitched, and an ugly look swept across his face. "Somehow I doubt that." For half a second, Rex feared the scientist would attack him; but then, out of nowhere, Rodger's evil look vanished, and he brightened up as though everything was right in the world. "I'm going into Redemption to get provisions."

"So that's why you're all gussied up." Rex sniffed him. "You bathed, and shaved, and you ran a brush through that kitchen mop you call hair. I'm impressed. You almost look normal."

"Thank you Rex," Rodger said, and smiled, and for a second it seemed to Rex that everything was 'good', that Rodger was the way he used to be.

As if.

"C'mon," he went on with enthusiasm. "It's a beautiful day for a carriage ride."

Rex wanted to go; instinct said otherwise—an instinct that roared hot because of a gnawing thought brewing in his head: *I'll never see Redemption. He'll kill me, and bury me on the side of the road.* "Naw, you go. Annabelle farts too much."

"Awe c'mon," Rodger whined.

The dog shook his dripping jowls. "I'll stay home and watch the mansion. I'll keep an eye out for intruders."

"Intruders," the scientist shot back, and storm clouds brewed in his eyes. "Aside from the McCluskies, there's no one within seven miles of us." He leaned over, his glare ridged. "What's the real reason you don't want to come?"

Rex decided the truth—*I'm afraid you'll kill me on the way to Redemption*—might not be the route to take with an insane man, and as he thought up a believable reply, the scientist twitched, and the evil in his eyes ran away, and he was normal again.

"I know we haven't been getting along of late," Rodger said sadly.

The dog sighed with so much exasperation snot flew from his snout. "Thanks for noticing."

"Don't be like that Rex," the scientist said softly. "You know I love you."

"I love you too," he returned, and hesitated. *Should I say more?* The thought lasted only an instant before fresh words spilled from the dog's mouth, "I love you enough to tell you that you're not normal anymore. Sure, you've always been crazy, always a few notches above what is normal, but you've never been like this. You are two people now, and I don't trust either of you."

Rodger twitched, his face aghast, a hue of redness spreading out across his freshly shaven cheeks. "You don't trust me? Rex, please, it's me."

"Is it?" the dog questioned. "I've read your copy of Robert Louis Stevenson's The Strange Case of Dr. Jekyll and Mr. Hyde, so I know you have a split personality."

"That's a work of fiction," he spat, appalled by the accusation.

"It's as real as your fucking time machine." He shook slaver off his jowls, collected himself, and since he had the Rodger he loved in front of him, decided to spit out the rest, to talk about the elephant in the room, the evil elephant that had turned the atmosphere a poisonous ugly and made him want to run away. "You're targeting the McCluskies." He pointed a paw at the windowsill. "You're watching them with your glass eyes."

"They're called binoculars."

"Call them what you want—you're still watching them."

"She's growing quite ripe."

A chill went down Rex's back, and he nearly wet himself. "You leave her alone—you crazy bastard."

Rodger twitched, and his look turned nasty. Mr. Hyde was back. "We'll have this discussion some other time." He motioned at the door. "Come on. It's a beautiful day."

The dog shook his head.

"I'm not going to ask again," Rodger said coldly.

A thin shiver of fear coursed through the dog, and he knew he had to change tactics, he had to get Dr. Jekyll back. "Listen crazy smart man," he said as pleasantly as he could. "Don't be offended, I just wanna stay home." He decided to add some 'punch' to his argument, and delivered the lie smoothly, "I'm still a bit bothered by what I saw yesterday."

Yesterday had been quite an event. The time machine, equipped now with a camera that could record sound with impurity, powered up, and Rodger pulled the cord twice with enthusiasm. He also set the cellar on fire.

The malice in Rodger's face melted. "Yesterday was upsetting."

"To say the least," the dog elaborated harshly, shaking off slaver. "Your last two cord pulls on your machine nearly made me puke, especially the last one." Rex cringed at the sight in his mind's eye. "His whole head blew away."

"Yes," Rodger breathed gravely. "The visions from the 1960's were most troubling."

"Troubling?" the dog questioned in wonder. "It was fucking horrific." He shook more drool off his jowls, and looked up with a quizzical glint in his watery black eyes. "And you think it happened in Texas?"

"I saw the state flag of Texas," he confirmed, nodding, still normal, still normal Rodger. "The president in the 1960s gets assassinated in Texas."

"It was sickening." The dog cringed again at the dark images, and found a bright spot in the entire gruesome episode. "The sound was good. Good work on that. I heard every gun shot."

"I counted twelve," Rodger disclosed. "From at least three different locations."

"It was a Texas turkey shoot," the dog said. "That crooked road is the perfect spot for an ambush. And there was no protection because the Buick had no roof." The dog's eyes glinted with sadness. "He was a good looking man."

"Will be a good looking man," Rodger clarified. "He hasn't been born yet."

"What about the musicians in the flying Buick? The musicians that ended up all over the cornfield? Are they alive now?"

He shook his head. "Those images were from the 1950s, and the men involved were in their thirties."

The dog breathed out something he shouldn't have. "Maybe there is still time to change all this horrific insanity."

Rodger twitched so strongly Rex thought he was about to have a stroke. The scientist soon recovered. "Yes, change things," he muttered evilly to himself. "I'm going to change things." He stared down at Rex, his eyes so full of craziness the dog felt light headed from fear. And then the mad scientist coldly confessed, "The saxophone is cursed."

Rex couldn't believe his ears. The crazy man was talking smart for a change; the problem was, he was still Mr. Hyde. The dog hoped a few 'choice' words would help bring him back to normal. "Thank you, Rodger. Finally, we agree on something."

"The evidence is overwhelming," the scientist conceded, his voice barely a whisper, his eyes blank as though in a trance. "The *Devil's Breath* played on the street before the president arrived, and it was at the Mason City terminal before the musicians took off." His eyes focused, and Mr. Hyde remained. "The *Devil's Breath* is cursed."

With lunacy still swirling in his owner's eyes, Rex stepped carefully with his words. "So, crazy smart man? What are you gonna do? Melt it down?"

"I haven't decided yet." The scientist looked down in shame. When he looked up the 'craziness' in his eyes were gone. "I'm not good at these decisions, my mind works differently."

"That's for sure," the dog said, touching Rodger's hand with his snout. "Good thing you've got me."

"Yes Rex, I believe you are Heaven sent. You are one of God's instruments, here to guide me."

Uh-oh, the dog thought.

"I know we've had this conversation before," he continued, still normal. "I've often wondered why implanting Mabel's vocal cords made you so smart."

"Was Mabel smart?"

"She could read, but her intellect falls far beyond the range of your scope. You're smart because God made you that way."

Uh-oh, the dog thought.

"I know you are here for a divine purpose."

Oh fuck, the dog thought, and tried to right the ship, to bring the conversation into focus. "When do you wanna talk about your saxophone?"

"I'm puzzled by that," Rodger admitted, a finger to his chin in pensive thought. "Somewhere in Time the *Devil's Breath* changes hands. Why? And a drifter named Craig plays the evil notes."

"Evil notes aside, the drifter played amazingly," the dog intoned, nodding with appreciation. "Once again crazy smart man, thanks for the 'sound'."

Those words brightened the scientist's mood and he nodded with agreement. "He played a wonderful song for the three musicians, melodic, pleasing to the ear, yet sad. And there were words to the song, you heard it too."

"*A long, long, time ago,*" the dog recited. "That's what the drifter sang, and then he started to play for them with your evil horn."

"They all applauded afterwards," Rodger said, thinking of yesterday's images. "The man named 'Buddy' asked Craig what the song was called, and he didn't know."

"That's cuz it was coming from your fucking horn." A thought struck the dog, and he quickly voiced it, "You know, I sense the drifter is benevolent, and you know what? Probably the woman who was blowing the horn first was benign to the evil as well."

As soon as the words left his mouth, Rex regretted saying them, for he had read Dr. Freud's works and knew about the ego. *Would Rodger's fragile ego shatter further now that the onus of blame fell entirely on his creation?* Then he wondered, *Would Mr. Hyde awaken to protect him?*

Rodger twitched, but Mr. Hyde stayed away, and the scientist dismally remarked, "Even putting the saxophone in the barn didn't help." He looked up in thought for a moment. "I wonder how the instrument ended up in the drifter's hands."

"Maybe a sun bomb fell on the woman with the nice fingers," the dog said with a laugh, hoping Rodger would laugh too. He didn't. The dog pushed on, "What are you gonna do about the *Devil's Breath?*"

"You're Heaven sent," he returned calmly. "What do you suggest?"

The dog spoke the truth, all the while wondering, *should I really say this to him?*

"Well, crazy smart man, even though you're all gussied up for town, before you go, you should handle the problem."

Rodger twitched, and he looked away. "The problem will be handled when I return." He turned back to Rex with an ugly maniacal glint in his eyes and coldly prophesied, "Like my other problem."

Instinct made the dog yelp, "What's that suppose to mean?"

Rodger twitched, his eyes on his dog, his lips bitter and straight. "If you don't want to come with me, you don't have to. However, tomorrow you can't say no. You have to come with me."

"Tomorrow?"

"I made some alterations to the inside of the time machine. There is a bench for us to sit on."

It took a second for the dog to process the information. *He wants to go for a ride in the time machine.*

"Are you fucking crazy?" the dog shot back, and regretted the words at once; regret or not, he kept talking. "Have you come unhinged?" He had more choice words for the scientist but stopped himself, instead adding, "It's too dangerous, and what about the fire the damn thing causes? It set the house on fire. Who is gonna put that out?"

"I made adjustments to the machine, there won't be a fire."

The dog raked his brain for something to say, and decided to stall. "Make a test run first crazy smart man. Send the camera one more time. If there's no fire, then, we'll talk about it."

Rodger thought pensively for a moment, and then slowly nodded. "Perhaps one more cord pull with the camera would be wise. You are, after all, Heaven sent and here to guide me."

"Someone has to," Rex said, and rolled his eyes. "Okay crazy smart man, see you tonight."

Rodger's eyes turned vicious, and he lunged with both hands at the dog. His hands were large and strong, and he seized the dog by the neck and the loose skin on his back. His actions, being so quick, kept the dog mute as his body roughly tore upwards. Drool flew from his jowls, and finally he screamed, "What the fuck!"

"Stay quiet you four-legged beast," he bellowed with a crackling evil laugh, and he charged across the room, swaying his dog with malicious intent. At the closet, he needed a free hand, but Rex squirmed too much to release his grip. He had to do something.

He callously slammed the dog's face into the wall. Rex squealed and barked, slaver and bloody snot flew from his snout. Rodger ran the dog's face into the wall again. Drool, snot and blood sprayed out on the wood in a crazy pattern. Changing tactics, he hammered the top of the dog's head into the wall, using his pet like a battering ram. The wall cracked, and Rex went limp.

Rodger removed his hand from the dog's hide and opened the closet door. A thick, moldy smell escaped. Rodger threw his animal inside with brute force and slammed the door. Rex bounced off the wall and fell to the wooden plank floor with jarring impact. His head swirled, no thought could lock in place. He lay stunned.

"I'm sorry," Rodger said, and tears spilled from his eyes. "Everything will be okay when I come home." He cried more, his forehead against the door in paralyzed anguish over what he had done to a defenseless animal. "I'm sorry. I'm sorry for locking you up, but I know once I'm gone you'll warn the McCluskies." He banged the door with his fist, and cried out in bitter pain. "You shouldn't have made me do it."

Rex sat up, his head groggy, his snout burning with pain; other than that he felt okay, and the shock was wearing off. He would be okay. Well, for now.

The dog heard his owner's footfalls fade, and then he heard the creak of the front door hinges opening.

Rex quivered in the dark and thought, *I'm in big trouble.*

*   *   *

Seconds seemed to last like minutes and minutes seemed to last like hours as Rex shivered in the dark gripped in an overwhelming fear, fear for his life, and fear for the lives of the McCluskies. He knew with certainty now his owner planned to kill Lucy McCluskie to terminate the evil spawn germinating within her. Would he kill Ian too just to be sure he wouldn't breed again? The dog was certain of it; and he was certain of this as well: *I'll be next on his 'hit' list.*

As the terrifying scenarios of what could happen blazed in his thoughts, he heard the hinges on the door squeak. His fear spiked. How long had he waited in the dark? Though it seemed longer, he knew with close accuracy Rodger had left only a half hour ago. With Annabelle slowing from age, it would take two hours to get to Redemption, and another two back. Four hours round trip. Thirty or so minutes had passed. Not enough time to go to Redemption; but enough time to dig a grave.

Footfalls echoed across the floor. *Not Rodger's.* The step was too soft. The 'click' of a heel meant a boot. *A woman?*

The door opened and sunlight flooded the closet. Rex squinted, looked away, and stumbled out. His snout worked fine, and he liked her scent. He circled her a few times before coming to a stop. He sat, blinked, and stared up at her. "Thanks for the rescue."

Rex considered her a beautiful woman. Her face was round, her cheeks high and curving into a slender rounded chin. Her lips were thick and coated with a red gloss lipstick. Her brown eyes glinted a pleasantness that made him feel good inside. Her black hair flowed over the raised collar of her coat. Her dress was not of the times: she wore a red leather trench coat that fell to her knees, black pants and a white shirt with a collar.

"I told Rodger I'd watch out for intruders. I'm glad I found one. And might I say, I sure found a beautiful one."

"Rex, you're going to make me blush."

"As if," the dog returned with piqued amusement. "You know something? I wondered when you'd come."

"You were expecting me?"

"I like your fingers. Though to be honest, I've never heard you play."

"The saxophone is my instrument," she flaunted with a confident swagger.

The dog raised a brow at her. "You look more like a banjo picker to me and, if you don't mind me asking—and please excuse my language—who the fuck are you? A better question might be, what the fuck are you?"

Her mouth hung agape for a moment. "You don't think I'm a human being?"

"Just a hunch pretty lady. See, there's a lotta craziness going on around here, and you and your fingers are part of it."

"So are you," she said bluntly.

"No kidding," he returned with a smirk. "After all, how many talking bulldogs do you know?"

"A bulldog with paramount aptitude," she added.

"Oh I like the way you said 'smart'. And if I was smart, would I be here?" As soon as the words left his mouth he thought: *Damn, I'm quoting someone who hasn't been born yet.*

"You are a most delightful existence."

"Oh please, stop, you're gonna make me blush."

She smiled, and he liked her smile. It was genuine. "You have a wonderful sense of humor."

"You should come by when I've got half a bottle of wine in me. Your stomach would be sore from laughing. Mind you, there is a downside when I consume alcohol: I lick my balls more." His grin widened. "I notice you're not laughing. I also noticed you haven't told me who or what you are."

She crouched down and put her hand on his head. "How badly did he hurt you?"

"I'll be fine," the dog said, and pleasantly rubbed his snout against her hand. "Well, at least until he comes back."

"It will give you time to prepare."

"Prepare?" he repeated smugly. "Even though I have a 'paramount aptitude', I'm still a bulldog. I am outmatched."

"The man in your dreams is always outmatched."

Rex paused, unsure how to respond. *Damn it, she knows about McCluskie.* "Uh, yeah, but he's got fingers and a gun that smokes green. I've got paws. And you still haven't told me what you are?"

"My name is Shannon, and I am the Deity Fate."

"Well I'll be damned," he said, his mind running down an unexpected course. "I never thought of that." He shook slaver from his jowls, careful to keep the spray off her boots. "If you don't mind, can you elaborate?"

"Fate and Time are hinged together to retain an orderly balance," she explained, gently stroking his head. "Bad things have to happen to keep in balance with the good things."

"Good things?" the dog questioned with a raised brow. "Are you trying to make me laugh? I've seen Rodger's crazy moments in Time."

"It's because of the saxophone."

"Tell me something I don't know."

"Your owner's machine is zeroing in on dreadful moments in Time because of the evil in the *Devil's Breath*," she informed. "The instruments evil notes are imprisoned within the goodness of Redemption, so it is using the machine to be heard."

"That sure explains a lot," the dog grumbled. "Though, I'm slightly puzzled. He's been playing it in the barn with the door closed. I can barely hear it. And it was in the barn when he used the machine yesterday."

"The escape route for the evil notes has been increased. They are weak when they reach the machine. It's the reason the casualty count was so low." She stood and asked, "You witnessed only five fatalities yesterday, correct?"

The dog counted them up in his head: *Three musicians, the guy steering the flying Buick and the president.* He looked up at her. "Five too many, including a president. And if you don't mind me asking, how did this thing get so evil? What did Rodger do?"

"Your owner did nothing," she said, and went on with, "Mankind's evil must be stored somewhere, and it was stored in the McCluskie's bloodline. When Ian McCluskie reached the town of Redemption the evil shed him—and ran to the saxophone."

Rex thought about it for a moment. "Ian McCluskie is my friend and a good human being."

"I agree," she said with a nod. "Mankind's cache of evil had to be stored in the McCluskie's bloodline. Remember, the 'good' has to balance the 'bad'. You've seen the 'bad' in the saxophone, and you dream of the 'good'."

The dog nodded at once. "Yeah, Jacob McCluskie is a compassionate man, or will be." He thought of something that made him grin. "Get this Mrs. Fate, he breaks into Heaven, shoots an angel named Envy in the face, and before he leaves, he puts her glasses back on and apologizes." He laughed. "Who the hell does that?"

His story made her eyes widen and her mouth hang open. She quickly recovered, smiled, and then looked off to the cellar. "Rodger brought the *Devil's Breath* inside?"

She made it sound like a question, which amused the dog, and with a shrewd nod he said, "He brought it inside right after yesterday's horror show." He rubbed his head against her leg, and glanced up at her. "Using my paramount aptitude, I've figured out you've come here to release it from its prison."

"The notes are in the Timeline, which means the notes need to be played." She grinned tightly at the dog. "Are you going to try and stop me?"

Rex backed away with a chuckle. "As if." He looked up at her with attitude glinting in his black eyes. "I'm insulted pretty lady, insulted you would think so little of my intellect to ask such a question."

"I apologize."

"You should be apologizing for taking the fucking thing."

"It needs to come with me." She crouched down and patted his head. "I'll take the bad thing and leave the good thing behind."

He sniffed her hand with his snout, liking the scent, and asked, "You think I'm the good thing?"

"I know you are the good, and you are here for a divine purpose."

"Awe shit, I've heard that before."

She ran her slender fingers down his back, rubbing him hard. "The residue energy brought back from the time machine is funneling into you. That's why you're dreaming of Jacob McCluskie."

The dog smirked. "I gotta say, McCluskie sure gets around."

"That will all depend on you." Then, quietly in his ear she added, "The Fate of Jacob McCluskie depends on a talking bulldog."

Rex laid his head on her knee. "I wish McCluskie was here to help me."

"Only you can make it happen." She patted his head, stood, and looked off to the cellar. "It's downstairs?"

"Why make it sound like a question?" he asked with a laugh. "You'll find it right next to the time machine. You can't miss it."

Her smile lit up his heart, and what she said made it glow, "You are a beautiful existence, Rex."

Even with the tender sentiment, he had to speak his mind, and did so with brazen callousness. "I wish I could say the same thing about you pretty lady."

"Please don't be bitter."

"Leave the fucking thing here," the dog spat, walking over to the cellar door. "I'll send the time machine for a ride, that'll set the place on fire." He glanced down at the cellar. "The problem will be solved."

"I wish it was that simple." She looked down at him. "It's time for me to retrieve the instrument and leave."

"Before you do, do you mind doing something for me?"

Her brows hedged slightly and her lips rose up at the corners. "Rex, are you asking for a favor?"

He rubbed up against her leg. "Well, you did show up without a bottle of wine."

Her soft laugh warmed his heart, and she said, "From what you've told me, I'm glad I didn't."

"There's another reason to do me a favor—I haven't licked my balls."

"Thank you for curbing your urge," she went on with a smile, "and Rex, I will do you a favor. I will do it simply because you asked." She crouched down. "What can I do for you?"

"Open the front door."

A coy smile touched her lips. "What are you planning to do Rex?"

"Warn the McCluskies. Make them leave." He cocked a brow at her. "How's that for some divine purpose?"

She walked across the room and opened the door.

*   *   *

The sight he beheld made him blink, and he wished in his heart it would all go away. His blink didn't work, his wish went unanswered, and fear crashed through him with the force of a train. Sweat broke out on his brow and glistened in the late afternoon sun. His stomach soured so tightly he doubled over on the seat.

The horse clumped up the driveway, unaware of Rodger's dire plight, and then the reigns tugged smartly, calling her to a halt.

The reigns jiggled in his hands for a moment longer, indecision gnawing in his brain. And then something in Rodger's head ruptured, it shattered like glass and fell away with such force he jumped. His eyes creased with a scowling wickedness. "Why didn't I kill the damn dog?"

Annabelle was forgotten, the elderly nag forced to wear the carriage until the problem was resolved, and now he feared in his evil heart there would be more than one problem. Three problems.

"Why didn't I kill the McCluskies?"

The reigns floated in the air as he jumped from the carriage; now he was running, and he cleared the steps in two strides. The door swung in the breeze and he charged inside to find, as expected, the closet door open.

He deplored foul language, most of the time. "Fucking dog."

He spotted a spade leaning in the corner. The shovel felt good in his thick meaty hands, the weight just right. He practiced swinging the weapon. "I wonder how smart you'll be after a couple of hits from this."

A smell caught his nose then, faint, but there, a subtle hint. He sniffed about for the odor, but soon the breeze from the open door made the smell go away; and away went the thought of the smell.

"Oh Rex…come here boy," he sang out.

He walked through the living room, headed for the kitchen, the floorboards groaning softly under his weight, and as his lips opened to sing out for the dog again, the smell returned, hot and heavy, and the words dancing about in the madness in his head got swallowed up with a gouging vacuum. "Gas."

The smell rolled up his nose with a suffocating thickness, mingling with his long white nose hairs, and he followed the smell to the cellar stairs. The fumes made his eyes water. *What has the dog done?* And without thinking, he crept down the stairs, the soft wood planks creaking eerily under his footfalls. His thoughts swirled around the dog, around Rex. *Where was the bastard?*

At the bottom of the stairs, he spotted his unnamed robot spinning about in the corner. The robot's head, (a metal bucket, all he could find) lay on its shoulder, the wires sprouting from its neck sparking brightly in the darkness.

Now the smell of gas and the dog were forgotten, and he ran to the button that turned on the lights, his feet splashing in huge puddles of gas, sounds not reaching the madness in his brain. His fist pounded the button hard. The lights came on. His eyes roamed the room, and a thought struck him, *the Devil's Breath.*

"Gone," he breathed, and cursed the dog.

Now his eyes watched his spinning robot with the broken head and a question blazed above the screaming craziness behind his eyes. *How did it get here?*

The dog of course, and he shook the shovel in his hands, and spotted a bucket near the time machine. With the lights on, he clearly saw the bucket was filled to the brim with what he suspected was petrol. He leaned the shovel against his work bench, crossed the room and picked up the bucket—it was an error in judgment.

As he lifted the bucket, the thin cord tied to it pulled tight, and three buckets filled to the top with petrol sitting atop the rafters tipped over and fell, drenching him in gas. He gasped hellishly, spraying gas out his mouth, and dropped the bucket in his hands. It landed by his feet, soaking his shoes.

He shook gas from his hair, and continued to spit, hating the taste in his mouth. As he did, Rex come down the stairs. In his mouth he held a long white candle, and Rodger's heart quicken, for the candle was lit and dripped hot wax.

Rex laid the candle on the last step, shaking his jowls. "Yuck, that tasted like shit, a lot like your cooking Rodger."

The scientist blinked, and the evil in him melted away, and he was normal again, and now the shock of being drenched in gas shook through him like an earthquake. He tried to speak, his mouth opening and closing, but no words came out.

"Have you gone mute Rodger?" the dog asked with a laugh.

"Rex…" he managed finally, and motioned around the room, gas dripping from the sleeves of his coat. "What have you done?"

"You have to ask?" The dog threw up his paws in exasperation. "I thought it was obvious—you're in my trap."

He twitched, gas droplets flying from his hair. "Trap?"

"The floor and walls are soaked in gasoline—and so are you." Rex smiled, his jowls dripping. "I would describe the situation as being highly 'inflammable'. Unless, of course, you wanna get rid of the 'in'," and the dog chuckled through his teeth. He motioned with his head at the burning candle on the stair. "All I have to do is roll this candle off." With that spoken, the dog bent down and picked up a yellow laundry cord in his mouth. Rodger had missed seeing the cord because the lights were off, but he saw it now, saw that the cord was tied to the laundry cord that worked the time machine.

"Why have you—"

"In case the candle goes out," Rex interrupted him. "As you know Rodger, your machine fires up real hot." The dog chuckled, and then coldly added, "How do you like me now?"

A million questions fired off in Rodger's brain: the question that broke the surface of the chewing insanity came out as, "How could you have done this?"

"Easy, I used my assets, just like Jacob McCluskie will do in the future."

The dog's words turned the scientist nasty. His eyes narrowed with vicious evilness, and he stepped over to his work benches.

"I wouldn't move too much Rodger. Cuz if you do, you're gonna be real crispy."

A strained evil creased his gas soaked cheeks, and he hissed, "How did you do this?"

"We'll get to that in a minute." A smugness shone on the dog's jowls, a glint of amusement in his eyes. "So, how was your trip to Redemption? I hope Annabelle didn't fart too much. Oh, by the way, what took you so long? Did you go to town by way of Vermont?"

The evil in Rodger shone through brightly. "The weathered old nag barely made it. I thought we'd eat her this winter."

"You thought wrong," he grumbled, his affection for an elderly horse glinting in his black eyes. "I gotta ask, even with a blazing headache—thanks for that by the way, you asshole— did you hurt or kill any defenseless animals on the way? And by 'animals', I'm including humans."

The goodness in Rodger bubbled up, tears filled his eyes and dripped down his cheeks onto the floor, steaming the lenses of his glasses. "Rex," he whispered. "I'm so sorry about what I did to you."

His words hit the dog's ears like hammer blows, igniting a hot vengeful anger. "Sorry about what you did to me?" the dog questioned with an eye roll. "What about Mabel? Are you sorry about what you did to her?"

He looked aghast at the allegation; his look soon turned to a wounded shame. "I did nothing," tumbled from his lips, and he looked at the floor.

"You are a terrible liar."

A silent moment of time ensued, harsh and unforgiving like the lights blazing above them, and Rodger looked up with a twitch, gas dripping from his hairy white eyebrows. "I can explain."

"I can explain too, you are a murderer."

His eyes were back on the floor. His shoulders conversed with deep sobs. "How did you know?"

"I have part of her in me," he explained with abrupt flair that shot snot from his snout. "I've always had this nagging thought you had done something bad, just like Dr. Frankenstein. So, to be sure, I asked an asset, and, even though she had already done me a favor, she happily told me the truth."

"She?"

"We'll get to her in a minute," he went on, a low growl in the back of his throat. "We're still talking about Mabel." He raised his snout at him. "Why did you do it?"

"I needed her vocal cords," he went on in defense as though his needs out weighed a person's life. "They were perfect for you. And it was easy to do because of Mabel's vast weight. A cut here, a cut there." He nodded at his accomplishment. "My calculations were precise. It all collapsed in the moment she sat down."

A thin desert breeze of complete bewilderment blew through the dog's thoughts, and after a long pause, he sadly admitted, "My God you are insane."

Rodger's ego needed protecting, and Mr. Hyde came back. He picked up the shovel.

The dog grinned coyly. "I know what you're thinking— maybe you can get to me—and if I were you, I'd be thinking that too, but shovel or not, everything is drenched in gas, even the shovel." Rex allowed his words ample time to be absorbed before adding, "You're gonna catch on fire. That can't be avoided. No matter how smart you are, you can't think of a way out. Cuz there is no way out. You are trapped."

Rodger hissed with ruinous compliance and dropped the shovel at his feet. His eyes twinkled behind his gas stained glasses. His good side returned, and now he looked appalled. "Rex, you've turned evil."

"You know something," the dog said at once, nodding, "I think you're right. I guess living with you has rubbed off on me."

The scientist regarded his dog in pensive thought before allowing, "So it's come to this. You're going to kill me."

"You picked a fight with the wrong dog."

"Is this because of Mabel?" he asked. "Is my talking dog passing a death sentence on me?"

"Your talking, ball licking dog hasn't decided yet. We haven't finished talking."

"What's there to talk about?" He twitched, and shuddered, and Rex expected Mr. Hyde to solidify in Rodger's eyes. But Hyde stayed away and the scientist asked, "Do you want me to beg for my life?"

"Oh fuck please, would you? Cuz that might be fun." Then the dog snidely added, "Rodger, even murderers should have some dignity."

Rodger twitched wildly, and a whirlwind of madness filled his eyes.

"Oh good," the dog said, "your Mr. Hyde persona is back."

Rodger picked up the shovel.

"C'mon Rodger, c'mon Mr. Hyde," the dog goaded, and pulled the laundry cord in his mouth taut. "Make your play so I can barbecue you right now." The scientist stood ridged, and after a few seconds, Rex said, "Good, we haven't finished talking yet."

"Who let you out?"

"An intruder," the dog replied, his lips set in a smug satisfied grin. "I guess you should have locked the front door." A chuckle came from the back of the dog's throat. "Does the door even have a lock?"

Rodger twitched and cursed under his breath.

"The intruder," the dog continued, "my asset, let me out of the closet, let me out of the house and, because she enjoyed our visit, gladly told me you were a murderer."

Rodger hissed. "I should have killed you."

"You should have, but you didn't."

"Who is this woman?"

"Are you interested in her, Rodger?" the dog asked with a laugh, slaver dripping from his grin. "To be honest, I thought you'd be more interested in the McCluskies. Cuz yes, you crazy asshole, I did exactly what you said I'd do: once my asset let me out of the house, I went over and warned the McCluskies."

He hissed between his teeth. "I should have killed you."

"You should have, but you didn't." The dog snickered, and used his snout to roll over the candle. Huge droplets of wax spilled out and sizzled in the puddle of gas by the stairs.

Rodger twitched with jittery unease.

The dog was back snickering. "Did that make you nervous Mr. Hyde? Don't worry, we still have lots to talk about—like your fucking saxophone."

"Where's the Devil's Breath?"

"The woman with the nice fingers came by for it."

"The sax player," he breathed out, his crazy mind glimpsing the images of her fingers dancing on the keys.

"Oh, and Rodger," the dog continued whimsically. "You are not gonna believe this, but guess who she is? I'll give you a hint, she's a deity. No shit, I'm not lying."

His eyes softened in wonder. "A deity has the Devil's Breath?"

"The Deity Fate."

Shock spread out across his face. "Dear God."

"After she let me out of the closet, we chatted, oh, you will be happy to know I did not lick my balls in front of her. I wanted to, but I didn't."

Rodger shook his head, mystified, and wheezed out, "Fate blows the horn."

"She sure does." The dog hesitated, and shook his head with regret. "Awe, damn, I forgot to ask why Craig the drifter ends up with the sax. That's gonna bother me."

Rodger ignored the dog and blurted out, "So the Deity Fate steals my sax and sets a trap for me."

"Not entirely correct," the dog put in. "She did steal your sax—oh, in the future, it's called 'jacked'." He chuckled at the word. "She 'jacked' your saxophone, but she didn't set the trap. I used another asset."

"McCluskie," he threw in, and between his teeth hissed, "I should have killed the McCluskies before I left."

"You should have, but you didn't. Oh, Ian owes me a coke. Do you know what that is? I'm told it's a drink. But get this, there is no alcohol in it." The dog's eyes glinted with mock anticipation. "I wonder if it will make me lick my balls."

The scientist twitched, and the madness fell from his eyes. Normal again, he weakly said, "Rex, please…"

"Oh, stop your fucking pleading." The dog rolled his eyes. "Geez I wish Mr. Hyde was back, at least he's got some balls." After a sigh, Rex said, "Anyway, Ian bets me a coke that you won't walk into the cellar, into my trap. He said, 'the smell of gas would make anyone retreat'. After I laughed, I made him shake my paw."

Normal Rodger remained, and flashes of ridicule shot through his eyes in pulsating waves. His lips curled up with scorn. "Are you mocking my intelligence?"

Rex snorted out the truth. "Not in the least. You are the smartest man in the world. You can build a sun generator, a time machine, fuck, if I asked, I'd bet you could build a space craft that could get us to the moon. But the small things in life you miss, and even with the cellar reeking of gas, I knew you'd come."

"You evil fucking bastard."

The dog laughed. "I thought you didn't like foul language? And you're still your normal self, crazy, but still your normal self. C'mon Rodger, watch your tongue."

"How did you become like this?"

"I had to," he replied with an ice cold edge in his tone. "You said it yourself, I'm here for a divine purpose. The Deity Fate said the same thing."

Silence ensued, and the dog cleared phlegm from his throat, hating the taste of the cord in his mouth. Rodger raised his chin toward the dog and quietly asked, "Saving the McCluskies is your divine purpose?"

The dog shook his head. "Not really. Saving the McCluskies and their unborn child is inevitable. No matter what you did, they would live, but would their great grandson?"

"Your divine purpose is him?" he questioned.

"Fate said something that bothered me. She was specific on who I had to save."

Rodger twitched, his lips quivering with disbelief. "You're mad. Jacob McCluskie won't be born for 77 years."

"I thought about that," Rex said, and the glint in his eye made the scientist shiver inside. "I also thought about the thing spinning around in the corner."

"The robot?"

"I had Ian carry it inside for me." The dog smiled wickedly. "I want you to know I pushed it down the stairs myself." After a chuckle, he added, "You should have heard the noise."

The scientist ran his hands through his gas soaked hair, puzzled, confused. "Killing my invention is your divine purpose?"

Ignoring his question, the dog continued with, "No shit Rodger, a few seconds after it landed at the bottom of the stairs, the damn thing climbed to its feet. Ian nearly shit his pants. Its head was a bit askew"—and he laughed—"and it spins around a lot, but it's still kind of working. You sure know how to build them. It took a licking, but it keeps on ticking." He paused, and then threw in, "Oh, by the way, it's drenched in gas as well."

"Rex, you've gone insane."

"As I said before, living with you has rubbed off on me."

"It's only an invention," he informed as though he couldn't believe he had to.

"What did you call it? Artificial intelligence? Something smarter than humans?"

The scientist hesitated, his thoughts torn apart by the dog's words. Finally, he blurted out, "It's only an invention."

"No one will be able to turn off your invention. It will kill Mankind. Your invention will take over before Jacob

McCluskie is born. So that's how I'm saving him. Sorry Rodger. You are too smart to live."

"Rex, please, think about this."

"I have Rodger," he said, taking a deep breath around the cord to calm himself. "I've thought about something else too. I always knew it would come to this. You and me. Our fight was inevitable."

The scientist thought about Rex's words, nodding, a hand to his chin in wistful thought. "Yes Rex," he calmly said. "Maybe you are right, you've read Dr. Frankenstein, you know how it ends."

"In the novel, it ends in the cold. This time it will end in the goodness of Redemption."

Rodger picked up the shovel, and Mr. Hyde came back. "You're right about one thing Rex, in matters like this, your intellect far exceeds mine. I walked into your trap. You're a genius, which means you're smart enough to know that you don't run up stairs fast." He swung the shovel like a baseball bat. "Even on fire, I'm going to bash your brains in."

"Come get me big boy."

Rex rolled the candle off the stair. It struck the floor at an odd angle, and spun up, spraying wax, and then it landed like a log in the puddle of gas, and sizzled out.

His heart froze, and then galloped with blinding fear as Rodger charged toward him. He swung the spade, and Rex bounced forward a scant second before the metal head struck the stair. The wood plank cracked with a deep finality, sending sawdust into the air. Rodger twisted about, looking for the dog.

Rex stood in a somewhat dry patch on the floor, the cord that worked the time machine still in his mouth. Pulling the cord would set off a fire; the problem was, now that he was off the stairs and in the room, the cord was too long, and there was far too much slack to work through his mouth to make it taut enough to send off the machine.

A crazed stillness glistened behind Rodger's gas stained glasses. "No where to run Rex, and your cord is too long." The corners of his lips curled up ever so slightly. "I'm going to bash your brains out."

"Gee, Rodger, I thought you loved me."

The shovel came down with blinding force, the metal striking inches from Rex. The slashing impact hurt the dog's ears, and he spat out the cord and scooted behind the spinning robot, its neck still spitting sparks.

"You can't hide Rex."

"I beg to differ you crazy asshole. I'm real safe here, and I'm real fast, faster than you."

The scientist lurched forward with a heaving hiss, and swung the shovel toward the dog's head poking out from behind the robot's legs. The spade's head glinted in the lights, and the dog saw it coming. His blow struck his robot, sending it spinning to the floor. Rex darted off between Rodger's legs. The dog was fast; so was the scientist. He spun about and swung his weapon. The tip of blade clipped the dog's back, sending him sprawling across the gas soaked floor. He yelped, the pain eating through his hindquarter, and climbed to his feet to see it happen.

The robot oscillated on its back in a pool of gas, and as Rodger went to right his invention, the sparks shooting off out its neck touched off the gas. A sizzling flare lit up the room. Flames spread out in all directions, eating the gas. The robot burned like a funeral pyre for a second, and then ignited with a blinding explosion. The air broiled—and a concussion wave blew through the cellar throwing Rodger onto his back.

The explosion stunned the dog as well, but being low to the floor saved him most of the savage fury, and he recovered enough to move. His ears rang and he was woozy—and then his heart sunk. The stairs were on fire. He'd never make it.

He thought of McCluskie, the man in his dreams, the man from the future. He would find a way out, and in the time it took Rex to blink, he knew what to do.

He snatched up the laundry cord in his mouth and turned to the time machine. Ian had looked inside the machine and had failed to close the door. *Good for me*, Rex thought, and jumped inside without hesitation. He spun about on the bench Rodger had built for their trip tomorrow, and used his back legs to slam the door closed.

An instant later, Rodger crashed heavily into the time machine's window. Flames ate up his face. His glasses melted off his nose. He pounded on the window with both fists and screamed the dog's name.

The sight sickened the dog. It was time to leave. He whipped his head about as hard as he could. The cord ripped away. The machine fired up—flames shot out the bottom.

Rex looked out the time machine's window, and the last thing he saw of Redemption Iowa was Rodger dancing about on fire.

And then he was gone.

The End

Seven Mourners
at Blackwells Corner

A cold dreary August rain fell.

Church bells clanged with a doomful ominous sound in the sorrow of Heaven's tears, and Jones hurried his pace up 50th Street, panting with excitement as he weaved in and out of the crowd. He squeezed between a huddled group, stepped out onto 5th Avenue and looked at the Neo Gothic grandeur of St. Patrick's Cathedral, shrouded now in a weeping drizzle and surrounded by thousands.

A baneful boom of thunder rumbled overhead and the rain fell harder. Someone yelled out, "Even in the rain, the Babe packs them in." And a smattering of applause rippled through the crowd.

Whistles blew sharply, and the policeman, many on horseback, moved the crowd away from the church stairs. A black limousine, its headlights lit, its wipers flashing, drove up through the parting crowd and stopped in front of the church. A minute later a hearse arrived and parked behind the limo.

A deep sorrow shuddered throughout the crowd when the pallbearers removed the coffin from the hearse. Even though it rained hard, every man in the crowd removed his hat in honor as the coffin was carried up the stairs. The Babe disappeared inside the church, the doors closed, and Jones waited on the street in the downpour.

An hour filled with heavy rain elapsed, and then the church doors opened. The pallbearers carried the Babe to the hearse for his last car ride. And within a minute, it was all over: the hearse drove off and the crowd began to disperse. But not Jones. He hung around, moving closer to the church, his eyes on everyone exiting the funeral.

His luck had been good of late. As much as he hated to admit it, the Babe's death proved it; for the Babe's death had provided him with the opportunity to meet the gambler. From what Jones had been told, this man loved baseball; above all, he loved Babe Ruth. Jones felt certain he would be in attendance today. The problem was, would he exit out another door? For that matter, *will I be able to spot him?*

The worry of that thought hungrily chewed into him, and he fished a crumpled, yellow-aged photograph from his pocket. The black and white image of the gambler was seared into his brain, yet, just to be sure, he studied the photograph again before shoving it back in his pocket.

The crowd leaving the cathedral slowed to a trickle, and a thin shiver of uneasiness washed through the pit of his stomach. *Had he missed him?* The question bubbled fiercely in his thoughts as time ticked by.

No one had come out of the church for the last few minutes, and a sick dejection seeped through him. He felt all was lost. All his effort was for not, and a sigh filled with an expletive rolled from his wet lips. As he turned to leave, a man stepped from the church. Jones's eyes nearly popped out of his head.

The man wore a long brown leather trench coat with a matching fedora. He paused at the top of the stairs and looked up at the black sky, allowing the rain to hit his face. Then he peeked inside his coat, and Jones saw his lips move.

The man's words were washed away with the sound of rain, but Jones knew who he was talking to. *Belvedere*, he thought. *The story is true.*

Jones's heart sped up. He had found him. He had found the gambler, and for an odd moment, his brain went blank. He didn't know how to act, what to say, how to approach him.

The gambler descended the stairs, his boots clicking on the concrete risers. At the bottom of the stairs, he turned and headed north on 5th Avenue. Jones remained in place, the shock of seeing him still messing with his thoughts. Yet, one thought did make it to the spot where decisions are made—*follow him*. And with his heart pounding with a fearful joy, he set out after him.

The gambler kept a steady pace down the sidewalk, his white ponytail bouncing on his back as he walked. Jones pursued, keeping what he thought was a good distance between them, trying to decide when to approach him.

At the corner of 56th Street, the gambler turned unexpectedly and Jones lost sight of him. He hurried ahead, and reached the corner within seconds; what he saw made his mouth drop open. "Where'd he go?"

Jones was running now, down 56th Street, desperation gnawing sickly through his stomach. Why hadn't he approached him sooner? Now he was gone—gone for good. The thought stuck in his head like an ice pick, and he swore bitterly, and was still swearing when, out of nowhere, a hand with a steel-like grip seized the front of his coat. Jones's world blurred, and the next thing he knew, he was pinned up against a wall inside an alley staring into cold brown eyes.

The gambler stood a foot taller than Jones, and he outweighed him by over a hundred pounds. His rain-lashed face rippled with a red anger that nearly made Jones wet his pants. The gambler's lips twisted bitterly, his white goatee shimmered with rain, and in a cold hard voice he said, "Christ said in His 'Sermon on the Mount' speech—'The rain falls on the 'just and the 'unjust'." The gambler leaned forward and through his teeth hissed, "What are you?"

Jones tried to speak but all that came out was 'uh… uh…uh…"

With annoyance, the gambler dropped him and stepped back. Jones fell to the ground, but quickly got to his feet and straightened out his coat, trying to reign in his thoughts.

"Why are you following me?"

Jones cleared his throat and as calmly as he could, said, "You're the gambler."

A voice sang out within the gambler's coat, "Ronald, he knows who you are?"

"Is that Belvedere?"

The question made the gambler pause, and Jones didn't like the look brewing in the man's eyes. "You sure know a lot about me." His words came out flat and curt, and he stepped up to Jones. "Who are you? And how do you know about me?"

Before he could speak, a muffled voice came from within the gambler's coat. "Can I get some air please?"

The gambler cursed under his breath, opened his coat, and a tiny blue and yellow macaw wearing an eye patch fluttered out.

Jones blinked in amazement. "You are beautiful."

The bird landed on the gambler's shoulder and, in a British accent as thick as oatmeal, dryly noted, "I wish I could say the same about you." He pruned his feathers and glanced about at his surroundings. "Ronald, I see we're in an alley. Do you remember what McCluskie said at our last poker game?"

"Yes I do," he returned with a hint of pique.

"If you do," the bird sang out, his beck raised with theatrical aloof, "then why are we still here in an alley talking to the Artful Dodger?"

"He doesn't look like the Artful Dodger. He's short, and his clothes are a bit baggy on him, but he's not bow-legged or wearing a hat."

"Who's the Artful—"

"He's a character out of Dickens." The gambler stared Jones in the eye. "Okay kid, what's your name?" Jones told him, and the follow-up question was, "What's your first name Jones?"

"I don't need one."

The gambler raised a white brow, thought about it, and then shrugged. "Okay kid, what do I care? Now why are you following us?"

"Can we discuss these matters elsewhere?" Belvedere threw in. "It's raining and we're in an alley, and you do remember what McCluskie told us about alleys."

The name had popped up twice in the conversation and now Jones had to ask, "Who's McCluskie? Is he a character out of Dickens too?"

The gambler laughed so hard his hat slipped forward and he had to adjust it. "McCluskie is real. Trust me on this, he's as real as you and me. No one in there right mind could make him up."

"That's a certainty," Belvedere cut in, and stared down from his perch atop the gambler's shoulder. "Mr. McCluskie hasn't been born yet. He traveled back in time to join us at our last poker game."

Jones blinked in astonishment, "Really?" and then added, "He must really like poker."

The gambler laughed around his growing smile. "He had no interest in poker. He only came for what was in the pot."

"He must have desperately needed it," the bird said, "No one in their right mind would have traveled back in time to join us at that game."

"The 1945 game wasn't that bad," the gambler said.

"I beg to differ, Ronald," the bird said, and turned his good eye to Jones. "The game was held in April of that year"— he paused for dramatic effect and added—"In a basement in Berlin, Germany, less than five miles from the advancing Russian Army."

The gambler scoffed at his bird. "It wasn't that bad."

"Oh please, Ronald." The bird rolled his one eye, stared at Jones and raised both wings to emphasize his point. "The game was under attack."

"It wasn't that bad."

"Dust kept falling on the cards," Belvedere complained. "And the table kept shaking."

"It wasn't that bad," he said, and grinned at Jones.

"Wasn't that bad?" the bird repeated mockingly, leering sideways at the gambler. "McCluskie told us the Canadians were bombing us." His good eye zeroed in on Jones. "And Ronald wouldn't move the game's location."

"Once the location of the game is set, it can't be changed," the gambler returned as though he couldn't believe such a thing had been mentioned. "And again, it wasn't that bad."

"I lost my eye," the bird squawked, and flew into the air. He fluttered about with hovering outrage and landed on Jones's shoulder, staring up now at the gambler. "If you recall, a German brute burned out my eye with a cigar."

"I came back for you," the gambler returned with a plaintive whine, and shrugged his white brows in defense at Jones. "When the Germans broke up the game, I forgot him in the rush to leave."

"We should have left when McCluskie left," the bird threw in.

The gambler nodded. "I can't believe he made it out."

"I'm not surprised," Belvedere said flatly. "The Nazis are no match for the Devil's dog. For that matter, neither are the Canadians."

"That was the nice thing about having McCluskie at the game," the gambler said, thinking of that time. "Since he was from the future, he knew exactly what country was bombing us."

"I should have left with him," the bird grumbled. "I'd still have two eyes."

"I think you look good with an eye patch," the gambler said with a smirk. "What do you think Jones?"

Jones glanced at the British talking macaw on his shoulder. "Uh…I think you look dangerous with an eye patch."

The bird thought pensively about that, and then dryly said, "Mr. Jones, do you feel that's a good look for me? After all, I belong to the gambler—not a fucking pirate!"

The gambler laughed, and stepped up to Jones. "Okay kid, how do you know about us?"

Jones fished in his pocket and held up the picture. "I won it in a poker game. Along with a real good story."

The gambler snatched the photo from Jones's hand, studied it for a second, and then held it up for the bird to see.

"Oh, Ronald, I think you look rather dapper in that photograph. Do you remember when it was taken?"

"1900," the gambler informed, "Redemption Iowa."

"That's what Wintergreen said," Jones spoke up. "He was the only mortal at the game."

The gambler's eyes narrowed in thought. "From what I remember, Wintergreen did rather well."

"A hundred extra years of life," Jones replied. "At least that's what he told me."

The gambler handed back the photograph. "Let me guess kid, you want in?"

"I want to play with the deities. I want to sit in at your next game."

He thought about it, his face reluctant. "I don't want a thrill seeker."

"I've played cards since I was fourteen," Jones boasted. "I'm thirty-eight now. I'm good at what I do. I love the game, and I need to step up the ladder. I need to play against the best."

The gambler considered his argument. "I don't know. The buy in is high.. Are you willing the pay the price?"

Jones nodded at once.

A deep reluctance remained in the gambler's eyes. "I don't know."

"Oh please Ronald, he found us," the macaw said, rubbing his green forehead underneath Jones's chin. "He deserves a shot, if he's stupid enough to take one."

"We have no idea what kind of gamesmanship he has," he told the bird. "I don't want to be embarrassed in front of Envy."

"The bespectacled angel won't care," Belvedere said. "She only cares about taking down the Deity Fate."

The gambler stroked his goatee in thought. "I don't know."

"I can beat you," Jones said with confidence.

The bird laughed. "Everyone beats Ronald."

"Not everyone," he returned in defense. "I'm in a slump."

"For fifty years," Belvedere sang out dryly, and then added, "Give the kid a shot. He deserves it."

The gambler nodded. "Okay. If you want in? Fine. My next game is in California on September, 30th, 1955."

Relief washed through him—now he had his shot at playing against deities, but his next thought came out as, "Seven years from now?"

"He's good in math, Ronald," the bird said with a laugh. "That's a plus."

"Now listen kid, if you repeat what I'm going to tell you, I will kill you."

"Pay heed to that Mr. Jones," the bird followed up quickly. "Ronald can be quite savage when annoyed. You should have seen what happened to the Germans when he returned for me."

"No one hurts Belvedere," the gambler said coldly, his attention on Jones. "So don't repeat what I'm going to tell you."

Jones nodded.

"The game begins at 5:43 am local time in Blackwells Corner, California."

"I can't believe we're starting that early," the bird griped. "I'll be cranky Ronald, at least for the first few hands."

The gambler ignored the comment and pushed on. "Go behind the Texaco station and look for an elderly black man seated in a rocking chair. His name is Mr. Isaac. You tell him, 'I'm expected'." He paused and added, "Don't be late."

Belvedere suddenly squawked, Jones recoiled and the bird flew away, landing a moment later on the gambler's shoulder. An odd look stirred in the bird's eye, and he delivered this:

"Seven will play cards with evil notes of hate,
Envy of Heaven will battle against Fate.
The Devil's Breath sings and warns her...
Soon there will be seven mourners
At Blackwells Corner."

"Holy shit," Jones muttered. "What just happened?"

The concern in the gambler's face quickly vanished and he tried to make light of the whole thing. "The bird has psychic events from time to time. Pay no attention to it."

He lifted his chin at him. "Remember, don't be late."

*   *   *

A dim orange glow lit up the black mountains in the star speckled distance, and Jones looked at his watch, cursing himself. He had overslept. On the most important day of his life he had overslept. How stupid could he be?

If his watch was accurate, he had a minute, maybe less. He ran around the Texaco station, panting hard with desperate excitement and his eyes zeroed in on the doorman. The elderly black man, dressed in a gray suit with a red tie, his head completely bald, rocked in the chair and looked out at the splendor of mountains awash in early morning light.

Jones ran up to him. "Mr. Isaac, I'm expected."

His eyes fluttered up to Jones, his dark lips pushed out with cold indifference, and in a deep voice he said, "Those are the magical words." He rose to his feet with the pace of an eighty year old, and an annoying urgency roared through Jones. He was late as it was, and now he had to deal with the archaic doorman.

"Can you—"

The stare in the old man's eyes made him stop mid-sentence. "You shouldn't ask that question," he cautioned, a thin gray eyebrow creeping up his forehead. "You should be asking yourself: should I go through with it?"

101

Douglas J. McGregor

"I've asked myself that question for a good long time, sir. The answer always comes up yes."

"You're a mortal playing against deities," he reminded him. "And they are a savage bunch, Mr. Jones."

"I need to do this."

He shrugged as though he could care less. "It's your soul," rolled off his tongue, and in a slow gaunt, he started off toward the tin shed building attached to the Texaco. "Don't be fooled by the surroundings," he told Jones. "The gambler hosts a lavish game."

"At least the Canadians aren't bombing us."

Mr. Isaac paused in stride and regarded Jones with a befuddled grin. "Helluva place to hold a poker game—in a city under attack." He shook his head with mystical disbelief. "And the damn bird lost an eye."

The man bitched more about the Berlin game, throwing in "I should have left with McCluskie", and grew silent as we reached the building. The wooden door with the hole-ridden screen creaked hellishly, and the old man stepped inside and started down a long hall, walking slow like time didn't matter to him. Right then, it didn't matter to Jones either, for a thought blazed in his head: *the building isn't this big.*

He considered mentioning it, something to talk about while they walked, but in the end he stayed silent, reasoning that: maybe some questions shouldn't be asked.

At the end of the hall, Mr. Isaac wrapped his knuckles on the door, and then gently opened it. Cigar smoke and idle chatter poured from the room.

"Boss, your last guest has arrived," the doorman announced, and stepped back, allowing Jones to see inside the room. He focused in on the green felt poker table awash in bright overhanging lights; then he zeroed in on a woman seated at the table.

Jones's heart skipped a beat. *The bespectacled angel,* he thought, a mild shock drifting through him. Her angelic face, highlighted with black rim glasses, radiated an alluring elegance he had never experienced before. Her brown eyes twinkled with delight behind her glasses and her celestial smile warmed him. He fell in love with her right then. Before the thought could truly take hold, the gambler stepped into his line of sight.

He looked as he did in Manhattan seven years ago. Today he wore a white button up dress shirt with a brown leather vest and saggy blue jeans. "Right on time, kid," he said, his smile bright inside his trimmed goatee. He shook Jones's hand, and gestured at the table. "Allow me to introduce you to everyone… this here is the Texan."

A thin man with wide shoulders turned in his chair, tilted up his cowboy hat and blew cigar smoke into the air before saying "Howdy," through lips hidden by thick shaggy gray whiskers.

Jones shook the Texan's hand, and the gambler gestured at the woman seated next to him. "This is the Deity Fate."

Fate rose from the chair with a confident flourish, a smile growing on her round face ringed with majestic locks of black hair that cascaded over her shoulders. A sweet, mild-mannered glint twinkled in her brown eyes, and that worried Jones, for beneath the glint brewed a cold evil only a blind man could miss.

"It's pleasure to meet you," she said, straightening out the cuffs on her white blouse before shaking his hand.

He wanted to respond 'likewise', but her cold, dead-fish handshake left him speechless. Fate filled in the silence with, "It's good to have a mortal at the game."

And that's when the mood turned ugly.

Seated directly across the table from Fate, the bespectacled angel rose abruptly to her feet. "Stop pretending to be nice, you bitch," she snarled at Fate, her glasses hedging up on her scowled cheeks. "You'd crush him like a bug the first chance you got."

"Fuck you—you four-eyed ugly nag," Fate fired back.

The Texan found that funny and spewed out cigar smoke with his laugh. He wasn't alone. The gambler laughed, and so did Mr. Isaac, who stood by the open door with his arms crossed.

"Fuck you right back—you pompous bitch," Envy barked.

"Do you want to do this right now?" Fate asked in a low evil tone, and motioned with both hands at Envy to approach.

Oh my God, Jones thought, *I'm gonna see an angel and a deity duke it out.*

Envy snickered with menacing intimidation. "You're going to look funny playing cards with a saxophone stuffed up your ass."

The Texan, once again, found that funny, and more cigar smoke spewed into the air. The gambler, on the other hand, had had enough: "Please ladies," he stepped in, motioning with his arms to get their attention. "We're at an event, in a beautiful moment in time, let's not spoil it with bitterness."

"No bitterness," Envy said, adjusting the collar on her blue jean jacket. "The evil bitch knows I hate her guts."

Fate went to speak but the gambler cut her off with a hard look, and turned to the bespectacled angel. "Now this beautiful creature here who just called Fate a pompous bitch is the Angel Envy."

Jones stepped around the table and reached out for Envy's hand. "Awe cool, an angel with glasses," he said. "You are so beautiful."

"She's a four-eyed asshole," Fate threw in, retaking her seat.

Envy ignored the comment, and the gambler introduced Jones to the huge deity stuffing his face at the buffet of cold-cuts and bread spread out on tables across the back wall. "This here is the Fat Turk." He was obese beyond the word, seven or eight hundred pounds easy. His red t-shirt was large enough to make a tent.

His huge face glowed with a warmth Jones liked, and the deity threw his beefy arm around Jones's shoulders, looking down at him. "You're real small."

"It's a good thing we're not playing football."

The Fat Turk laughed, gave Jones a gentle squeeze, and sat at the table. The gambler gestured at his bird, now perched on the edge of the table behind a stack of black, white and red chips. "Of course, you know Belvedere."

The bird nodded, and Jones went over and lightly stroked the bird's head. "I still think you look dangerous with the eye patch."

"Thank you Mr. Jones, and I still think you look like the Artful Dodger, only older."

"You're drunk," the gambler said with a laugh, guiding Jones to a chair between Envy and the Fat Turk.

"I'll have you know Ronald, I'm only into my first martini," and the bird leaned over and sipped from the martini glass beside his stack of chips.

"I don't like it when you drink gin," the gambler told the bird. "You slur your words."

"I notice you have a vodka with cranberry in front of your chair," the bird said with a mocking ha-ha. "Maybe if you stopped drinking Vodka you'd get out of your slump."

The Texan spoke up from around his cigar, "Hey Ron, I'd like to know if you're in a slump or not. Are we going to talk or play cards?"

The gambler nodded and turned to Jones. "I have a stocked bar."

"It's not even six in the morning," Jones returned.

"Yeah so, what's your point?"

Jones thought about, but not for long. He stepped over, dug a cold Bud from the ice cooler beneath the buffet table and opened it with a can opener on the cooler's lid. The gambler directed him to his chair.

"You can sit between Envy and the Fat Turk." The gambler pointed at the stacks of red, white and black chips in front of the empty chair. "I knew you would come, so I prepared your chips in advance."

Jones thanked him, and knew what was coming next.

"Now for the buy in," the gambler said, and asked, "Are you sure?" Jones nodded and the gambler waved his hand in front of him. "I now have your soul in the bank."

"I don't feel any different," Jones admitted.

"You will after I take all your chips," Fate threw in with a quiet laugh. Jones waited for Envy to comment, but she stayed quiet and absently ran her fingers up and down her stacks of chips.

"At the end of the game," the gambler continued, "all you need is one chip to redeem your soul. The more chips you have at the end, the more time you have to live."

The gambler walked around to his chair at the table, gently stroked Belvedere's head, and said, "Let's play cards."

"Finally," the Texan said.

*   *   *

The ante was a red chip, and Jones anted up and the gambler dealt first. Jones ended up with a two of hearts and a five of diamonds and discarded the moment he could. Envy, Fate and the Texan stuck around to see the 'flop'. The Texan sure liked seeing the two red sevens; Envy and Fate not so much. After some name calling, they discarded. The Texan scooped up the pot and glanced at the gambler. "You should have kept your doorman around in case these two go at it."

"Mr. Isaac is available if we need him," the gambler noted, glaring at Fate.

"We almost needed him at the Berlin game," Belvedere threw in lightheartedly, hoping to brighten the mood. "McCluskie had a few choice words for the German general." He sipped on his martini, his head tilted upwards in thought. "What was his name again? Ludwig 'something or other'. Anyway, I felt certain that General Ludwig was going to leap across the table and strangle him."

"McCluskie can be damn funny, and insulting," the gambler threw in with a laugh, his smile bright.

Envy looked Fate in the eyes. "I wish he was here now to insult your ugly bitch face." And she anted up.

Fate threw a red chip into the pot as well, stared at Envy, called her a 'four-eyed bitch' and added with dripping implication, "Be careful what you wish for."

Envy shot out of her chair with such force Jones fell sideways into the Fat Turk's lap. Fate flew out of her chair too, knocking over the saxophone leaning against the leg of the table. The gambler yelled for Mr. Isaac, the bird flew off and landed on the buffet table, and the Texan yelped, "Holy shit, a cat fight."

"Please ladies, be civil," the gambler pleaded, and leaned over the table, waving his arms to get their attention.

"What do you know about McCluskie?" Envy demanded.

Mr. Isaac burst into the room, pushed aside the Texan, and stepped up to Fate, their noses only inches apart. "I can take you out easy," he told her through clenched teeth, and swung his attention to Envy. "And I can sure give you a hard time." His eyes were on the gambler then, waiting for instructions.

"Thank you for rectifying the problem Mr. Isaac," the gambler said. "You may return to your post."

The old man nodded, yet before he left, he coldly threatened, "If I have to come back, you two will have a problem neither of you want." He closed the door, and the gambler said, "It's your deal Texan."

The Texan dealt, and Jones got about the same as the first deal, a three of clubs and a nine of spades. He discarded, and that's how it went for him. In a couple of hands, he hung around long enough to see the 'flop', but discarded when the betting went wild.

His chips dwindled, and he began to worry.

When it came time for him to deal, he dealt himself a pair twos, and wanted to play, but so did everyone else, and the betting went wild, and he tossed away his cards when it came time for him to bet.

Aside from the occasional insult, Envy and Fate stayed quiet and played cards. The gambler remained rooted in his slump, and had less chips than Jones when it came time for Belvedere to deal.

The gambler dealt for the bird, and dealt Jones two black aces. He struggled to contain his smile. Now he wanted to play, and so did Fate and Envy.

The 'flop' came down: the six of hearts and two black eights.

Fate liked the 'flop' so much she quietly gasped. Envy liked it too, but she was too shrewd to show her emotions. She stared down at the cards through her glasses, saying nothing, playing with her chips.

Jones had studied their behaviors since he arrived, and had a good idea what each of them had. He figured Fate had an eight, and that worried him. Envy had a run, maybe a four and five, or maybe a nine or ten. She needed help; Envy didn't. And Jones had two pair, aces high.

Betting resumed and Fate, chuckling under her breath, pushed an entire stack of black chips into the pot. Envy matched the bet and added a subtle, yet tasteful, "Bitch," as she leaned back in her chair.

It was Jones's turn to bet, and the aces in his hand did all the talking; he pushed out his stack of black chips, and grinned at the gambler. "Be kind."

Fate shot Jones a bitter look. "You stupid mortal, you're playing with fire. Get out while you can."

Jones said nothing; Envy, on the other hand, added, "Disrespectful bitch."

Fate's reply scorched everyone's ears, and after the gambler cautioned them both to keep it civil, mentioning Mr. Isaac's name in passing, he flipped over the 'turn' card. The jack of diamonds stared up at everyone.

A scornful distaste brewed in Fate's eyes. She cared little for the jack. Envy cared little for him either. It was her turn to bet, and she checked.

Jones checked as well. Fate decided to make it hard. She stared across the table at Envy. "Got no balls, bitch?" and she threw a red chip into the pot.

Envy smiled wickedly. "I'm a female, so no, I have no gonads." She threw a red chip into the pot. "I have breasts, unlike you—you flat whore."

"Do I have call Mr. Isaac?" the gambler asked quietly.

With an evil smile brewing on her face, Fate stared across the table at Envy. "If you win this, I'll tell you a good story. A McCluskie story."

"Oh, I'd like to hear that," Belvedere spoke up suddenly, and sipped at his martini. "I'd love to hear a good McCluskie tale. And to think, he's not even born yet."

The gambler shushed the bird and looked at Jones "It's your bet."

Jones threw a red chip into the pot. The gambler sipped on his drink, paused to build up the growing anticipation, and then turned over the 'river' card.

The ace of hearts stared up at everyone.

The three aces and those cold black eights made his heart speed up, and now his thoughts were on his soul. *Is the hand strong enough?* he thought darkly, and the answer came back quick. He pushed all his chips into the pot. "I'm all in."

That sure got everyone's attention. The Texan choked on his stogie, the bird muttered, "Dear God" and the Fat Turk stopped chewing on his bagel long enough to say, "I'm going to need a scotch after this".

The gambler stared Jones in the eye. "Are you sure?" and then excused himself saying, "none of my business."

Envy turned to Jones. "You sure like that ace."

"Enough to bet my soul."

The gambler leaned across the table and counted Jones's chips before turning to Fate. "You have enough to match him and stay in the game."

She sighed under her breath. "Damn mortal. What an annoying species."

Playing cards for thirty years had taught Jones a lot, taught him to keep his mouth closed in times like this, still, his soul was on the line, and well, *fuck her.*

He looked at the gambler. "I don't want Mr. Isaac to show up but"—he turned to Fate—"Fuck you—bitch!"

Envy laughed so hard her glasses slipped to the end of her nose; and the Fat Turk stopped chewing. Even Belvedere, in mid sip at the time, was unable to suppress his laughter, and a snorting spray of gin and vermouth hit his chips. Fate glared angrily at Jones. "You are a mere speck of existence to me."

"That may well be, and you don't have to respect me because of it, but this mere speck of existence has you right where he wants you." He motioned at her. "Match my bet or fold."

She sighed with annoyance, and her eyes turned to the gambler. "In all your games you have welcomed assets," she said, her lips twisted out bitterly. "If I recall, the weapon in the pot brought McCluskie to your Berlin game."

"I wish we were back at that game now," Belvedere threw in whimsically. "Even with the Canadians bombing us, the mood was lighter." He chuckled and added, "We don't normally see Mr. Isaac this often."

"Will you shut up?" the gambler cut in, and turned to Fate. "Assets are welcomed at my game."

She plunked down her saxophone into the pot. The tarnished brass glinted dully beneath the lights, and Jones read the inscription on the dented bowl. *Redemption Iowa, 1900, The Devil's Breath.*

"Is it enough to equal the bet?" Fate asked.

The gambler nodded, but Jones took exception. "Why would I want with your fucking saxophone? I don't play. Put your chips in the pot."

"It's a special horn," she said.

"Special or not, I don't want it," Jones fired back. "To be honest, right now I wished the Angel Envy had stuffed it up your ass. You'd be sitting funny but at least your chips would be in the pot."

"Maybe I'll shove it up your ass," Fate barked, and rose to her feet with a hostile snort. She clenched her hands into fists. The Texan yelled, "Holy shit, not again!"

Jones was on his feet in a flash, and he picked up his chair in both hands, ready to bash her. The gambler yelled for Mr. Isaac and the bird flew away, nattering about there being less excitement at the Berlin game. Mr. Isaac burst into the room a second later, a nasty look on his face, and the gambler intercepted him before he could reach Fate.

"It's Jones," the gambler said, motioning at him.

The doorman turned to Jones, and his lips slowly rolled upwards over his teeth into a beaming smile. "Oh c'mon, please. Not you. Not the mortal. I would have been less surprised if the bird had been the problem."

"It's nice to see you too Mr. Isaac," Belvedere sang out from the buffet table. "I believe this is a record for you for appearances at a game. And to think, the day is young. We may see you five or six more times."

"You better not," he cautioned gruffly and looked at Jones. "What is your problem mortal?"

Jones gently placed the chair on the floor. "I'm sorry Mr. Isaac, I got caught up in the moment."

"I'm sure you had help," he muttered, and looked around the gambler at the deity Fate. "Try not to look so innocent." He quickly glanced at everyone. "Okay, I've had enough. So listen, if I have to come back, it's going to be the 'end' for someone at this game, and I'm not counting the mortal in this because he's too easy to take out." He backed away to the door, his eyes on the gambler. "Boss, your Berlin game had less excitement."

"I just mentioned that," Belvedere cut in.

Mr. Isaac pointed his finger at the macaw. "Bird, if I have to come back because of you, I'm going to poke out your other eye."

As he exited the room, Jones took his seat and looked up at the gambler. "Sorry for interrupting the game."

The gambler ignored the apology. "If you had given me a chance, I would have told you that I will give you fair value on the horn at game's end." Before Jones could respond, the gambler looked at Envy. "Your bet, angel."

Envy tossed away her cards, and turned to Jones. "Kick her ass."

"What do you have, Fate?"

She stared Jones in the eyes. "You seem awful confident."

"Confident enough to know I'm gonna need to take saxophone lessons."

The gambler took matters into his own hands, and he leaned over the table and turned over Fate's cards. She had a seven of hearts and an eight of diamonds. He turned Jones's cards over then, and the black aces made the Fat Turk gasp.

"Full house, aces high," the gambler said, and pushed the saxophone and mountain of chips toward Jones.

"Ronald," the bird sang out. "Did you notice? Jones has the Deadman's hand."

"What the hell are you talking about?" the Texan asked.

"When Wild Bill Hickok got gunned down in 1876, he was holding black aces and black eights. It's now called the Deadman's hand."

"Thanks for the history lesson," Fate grumbled, and stared at Jones. "Deadman, indeed. How apropos."

And that's when Belvedere shot into the air. He fluttered about the room in a panic and landed at the edge of the table near Envy. He squawked once and coldly delivered:

"Evil notes sing a song so mean
It blows a movie star off the silver screen.
The Little Bastard,
Is not mastered,
And it gets plast—"

"Ron, can you shut that damn thing up?" the Texan barked. "He's giving me the creeps."

The gambler rose to his feet. "Maybe we should take a break."

*   *   *

The break lasted thirty minutes, and everyone but Belvedere and Jones left the room. Jones downed the rest of his beer and got another one, needing the drink badly. He resumed his position at the table and leaned back in his chair, his thoughts all over the place, revisiting glimpses of what just happened. And now he was scared.

The funny thing was, he had always known his soul would be on the line, and it never bothered him. Not in the least. But now it did, and he wanted out. This was not a friendly game. This was hostile, this was war with cards and chips, and he had an enemy, a real bad one; and he took another guzzle of beer hoping it would settle his nerves.

"You did well Jones," the bird sang out, breaking the silence. "And now you own a saxophone."

"Lucky me," he muttered, and leaned the saxophone against the leg of the table. "The Devil's Breath—it sounds evil."

The macaw chuckled. "Not only does it sound evil, it is evil, and that would be a gross understatement."

"Considering who I won it from, I won't argue the point." Jones went back to his beer, and counted his chips. His nerves settled slightly when he tallied up what he had: not counting the saxophone, he was up a dozen chips. But the game was young.

Belvedere sipped at his martini, chewed on a cashew, and reminisced about the last hand. "When the ace popped up, the look on your face was priceless."

Jones took a hit of his beer, and he laughed at himself. "I tried to conceal my joy."

"You failed Jones," the bird replied. "Miserably. Most likely even Mr. Isaac, posted in the parking lot, sensed your glee." He bent over, his beck above the rim of his martini glass, and in a serious tone added, "Everyone in the room knew you had aces, which begs the question…"

"What question?"

"Think Jones," the bird said, and took a sip from the glass. He was back looking at Jones. "Why did Fate play on?"

Jones thought about it, still not understanding. "What are you getting at? Three eights is a pretty strong hand."

"Not against three aces," the bird said, "and as I mentioned before, the entire room knew you had aces."

"What are you getting at?"

"Isn't it obvious?" the bird said with an eye roll. "She wanted you to have the Devil's Breath. The question now is, why?"

"Maybe she thinks I'm musical."

"I admire your wit in such dire times."

"Dire times?" he questioned, and motioned at the sax. "It's only a saxophone." He picked it up and, on impulse, blew into the mouthpiece, blowing a fluttering 'run' of shrill notes.

"Will you stop that," Belvedere snapped. "You're blowing evil notes."

"As if," and Jones blew out another string of sour notes for fun. He placed the saxophone against the leg of the table, took a hit of beer to rid the taste of the mouthpiece from his tongue, and turned to the door as it opened.

Envy entered the room. Jones's eyes were on her—and he saw something that made his jaw drop: a wine glass, filled nearly to the brim with red wine, hung suspended in mid air. Standing next to the hovering glass, Envy cleaned her glasses on the shirt tail of her pink blouse. Once the glasses were shinny clean and back on her face, she plucked her wine glass from the air and took her seat beside Jones.

"Thanks for the magic."

"Thanks for making me laugh," she said, her smile bright. "You couldn't believe how much I was laughing inside when you picked up your chair to hit her. You have no shortage of courage."

"To be honest Envy, I was happy to see Mr. Isaac."

Her smile was back, even brighter this time, and she leaned over and whispered in his ear, "You had nothing to worry about. If she had moved on you, I would have torn her to shreds. Mr. Isaac would have carried her out in a bag." She leaned around Jones. "Did you hear that Belvedere?"

"Yes I did. My hearing is quite good angel." The bird snickered. "I'm glad that didn't happen. I think we've seen enough of Mr. Isaac for one day."

The bird got a smile from the angel and Jones threw his arm around her shoulders and hugged her. "Thanks beautiful angel. Thanks Envy. You are so special." He paused, his eyes wide. "Listen, I have to ask you something. Why didn't she fold? She knew I had aces. The whole fucking room knew I had aces. Why does this bitch want me to have her saxophone?"

Envy leaned over, her cheek against his. "Try to draw out the reason from her subtly, without her knowing. Use the horn to your advantage." She moved her head back, placed both hands on Jones's cheeks, and kissed him hard on the lips.

His cheeks flushed red and he grinned at Belvedere. "I got a kiss from an angel."

"I got a high-five from McCluskie," the bird boasted.

"What's a high-five?"

The bird raised one of his talons in the air. "McCluskie placed his hand against my talon. It was a pleasant gesture."

Envy glared at the bird. "What do you know about McCluskie?"

"Not much angel. His stay was under an hour."

"What did he say about dark alleys?" Jones asked.

Belvedere looked at the angel. "Seven years ago, we came upon Mr. Jones in a dark alley, and I mentioned that McCluskie warned us dark alleys are no place to be—the Devil tells him that all the time." The bird eyed Envy. "Always heed advice from Lucifer, don't you agree, angel?"

The question took her by surprise, and she sipped at her wine until, "He is an archangel." She raised her chin at the bird. "Anything else?"

"What are you fishing for Envy?" the bird asked, chewing on a cashew. "You know most of the story. McCluskie is tethered to the Devil, and he showed up at a poker game under attack to get a weapon that will kill a Horseman. That alone should tell you everything. And if it doesn't, allow me to share my opinion, he is an extremely capable individual, and extremely dangerous."

"He's only a mortal," Envy grumbled, looking away.

"Tethered to your enemy," the bird reminded her. "No matter who you are: angel, deity, Horseman, take your pick, I wouldn't want to be on McCluskie's 'bad' side."

Envy's eyes grew hard. "He's going to be a problem."

"I would think so," the bird said without hesitation. He sipped at his martini, and looked at the angel, "Here's something that might interest you Envy, as he played cards for the weapon in the pot and insulted the general, he casually mentioned he had killed a Horseman."

Her eyes grew large behind her glasses.

"He never mentioned which Horseman," the bird went on with a good measure of exasperation. "Ronald and I have a fifty dollar wager on who it will be. He thinks it'll be the Angel of War; I bet on the Horseman Pestilence." The bird chewed on his cashew and threw in, "McCluskie also casually mentioned he had killed an angel."

She gasped, and as she did, the gambler entered the room, a fresh vodka and cranberry in his hand. "What's going on?"

"The bespectacled angel just kissed Jones squarely on the lips," Belvedere piped up. "It was quite passionate."

The gambler raised a brow at Jones. "At least you're not hitting anyone with a chair."

"The day is still young Ronald," the bird sang out. "I fear we will see Mr. Isaac again."

"I hope not," the gambler said wearily. "He looked angry the last time we saw him," and he paused, adding, "What word did McCluskie use for angry?"

"Pissed," the bird answered. "From what I hear, the Devil is always pissed at McCluskie."

"No surprise there," the gambler noted with a smile. "Mr. Isaac is pissed, and"—he glanced at Envy—"please angel, no fighting."

"Why are you looking at me, Ronald?" Envy asked, barely able to contain her smile. "I'd be more worried about Jones."

The Texan and the Deity Fate entered the room then, and everyone resumed their position at the table. The gambler opened a fresh deck of cards. "Okay, we're only waiting on the Fat Turk. We'll change decks. Belvedere's talons have made a few holes."

"Stupid bird, shouldn't even be in the game," Fate said, looking down at her chips, but soon she was looking at the gambler.

His cheeks creased with red, evil intent, and he leaned over the table, his eyes burned into Fate, "If you ever insult Belvedere again, you better prey someone calls for Mr. Isaac, because you are going to be in a fight with me."

Fate tossed her head in a huff. "Can't take a joke?"

The Fat Turk burst into the room then, waving a scrap of paper in his meaty hand. "You are never going to guess who I just met in the parking lot." He waved the paper about. "James Dean—the movie star! I got his autograph."

"Who cares?" the Texan grumbled. "Let's play cards."

"He's driving his Porsche to a car race," the Fat Turk continued. "He stopped here for gas." He showed the autograph to the gambler. "What's it worth as an asset."

He shook his head. "No value."

"He's a movie star," the Fat Turk pleaded.

"Maybe so," the gambler said, "but right now his autograph is worth the price of the paper." He glanced at everyone. "Ante up, my deal."

*　　*　　*

Everyone anted up and the game resumed.

Jones's good luck hung around, and he won the pot with three threes. The Texan dealt next, and Envy and Fate squared off. The flop came down: jack of clubs, queen of hearts, nine of spades. They checked, called each other a bad name, and the Texan dealt the turn card. The seven of hearts stared up at everyone and Envy pushed a mountain of chips into the pot.

Fate stared her down, and then swung her attention to the gambler. "It's all I have."

"Bet or fold," the Texan said impatiently.

Fate hesitated, looked at her 'hole' cards, and pushed all her chips into the pot.

"No insult?" Envy asked, her brows raised above the rims of her glasses. "I was hoping for a good one."

"So was I Envy," Belvedere said in a drunken slur.

Fate glared at the angel. "Let's play cards, you four-eyed nag."

The river card came up the two of diamonds, and Fate turned over her cards with a laugh. Two black twos stared up at everyone. Fate had three of a kind, all twos; Envy turned over her black sevens. She had three of a kind, all sevens.

"You lose, bitch."

Fate said nothing, staring down at the cards. The gambler rose to his feet, cleared his throat. "You're cleaned out Fate. You have to go."

"You better call Mr. Isaac," Belvedere threw in quietly. "This may get ugly."

Before Fate could speak, Envy waved her hand, and half the chips in the pot moved in a tumbling wave toward Fate.

The bird blinked at what just happened. "More magic for you Mr. Jones."

Envy glared Fate in the eye. "Half the pot for the McCluskie story."

"Are you sure you want to hear it?" Fate asked, her smile growing smug. "You may not like what you hear?"

Belvedere turned to the Fat Turk and laughed. "I bet I'll like it."

Envy rose to her feet. "I'm waiting."

Fate answered with, "Beware of the Devil's dog."

Belvedere was back looking at the Fat Turk. "I already told her that."

A thin hue of red emotion washed across Envy's cheeks. "I'm going to need more for your end of the pot."

Fate stood and stared the angel in the eye. "In the future, in a place you feel safe, you are going to run into Jacob McCluskie."

"Envy," Belvedere sang out at once. "When you do, please say hi for me."

Fate turned to the bird. "She won't get the chance."

"What does that mean?" Envy demanded, her hands clenched in fists.

The Fat Turk leaned toward Belvedere. "A black chip says we're going to see Mr. Isaac real soon."

The bird scoffed. "I'm surprised he's not already here."

"Ladies, please," the gambler sang out. "Let's not bother Mr. Isaac again."

"What does that mean bitch?" Envy snapped, and stepped around the table. "And how do you know it?"

Everyone stood, and Belvedere said, "My God, poor Mr. Isaac is going to be exhausted after this game." He eyed the Fat

Turk. "We might as well have him sit in at the game. It would be easier on him."

The gambler snapped, "Envy," and as he did, Fate defused the situation by retaking her seat. She crossed her legs, and stared up at Envy. "Throw me a black chip and I'll tell you about Rex, the talking dog."

"A speaking canine?" Belvedere managed in a drunken slur. "That's utterly preposterous. The only speaking dogs I know of are in cartoons." He went to add more, but Envy shot him a mean, vengeful look, and Belvedere closed his beck.

"A black chip for the story, you four-eyed nag."

Envy sat and, without hesitation, tossed a black chip at Fate.

Everyone resumed their positions at the table and Fate said, "I ran into good ol' Rex back in 1900. His insane owner made the Devil's Breath—and that's what I was there for. Before I left, he told me a story, a story about the man he dreams about—Jacob McCluskie. And in the story there was an angel who wears glasses."

Fate grew silent and anted up with a red chip.

"I need more," Envy said.

"The game is young," Fate said. "Let's play cards, we'll talk later."

Belvedere glanced at the Fat Turk. "I should have bet you that black chip."

Fate took the deck from the Texan, and as she shuffled, the low whine of a siren drifted through the room.

"We heard plenty of sirens at the Berlin game," Belvedere noted with a drunken laugh. "Never expected to hear one here. Then again, I never expected to see so much of Mr. Isaac today."

"There's more than one siren," Envy said with a hint of concern.

"I hear them too," the gambler said, and stood, calling for Mr. Isaac.

He burst into the room a second later and the gambler stood at the doorway, hands up in defense. "No issues here, Mr. Isaac, we only wish information. Why all the sirens?"

"Ambulances, boss," he replied, his face serious, and looked at the Fat Turk. "The movie star you were chatting with in the parking lot rolled over his Porsche, the Little Bastard."

The Fat Turk gasped, and Fate stared at Jones. "Did you play the horn?"

"Uh…"

"You shouldn't have done that."

"I told you it was evil," Belvedere said softly.

"Is there anything else Mr. Isaac?"

"Yes, it's safe to say the movie star has made his last movie."

The gambler looked at the Fat Turk. "Sixteen black chips for the autograph."

The Fat Turk placed the piece of paper in front of him and the game resumed.

*   *   *

Jones's luck ran hot and cold all afternoon. He won a few hands, and had the savvy to get out of a hand before he had lost too many chips. He still had a good sizeable mountain of reds and blacks, but so did Fate and Envy.

The gambler remained in his slump, and went out first. Then, the Texan, believing a straight flush was unbeatable, ended up going home when Envy revealed her four eights. The Fat Turk went next, unable to believe a talking macaw had knocked him out of the game with a pair of fours.

"Ace high won't cut it in this game, Turk," Belvedere said, eyeing the gambler as he scooped up the winnings.

"I was bluffing," the Fat Turk informed, downing the rest of his scotch. "If you had any manners, you would have realized that and thrown away your measly fours." He thanked the gambler for having him and then disappeared.

Four players remained: Belvedere, Jones, Fate and Envy. It was Belvedere's deal and the gambler dealt for him. Jones liked his red jacks. Fate liked her hole cards too, and hung around to see the 'flop'. It came down: the three of hearts, the four of spades, and the queen of clubs. Jones hated the flop, so did Fate, and they both checked.

The turn card came down the jack of spades. Jones struggled to suppress his joy, and he pushed out half his chips into the pot. She matched his bet at once, and a thin shiver of fear rippled through Jones's gut. *What does the bitch have?* he wondered.

The river came down: the four of hearts. Nothing for Jones, but Fate liked it, and a smug smile brewed on her face. "What do you have in front of you Jones, because that's the bet." She tapped the table with her finger. "Put the horn in the pot too."

He hesitated, thinking.

A few seconds elapsed, and then Fate snapped, "Are you going to bet or fold?"

"What's your rush? Do you have another game to go to?"

"I believe McCluskie said that to the German general at the Berlin game," Belvedere piped up, gin and vermouth slurring his words. "Everyone laughed but the German general." The bird looked at the gambler. "I wonder what happened to him."

"Nothing good," the gambler said, and turned to Jones. "What's your play?"

Jones pushed his chips into the pot, and turned over his cards. "Full house, lots of jacks and two fours on the table."

She turned over her hole cards and Jones gasped. The four of diamonds and the four of clubs stared up at everyone.

"You lose," she said, raking in the pot.

The gambler stood. "Sorry Jones. You're cleaned out." He nodded with admiration. "You played damn well. Sorry about your soul."

Jones stood, and Envy was on her feet in a flash. She hugged him tightly, kissed him, and told him she loved him. He gave the macaw a high-five, walked around the table to Fate, and handed her the saxophone. "Why did you give it to me in the first place? You knew I had aces."

"I wanted you to hold it," she told him, rising to her feet. "And I want you to hold it now." She placed the Devil's Breath back in his hands. "Carry it for the rest of your life." She fished a black chip from the mountain of chips in front of her and threw it at the gambler. "I don't want his worthless soul. Give it back to him."

The gambler waved his hand. "Good for you Jones. You have your soul back."

"And an evil saxophone," Belvedere said with a chuckle. "You failed to mention that Ronald."

As Jones reached for the doorknob, Fate added, "Oh Jones, I wouldn't play it too often." Her laughter echoed down the hallway as he walked away.

It was Envy's deal, and as she shuffled the cards, she asked, "Why did you give him the instrument?"

"I don't want to carry it around until 1959," she said. "Jones can do it."

"That's the end of his life?" Belvedere asked with concern.

"Hardly," Fate said with a laugh. "He'll run out of money in Mason City Iowa and pawn it." She grinned. "I have someone coming to pick it up."

Envy stared at her. "You know something, you are quite a bitch."

The End

The Devil's Breath

The drifter pulled down his black toque over his ears, pulled up the collar on his olive green army coat to hide his long hair and walked out to the road.

A cold February wind bit into his cheeks and whistled with a sinister rage down the lonely stretch of highway. The metal sign that read **North** fluttered wildly in the wind, clanging like a church bell. His boots crunched on the gravel shoulder and he stepped across the white line onto the frozen cracked pavement of route 65.

He scanned the horizon through the pallor of his icy white breath. Empty. And so, with no traffic in sight, he buried his hands in his pockets, shivered in the gnawing teeth of a raw winter gale and thought about why he had come to Iowa.

His thoughts peeled back seven years to Korea.

The thick splash of army boots striking mud washed in a low murmur below the sharp ping of rain bouncing heavily on his helmet. The leaves and branches chattered with rain, and wisps of fog drifted like sluggish snakes, mingling in the thick brush and across the path.

Craig walked third in a line of twenty, bent over slightly to shield his Browning rifle from the rain, his eyes shifting from side to side, scouring the woods for signs of movement, signs of the enemy.

Time marched on, and the rain fell, and then, far off on their left, deep in the bush, a bird cried out, and everyone froze.

A short tense moment of time ensued. Everyone waited for something to happen, but nothing did.

Finally, the sergeant, standing behind Craig, cleared his throat and stepped out of line. Sergeant Greene was an old timer, if you wanted to call thirty-eight old. It was his second war and all he wanted to do was get out alive.

"It's only a bird," he said gruffly. Someone at the end of the line made a funny comment Craig couldn't hear and laughter rolled through the platoon. The sergeant glared angrily in the direction of the comment but said nothing. Then his brown eyes shifted to Craig. He looked up at him through the rain dripping off the rim of his helmet. "C'mon music man, we'll lead the way into camp."

A sick knot of fear squirmed in Craig's belly—walking 'point' was never good, and his cheeks paled slightly and he wished he was anywhere but where he was.

"It'll be fun," the sergeant added with a laugh. "And when we're close to home and safe, you can play your harmonica for the boys." He went to say more, perhaps to request a song, his lips beginning to move, but he never got out the first word.

His face exploded in a violent splashing red that shot out across Craig's chest like a whip. For an instant, time froze, and Craig saw the remains of the sergeant's shattered face: his chin and nose were missing, and his tongue, now only a stub, thrashed and spewed blood like an unattended garden hose.

Time hiccupped then and reality filled in: the sergeant's smoking face fell away from his sight and the woods exploded with red flashes. Bullets whizzed by him.

An air-horn jerked him away from Korea's horror and back to the present, back to Iowa and Route 65. An eighteen wheel truck, its silver skin gleaming in the sun, barreled up the highway. He stuck out his thumb. The rig zoomed by, its wake nearly blowing him off the road, and then the brake lights went on. Craig hurried to the truck and climbed into the cab, thankful for the ride and happy to be somewhere warm.

As he settled into the passenger seat he assessed his new companion. The trucker looked normal (and you had to be careful these days). He was bleary-eyed from driving, unshaved, and thick in the shoulders and so fat in the waist a bulge of stitching on his blue sweater had popped loose. He was as young as Craig—early to mid twenties. Craig liked his smile.

"Are you headed to Mason City?"

"You know it," Craig replied, and cordially introduced himself.

The trucker stuck out his meaty hand. "I'm Roy."

With the pleasantries over, Roy geared down, and soon they were speeding down the highway. For a good long minute, Roy never spoke. He drove with his eyes on the road as though he had no passenger. Craig relaxed in the seat, happy he didn't have to talk, not that he minded, it was worth the price of the ride, still, a quiet driver meant he could think, think about what awaited him in Mason City.

Roy finally broke the silence. "Are you a war vet? Cuz you're wearing an army coat." He shook his head, his chubby lips turned out with distaste. "It's too cold to be walking around in that. That's good for the fall and spring. Not winter."

"I like wearing it," Craig admitted. "I feel blessed with it on." Then he quietly added, "It's a keepsake from Korea."

Roy nodded with admiration. "Did you see lots of action?" His eyes narrowed and focused on Craig's coat. "Are those bullet holes?"

Craig's fingers played with the holes in his coat: seven in all; some large, some small; the holes ran in a half moon shape across his chest.

"Not bullets," Craig said. "Teeth."

The word hung in the air with acute shock, and Roy weakly managed, "What do you mean?"

"My sergeant only stood as high as my chest," Craig went on. "It's funny, he always used me as protection, walking behind me because I was so much taller than him." He shook his head sadly. "It didn't matter. His whole face got shot off."

Roy paled, and the odd guise in his eyes worried Craig. He put his hand on Roy's shoulder. "Are you okay?"

It took a moment before Roy nodded, and then words stained with a thirsty fascination spilled from his mouth, "What happened?"

"As you can see I got away, the only one in my platoon that did. The only reason I survived was because of my sergeant—his body protected me from the Chinese onslaught."

"How'd you get away?" he asked at once.

How much should I tell? Craig thought, and decided the truth, at least for awhile, would do. "I returned fire." He regarded the trucker with an ardent stare. "It's weird, but in times like that, in firefights, twenty rounds seem to shoot off real fast."

"I bet," he wheezed out as though in a trance.

"I reloaded twice," Craig went on, looking out the window at the frozen Iowa farmland, collecting his thoughts. "When I ran outta ammo, I threw away the rifle and used my pistol." He turned to the trucker and shrugged with a conceded helplessness. "Within ten seconds all I had left were two grenades and a knife, and the Chinese were coming out of the woods. There had to be a hundred of them."

"What did you do?" Roy asked breathlessly.

"I threw both grenades and ran."

The trucker nodded with a tight, satisfied grin. "Good for you—and you out ran the suckers."

Craig nodded, but it was a lie, and he looked out at the Iowa farmland, waiting for Roy to ask follow-up questions. But the trucker stayed silent, his eyes on the road, mulling over a horror story from seven years ago, and Craig thought about what had really happened.

His thoughts returned to Korea.

Bullets whizzed by his head like angry wasps, and he threw himself down onto the cold mud. Screams of his friends rang in his ears, and he inched forward toward the sergeant. The veteran of two wars had run out of luck, and he lay on his back in the mud, his hands twitching in grisly spasms as Chinese bullets pulverized his body. Bits and pieces of bloody raw flesh flew up in vicious splashes like serpent's tongues in front of Craig's eyes.

Fear gripped his thoughts, and he froze, unsure as to what to do; but his indecision only lasted a second, for a bullet ricocheted off his helmet, spinning it sideways on his head. A thought screamed in his head: *Protect myself.* He calmly corrected the position of his helmet and reached for a weapon.

The rifle he had been so careful to keep dry now lay in the wet mud beneath him, and he worked it free, steadied his nerves and rested the dripping barrel on the sergeant's leg. He squeezed the trigger, and as he had told Roy, twenty rounds shoots off fast. By the time he clicked his third magazine into place, he realized something that sent a sick shiver of terror through him—he was the only one in the platoon firing. His eyes twitched from side to side. What he saw through the driving rain sent a scorching flame of terror up his throat. Everyone in his platoon was dead, their wet olive colored clothing stained with gurgling blood.

His eyes were back on the forest, and ahead through the downpour, he saw the enemy in the bushes. The Chinese stood out like evil black scarecrows in the misty dripping green and brown of the forest. He squeezed the trigger with frenzied desperation until the weapon clicked dry, and then tossed it away, drawing his pistol. The .45 was for close engagement. Craig didn't care, and he pulled the trigger over and over until he ran out of ammo.

His heart pounded like a bass drum, and over the sergeant's leg, he saw the Chinese advancing. Instinct took over.

He threw the .45 into the air, and his wet hands pulled free the grenades pinned to his coat. Using his thumbs, he popped the pins free. He threw back his left arm and tossed the grenade; before it had landed, he tossed the other one.

The explosive concussions fired off back to back—and now he was running, his arms crossed over his face as he crashed through the underbrush, his breath coming out white and horse.

Bullets zinged by his head, and he kept running and soon he was out in a clear spot in the forest. He gathered speed over the carpet of wet pine needles and his hopes soared. Maybe he could out run them. And then the forest came to an end, came to a cliff. The drop was a hundred feet, probably more, and he turned back to face his destiny.

Blurry black shapes advanced slowly through the bushes toward him, and he drew his last remaining weapon. The knife was useless against Chinese machineguns, but it was all he had, and he darkly wondered, *did the Chinese take prisoners?*

As he thought this, he noticed something odd. The Chinese soldiers, fifty at least if not more, were dropping from sight one after the other.

And soon there were none.

"What's going on?" Craig breathed out, and then the underbrush shook, and parted, and a man in a gray trench coat stepped out.

He was tall, taller than Craig and Craig stood six-foot three. He was thin like Craig too, yet much older. He looked to be in his eighties.

With a pinched bitter look, he shook rain off his fedora, straightened his tie, and turned to Craig.

What seemed like a million questions fired off at once in his head, and he stepped forward a few feet, slashing the knife in front of him. "Stay away."

The man's thin lips curled out with aloof exasperation. "Oh, for the love of God." He placed the back of his hands on his hips, his face creased with a stinging 'are-you-kidding-me' look, and shook his head in disbelief. "Put that fucking thing away before I shove it up your ass."

Craig held the knife in front of him. "Don't come near me."

"Listen asshole, I'm not in the mood." The man sighed rain off his lips. "I should be in the present Timeline, in the year 2016, but I'm paying off a debt. That's why I've traveled all the way back to Shitsville, Korea circa 1953. So put the knife away so I can talk to you."

Craig lowered the knife to his side, a nervous glint in his eyes. "Who are you?"

The man threw up his hands in mock ire. "I would have thought by the dead Chinese you would have figured that out by now. You're a Catholic boy, right? You've leafed through the Bible from time to time. Maybe you've read some of Revelation. I'm suppose to have a pale horse for some reason."

Craig blinked in astonishment and quietly managed, "The Angel of Death."

"Thank you for getting it." The man bowed slightly. "That prick McCluskie got it right off. When I asked him if he knew who I was, he said, 'if I had to cast the Angel of Death in a movie, I'd pick you'." He motioned at himself. "A star is born."

"McCluskie? Who's McCluskie?"

"He hasn't been born yet," Death informed. "He's indirectly responsible for me being here."

"From the future?"

"Thank you for paying attention," he returned abruptly. "Yes, from the future. See, I owe McCluskie a favor, he owes the Deity Fate a favor. Being the prick that he is, he passed my favor over to her as payback. As usual, I get the short end of the deal, ultimately winding up in a Korean rainstorm talking to snot-nosed eighteen year old."

Craig shook his head in despair. "I don't understand. Why is this happening? Who is the Deity Fate?"

"She is the reason you are alive," he snapped. "Because of her, I saved your ass."

"Why?"

He pointed at the harmonica poking from Craig's pocket. "I understand it's not your instrument."

"It's too hard to lug around a saxophone on patrol."

"Don't get smart with me," Death said gruffly. "I have to take it from that asshole McCluskie because he's tethered to the Devil, but I don't have to take it from you."

Craig's eyes grew wide. "Sorry?"

Death waved his hand at the apology, and came forward a few feet, standing no more than a yard away from the private. "Now listen, and listen good, I don't care what you do for the next seven years, but on February 2nd, 1959, you make sure your skinny ass is in Mason City, Iowa."

"Why?"

"Go to the pawn shop."

"Why?"

"It will cost ten dollars," he said. "The money will be provided before pick up."

A short silence ensued with only the sound of falling rain. And then Craig spoke his thoughts, "I don't understand any of this. Why?"

"Fate has chosen you to play the Devil's Breath."

"The Devil's Breath," Craig whispered, and suddenly someone was shaking him. He looked over to see Roy's meaty hand on his shoulder. He was back in a truck in Iowa motoring north on Route 65.

"You were talking in your sleep."

"I fell asleep?" he asked. "I don't remember."

"Yeah, and you were muttering." He looked Craig in the eye. "By the way, what's the Devil's Breath?"

*   *   *

The air-horn on Roy's truck blasted out a friendly 'goodbye' and with heavy diesel fumes in his nose, Craig walked down the street to Bob's Pawn Shop—the only pawn shop in town according to Roy, who drives through Mason City all the time.

A small poster taped to the inside of the pawn shop's frost-coated window caught Craig's attention and he paused long enough to read it before going inside. The bell above the door jingled, and a warm musty smell greeted his nose. Craig took off his hat and shook his head; his hair spilled out over the shoulders of his coat. And now his eyes were on the proprietor at the end of the room seated behind the wood counter.

The man (and Craig assumed it was Bob) looked to be about forty, and his cold blue eyes tinted with a quizzical glint behind the thick lenses of his glasses. His eyes hardened. He ran his hand across his buzz cut short hair and rose to his feet with military abruptness and stormed around the counter.

Awe fuck, Iowa Bob is a tight-ass zealot, he thought, and as the proprietor approached, Craig's eyes quickly roamed over the store's merchandise. Being Iowa and farm country, tools of all varieties took up most shelf space, but not all, and the pawn shop had a music section, a small one.

"Hey," the proprietor began, and he came to a stop in front of Craig and crossed his arms. "Are you a woman? Cuz you have long hair like a woman."

Craig had dealt with bigotry before, and decided to ignore it. All he wanted was the saxophone. And now a sweet smile curled onto his lips. "I'm between haircuts, sir," his words dripping with sincerity, "and I'm a bit sensitive about it."

The proprietor's cheeks hedged, pushing his glasses up on his nose, and then his expression froze, unsure how to respond. Finally, after a few seconds, he managed, "Oh," and he laughed awkwardly, straightening out his thick red corduroy shirt. He cleared his throat. "Are you in town for the show tonight?"

"The one at the Surf Ballroom?" Craig asked, and motioned with his head at the door. "I saw the poster in the window."

"Buddy Holly is performing," Iowa Bob said, "and Richie Valens and the Big Bopper. It's great they came by. It'll help local business."

Truckers play lots of music, and Craig was familiar with all three musicians, and he liked what he'd heard. "To be honest sir, I didn't know they were in town."

"I'm not surprised, it was a last minute decision to put the Surf Ballroom on the tour." The proprietor pushed his glasses up on his nose, that quizzical glint back in his eyes. "So? What can I help you with today?"

"I can't leave Mason City without a souvenir."

A glint of dollars signs glistened in the proprietor's eyes. Long hair or not, business was business. "You've come to the right place young fella. What can I interest you in? Perhaps a coat? It's too cold to be walking around in what you're wearing." He gestured with salesmen glee at his rack of coats.

Craig shook his head and lifted his chin at the music section. "I see you only have clarinets, guitars, tambourines, and a crooked-neck banjo—but no saxophones."

The proprietor eyed him keenly. "You're looking for a sax?"

Craig held up his harmonica. "I've decided to change instruments." He stepped forward, looking down into Iowa Bob's eyes. "Any saxophones?"

The money glint was back in Bob's eyes. "I have a dozen." He focused in on his music display, shaking his head sadly. "I don't put them out often because I've got no stands." He directed Craig to the stairs near his counter. "I store them in the basement, so if you'd like to follow—"

Craig stopped him with a raised hand. "I don't need to. I'm looking for a particular saxophone. A saxophone named the Devil's Breath. So that's the one to bring up from the basement." The words struck the proprietor with such impact, he gasped and stepped back as though needing more air to comprehend the idea. "I can't believe it." He looked away in dismay, and finally, after a deep breath, turned to Craig. "Wait here."

He was gone in a flash, scooting around the counter. He by-passed the basement stairs and went instead to a backroom. Craig leered around the counter and watched what Iowa Bob did.

A minute later, the proprietor returned carrying a saxophone. He shinned up the instrument's rim with his shirt tail and handed it over the counter to Craig. "I believe this is what you want."

Craig read the engraving on the bowl: *Redemption Iowa, 1900, The Devil's Breath*. He had the right instrument, and he inspected it quickly before hanging the thin leather strap around his neck. "I'll need a mouthpiece to test it."

And that's when things took an interesting turn.

The 'salesman' in Iowa Bob vanished and his expression turned as cold as ice. "Who are you Mister?"

"Excuse me? I'm the man who has come to buy a sax."

"Give me the truth," he hissed, his eyes narrowing. "How did you know it was here?"

Craig considered who had sent him, and eventually said, "That's a confidential story sir. Now, how about that mouthpiece?"

"It doesn't come with a mouthpiece." And he coyly added, "I can sell you one, but that's extra."

The word *extra* bounced around inside Craig's head. Death had promised the money for the sax would be provided before pick up, and true to his word, Roy passed him a ten dollar bill as he was climbing from the cab, wanting Craig to use it to buy food. He wondered now if he needed a mouthpiece, but the thought quickly went away when he remembered Death's parting words, 'Fate has chosen you to play the Devil's Breath'.

"Do you want it?"

Craig asked the brewing question. "How much?"

Iowa Bob licked his lips, set his glasses further up on his nose, and flatly said, "A thousand dollars."

Did he really say that? And now Craig's thoughts were back in Korea, back on the Angel of Death, and a grin broke out across his face. "I hope you have a little wiggle room in that price. After all, even in mint condition, this horn would only retail for two hundred."

"It's a special sax," he informed smartly. "It's a horn that's been involved in lots of crazy stories."

"Stories?" Craig's heart sped up. "What kind of stories?"

Iowa Bob flashed him a grin. "Those are confidential young fella," and now he was snickering. "Rest assured, the sax is worth every dime. Remember, you're paying for pedigree."

"Pedigree? It's a fucking saxophone."

Craig's expletive fired up the ire in Iowa Bob's eyes. "Mind your tongue, long-hair," he advised coldly, and after a deep breath added, "The fella that sold me the sax told me all about its provenance. I didn't believe a word of it, but now you're here, and now I'm starting to believe him."

Craig stared him in the eye. "What did he say?"

"He told me it's been played by deities."

His words made Craig pause, and he thought about it, but not for long, deciding it didn't matter. He pushed on with, "That may well be, but I was told it would cost ten dollars."

"Who told you that?" Iowa Bob demanded. "This is my store. I set the prices."

Awe, this is not going well, Craig thought, and scrambled for something to say. "You know, you planned to throw it out. It was sitting in the garbage can."

The proprietor chuckled, and soon his chuckling turned evil; and then Craig heard a loud click, and his eyes focused in on the revolver shaking slightly in Iowa Bob's hand.

Craig's heart quickened, his cheeks flushed, and he stepped back trying to think of something to say, but all that came out of his mouth was a meek sigh.

Iowa Bob held the weapon at his side. "Take it off," he said, each word delivered sharp and cold like a knife blade. "Put the sax on the counter and step away."

Craig did as ordered.

"I know you want it. And I know you have money to buy it." Using the hand holding the revolver, he motioned at himself. "Why shouldn't I make a few dollars?"

"I don't blame you for trying to gouge me, it's Mankind's way. But ten bucks is a good price, and it was the price I was told to pay."

"Who told you that?"

"You want the truth? I mean, really?" And he pushed on with, "Okay. Here goes." He looked him in the eye and cryptically whispered, "The Angel of Death." Craig let his words absorb in before adding, "Seven years ago Death saved my life in Korea. He told me Fate has chosen me to play the Devil's Breath. He told me to pick the horn up here at this time." Craig held up the ten dollar bill. "I was told to pay this." He slapped the bill down on the counter.

After a long moment, Iowa Bob sighed harshly, "It's not enough."

"Sir, you seem like an intelligent man, so you have to ask yourself, if I leave the store without the sax, what do you think is going to happen?"

It took Iowa Bob no time at all to think about it. He pushed the instrument across the counter. "Take the damn thing."

"Mankind never fails to impress me."

*   *   *

Iowa Bob had more to say, a lot more, and what he said scratched with frenzied malevolence in Craig's head all the way to the Mason City Airport Hotel—a two-story eyesore in need of a fresh coat of white. He needed a place to hold up, to think.

A savage blast of winter wind screamed at him as he reached the door, and away went his hat, blowing into the small reception area. His whipped-up long hair sure got the attention of the elderly clerk behind the counter. The old man's eyes bugged out, and a scornful bigotry puckered on his wrinkly face. He straightened his bolo tie, ran his thin age-spotted fingers over his bald head and pretended to act sad. "Sorry. No rooms. Try back next week."

For half a second, Craig considered dropping the Angel of Death's name into the conversation; yet in the end, he dug a twenty dollar bill from his pocket, the last of his money, and held it up to the clerk. "Are you gonna disappoint our 7th president, Andrew Jackson?"

The clerk turned out to be a patriot, snatching the twenty from Craig's hand without hesitation. "He was the 7th president?"

"Right between Adams and Van Buren," Craig informed smartly, and wanted to add, 'don't you remember voting for them?', but kept the insult to himself.

"You don't say," the clerk returned, nodding in thought, and he placed a brass key on the counter, a smug smile brewing on his timeworn face. "Lucky you, you're staying in the presidential suite."

"I hope so," Craig threw in. "I'm paying triple the price."

The clerk's eyes hardened. "You're lucky I didn't want a Ulysses S. Grant." And then he snidely inquired, "What number president is he?"

"The eighteenth."

"Good to know." He jerked his thumb over his shoulder. "The presidential suite is on the ground floor—way in the back." His smile widened. "You can watch the planes take off."

Craig didn't care, a room was a room, and he snatched up the key. "Please register me under Jackson. Party of one."

He went outside into the frozen breath of a bitter wind, walked around back, staying on the concrete deck and stopped in front of room number 7. The room lined up perfectly with the end of a runway, which Craig estimated to be no more than thirty yards away. A short snowy infield and a chain link fence separated the airport from the hotel property. *It might be loud,* he thought, and quickly decided he didn't care. He had slept in worse places.

The room smelled liked mothballs and, as the old joke goes, it was so small you'd have to go outside to change your mind. "The presidential suite my ass," Craig muttered, and leaned the sax next to the nightstand. Then, after kicking off his shoes and socks, he stretched out on the bed, thinking of Bob's Pawn Shop, thinking of Bob.

In his thoughts, he saw Bob's bitter face, his cheeks crimson. In his hand he held the ten dollar bill. "It's not enough."

"Ten bucks is ten bucks." Craig raised his chin at the owner. "And I still need a mouthpiece."

Without having to mention the Angel of Death, Bob placed a mouthpiece on the counter. Craig picked up the sax, dropped the mouthpiece in his pocket and started for the door. Bob yelled out, "You are running into a mess of trouble young fella. Why do you think that thing was in the garbage? It's evil. Pure Evil."

Craig reached for the door handle, and then turned back. "What do you mean?"

"It played at Blackwells Corner." He raised a brow at Craig. "Have you heard of James Dean?"

He crept forward a few feet. He had seen all three of Dean's movies and had read the account of his death. He knew about Blackwells Corner. "The sax was there?"

"From what the fella who sold it to me said, the sax played a merry tune while Dean gassed up his Porsche and ate lunch. Minutes later he was dead."

"You're making this up."

Iowa Bob laughed. "Ask the Angel of Death."

"What else have you heard?"

"A whole lot young fella," he returned darkly. "Enough to know you're as cursed as the instrument."

The buzz of a small plane landing brought him out of his thoughts, and he sat up on the bed and looked at the instrument. It looked harmless. Still, he feared the worst from it, and decided not to play it—to keep it mute.

Satisfied with his plan, he lay back on the bed and closed his eyes. As soon as he did, saxophone notes played in his head. The melody touched his soul, and he fell asleep with the song resonating in his thoughts.

Hours passed with blessed dark nothingness, and then: lights shone in the window and the slam of car doors aroused

Craig from sleep. He was at the window in a flash. A car idled at the end of the runway, its headlights burning, illuminating four men.

A rattle on his left made him whip his head about, and he watched in horror as the saxophone knocked against the nightstand.

"…it's alive," he breathed out.

A mild shock fell over him, and without knowing he had done it, he crossed the room, picked up the instrument and placed the thin cord around his neck. The instrument vibrated in his hands.

"Dear God," he muttered, and dug into his pocket for the mouthpiece. He slid it into place, and then, without realizing it, he was outside. A light snow fell, and his bare feet crunched over the snowy infield. He walked up to the fence, its frozen gray interlacing glaring in the beams of car lights. All four men turned to him.

Craig gasped in shock—he recognized one of the men. Buddy Holly was tall and thin and dressed in a thick winter coat. He wiped the fog off the lenses of his glasses with a finger and walked closer to the fence. "What's your name?"

"Craig."

"I'm Buddy," he said, a hint of Texas drawl in his frozen breath. "Are you gonna play us a song?"

Craig cleared his throat, got the note in his head, and hummed it, and then he sang, "A long, long time ago…" and he took a deep breath and blew into the sax. His fingers danced on the keys as the notes came to him. The others joined Holly by the fence as the song played into the snowy Iowa night. The men listened in utter fascination.

As he delivered the notes with precision, he heard the song's words in his head. They flowed beautifully, just like the melody. Yet, the song's meaning was lost to him, he understood none of it; well, except for the line '…the day the music died'. Those words he understood well; those words made his blood run cold.

When the song came to an end, the horn went dead in his hands. They all applauded, and one of them said, "That was amazing."

"You're right Richie," and Holly came right up to the fence. "What was that song called?"

Craig sadly shook his head. "I don't know."

Before Holly could speak, a plane taxied up toward where the men stood. Holly looked Craig in the eye. "You are one talented sax man. You played the devil outta that thing." He turned, and caught up with the others. Craig watched them board the plane. Then he went inside, took off the sax, lay down and went to sleep.

It would be late afternoon the next day when he would hear the news of the plane crash.

He was not surprised.

* * *

The newspaper shook in his hands. And soon tears dotted the newsprint, lots of tears, and the headline in his vision blurred. Not that he needed to see it—the words were seared into his brain.

An overwhelming grief chewed into him, tiny teeth ripping into his soul, and he screamed in anguish until his throat grew raw. His screeching howl echoed in the alley, and he leaned over and cried some more.

When his tears ebbed, he straightened up and tossed away the newspaper. Its pages spilled apart and tumbled away in the light July breeze. His eyes were downcast now, focused on his only possessions: a timeworn army coat and a saxophone.

The Devil's Breath lay atop the coat, the slant of the sun striking the alley just enough to nick its bowl, and the glint teased Craig. He heard a mocking 'ha-ha' in his head, and anger spiked through him. He snatched up the horn as though seizing a snake and screamed at it, "You fucking thing!"

The 'ha-ha' was back in his head, taunting him, and with a loud heaving sigh, he savagely threw it down the alley. It bounced twice and slid across the asphalt into the wall. A few fluttering newspaper pages clung to it.

"It ends now." His words echoed empty and flat, and he whipped about, his long gray hair sweeping out like a curtain behind him as he stormed from the alley.

His thoughts were clear, maybe the clearest they've been since Death showed up in Korea. He knew exactly where he had to go and what he had to do.

The construction site he had passed earlier was empty now, the workers on break, and no one saw him slip in through the gate. The sledgehammer leaned against the tractor tread of a dozer, and he picked it up, liked the weight of it in his hands. "This will do just fine," he said evilly, and quickly returned to the alley.

He dropped the sledgehammer on the asphalt, marched up to the instrument and kicked it away from the wall into a sunny spot. He stared at it for a long moment, and had to admit, aside from a few dents and scraps, it looked the same as when he picked it up at the pawn shop in Mason City, Iowa eighteen years ago. Thinking of that brought tears to his eyes.

Eighteen years, he thought, and for a moment, he couldn't remember how old he was. When the answer came to him, his mouth opened and he sadly muttered out the truth, "Forty-three years old, and my life has come to this: no family, no friends, only a sledgehammer and a saxophone."

He kicked the instrument out into the middle of the alley and leered down at it. "You're finished. You've played your last evil note." His eyes swept over to the sledgehammer, and beside it stood a woman.

She looked to be in her thirties, bright brown eyes, high cheeks, and a slender rounded chin. Her black hair was tied back in a tight bun. She wore a snug fitting white blouse and dark pants tucked into her boots. She smiled. "Hi Craig, my name is—"

"I don't need the introduction," he barked at her, flicking his head back to get the hair out of his eyes. "I wondered when you'd come by."

She tilted her head a bit to the side in curiosity. "You expected me?"

"Either you or the Angel of Death," he told her. "I'm glad it's you. Death looked pissed off the last time I saw him."

"My name is Shannon, and I am the Deity Fate."

He nodded at her, a smile brewing on his face. "Hey, you wanna hear something funny? I thought you'd be taller." He walked up to her and stared down into her face. "My name is Craig, the drifter, and I'm the guy you cursed." She went to respond, but he bent down and picked up the sledgehammer. "Did you come by to pick up your evil saxophone before I smash it flat?"

"You don't need to do that."

He laughed at her. "I beg to differ. For the last eighteen years I've seen what that fucking thing has done. It has to go."

"The evil has been exhausted."

"Again, I beg to differ." He walked over to the horn and kicked it a few feet.

"Craig, please, let's talk—"

"Talk!" he screamed, and with a surge of savage fury, he turned to her. "What do you want to talk about?" And in an evil dark tone he pushed on with, "Do you want to talk about the day—the fucking music died?"

"It was tragic."

"Oh fuck please—tragic? Is that the word you want to use? I was thinking more along the lines of 'horrific'. Then again, I started the 'tragic' event, so maybe I'm just embellishing."

"Craig, you don't need to be like this."

"Like what?" he barked, and with the same fury added, "Your horn and I killed the president!" He started to cry, and walked toward her. "In case you're unaware, I was in Dallas Texas in November of '63. I played a great song for everyone only minutes before the president came by. I don't need to tell you what happened after that."

"I'm sorry."

He laughed through his tears. "I sure hope that's not your apology, cuz if that's it, it sucks. Oh, in case you're unaware, a few years later, your horn and I drifted out to L.A., and killed the president's brother."

She looked down and sighed, "It was terrible."

"Do you know what else was terrible?" he asked her, and quickly added, "I drifted into Memphis Tennessee in April of '68 and played a song in front of the Lorraine Hotel. As I was playing, Martin Luther King Jr. stepped out of his car and listened, nodding in admiration at my performance." He glared down at her. "I don't need to tell you what happened after that."

She motioned with her hand. "Please put down the sledgehammer."

He came toward her. "You're a deity, so you must have all kinds of powers." He sniffled back tears. "Are you gonna make me?"

She shook her head at once. "You're free to do what you wish, but as I said before, the saxophone's evil has been exhausted."

"Oh fuck, please, are we back to me 'begging to differ' with you?" He motioned with his head at the saxophone. "Do you know what that thing did yesterday?"

She nodded, and went to speak, but he was too angry to let her get out her words. He wanted to talk, he wanted to get his words out, eighteen long years of words that had culminated in yesterday's horror in a maternity ward.

"All boys," he said. "The nurse killed all the boys in the maternity ward."

"She was looking for Jacob McCluskie."

He went to speak, but hesitated. "McCluskie? I've heard that name before. Death mentioned him."

"He was supposed to have been born in the 2nd Avenue Med Center in Queens, New York, in the building you played in front of yesterday. Someone, however—and I have my suspicions—prevented that from happening. Jacob McCluskie was born yesterday, July 7th, 1977 in North Carolina."

"Good for him. Do I get a cigar?" he asked with a laugh, walking back to the saxophone.

Fate pushed on with, "All of Mankind's evil was stored up in the McCluskie bloodline. When his great-grandfather went to Redemption Iowa in 1900, the evil shed him and went into the horn. It would play evil notes until this date, until Jacob McCluskie was born." She came forward, right up to him, and gently touched his arm. "The evil is gone from it. It's benign."

"Benign?" He looked down at the instrument, gleaming in the sun. "Maybe I should play a few notes. Test it out. See what happens to you."

"I would love to hear you play."

He shook her hand from his arm, stepped back and threw the sledgehammer away. Tears bubbled up in his eyes. "Why did you curse me?" He stared down into her eyes. "It would have been far more humane to let the Chinese kill me."

"I refused to let that happen," she told him, her tone harsh. She stared hard into his teary eyes. "I saw you play the saxophone at a high school concert. As I watched you play, I saw your 'fate'—killed in Korea—and that hurt me deeply." He went to speak, but she cut him off. "Yes, I feel too, and that's why I did what I did. I needed a proxy to play the horn. And I chose you."

"You damned me for eighteen years."

Her expression remained ridged, and she said, "Like it or not, you're alive."

The words brought tears to his eyes, and he looked away, not knowing what to say, not knowing what to do.

A quaint smile touched her lips, and she came over and wrapped her arms around him. "I'm sorry about the last eighteen years, I'm sorry about the hell you went through, the torture you endured, but Craig, I'm not sorry for saving you."

He hugged her tightly. He needed to hug someone then, deity or human, it didn't matter, and he cried in her ear. "I don't know what to do now. I'm scared."

"Don't be scared." She squeezed him hard. "It's all over now."

The End

The Out of Towners

'Baby please don't go down to New Orleans...
You know I love you so—baby please don't go.'

A dead blackness squeezed the hunter with vice grip force and he fought against it, desperately clawing his way upwards, struggling to reach reality's surface before it was too late. The wind's howl rattled around in the back of his head and he heard pelting rain; and he felt a moist pressure on his face—then his eyes exploded open. He jerked backwards, scaring the skinny black kid holding the white beach towel to his face.

The kid fell over on his ass, but quickly got to his feet, adjusting the straps on his school backpack. Kody thought the kid looked about eight or nine. He also thought the kid looked terrified. Eyes were not supposed to bug out that much.

Kody sat up with a painful sigh, his face on fire and his head throbbing. The kid kept his distance, six feet away, hands at his side, holding the bloody white beach towel. "Are...Are you okay, mister?" the kid asked, nervously running his hand across the front of his yellow rain sleeker to straighten out the folds.

The question got him thinking, and the broken-glass memory of how he ended up here fell into place with jarring force and now he had a few questions of his own. Why was he still alive? He should be dead, torn to pieces. Not that he was complaining, but still…and who was this black kid? Where did he come from? And where was Apollo?

"Have you seen a cat around here?" Kody asked. "He's gray with a white belly and face. Oh, and he's kind a fat."

The kid shook his head.

"Okay, that's a problem," Kody muttered with a sigh, and looked at the kid. "You don't have to be scared of me."

The kid hesitated, and then, with his voice filling with suspicion, he said, "You're bleeding green, mister."

"Do you have something against people with green blood?"

"No sir."

He considered lying to the kid, giving a bullshit story like 'I've got a rare condition that turns my blood green', but he didn't have it in him to lie, not to this kid. The kid had come to his aid; maybe the kid had saved his life; so the kid deserved the truth. "I'm not from this planet."

If it was possible, the kid's eyes bugged out further. "Like Star Trek?"

"Awe, don't be comparing me to that." Kody started to climb to his feet, but the wooziness swirling in his head kept him on the floor; and he listened to the ferocity of the rain for a moment before turning to the kid. "I live on this planet from time to time."

"You live in the Ninth Ward?"

"Not New Orleans. I live in Redemption Iowa."

"I've heard of Iowa." He shrugged. "I've never heard of Redemption."

"Nicest place on your planet, no evil."

The kid thought about it, but not for long. "There's lots of evil around here."

"There sure is kid." Kody made another attempt to get to his feet, and this time he succeeded, overpowering the grogginess that had sucked him down each time before. He leaned against the cinderblock wall for support.

"Wow, men from outer space are sure big. How tall are you?"

"Six-foot-seven." He grinned at the kid. "You'll catch up one day."

The kid looked over Kody' hardware: double barrel shotguns strapped to each thigh, four holstered pistols strapped across his chest. And the kid suspected he had more weapons inside his coat. "You sure have a lot of guns."

"Trust me on this kid, I need them."

The kid nodded without hesitation and held out the towel. "I didn't know what to bring, except the towel, cuz I knew I'd be wet. Take it mister. Your face is still bleeding."

"Thanks kid." Kody pressed the towel against his cheek and fresh green blood squeezed between his fingers. The gash felt deep and long. It hurt like a bitch, as did his head, and with his other hand, he reached through his long blonde hair and gently touched the bump. His blue eyes were back on the kid. "What happened? Why are you in an abandoned brick factory in the middle of a hurricane?"

"I'm trying to get to the Superdome," he explained, tears moistening his eyes. "It'll be safe there, and maybe there'll be food." He shook his head helplessly. "The water is rising." His voice broke. "It was up to my waist, and I can't swim. So I came in here, but this place doesn't seem like it'll last long either."

Kody cocked his ear and listened. "Storm is getting worse." As those words tumbled from his lips, the submerged, yet burning question plaguing him since meeting the kid finally broke the surface. "Where are your parents?"

"I don't have a dad." He shrugged sadly. "And my mom never came home." Tears moistened his eyes. "I can take care of myself."

His last sentence stung Kody' heart. "How old are you?"

"Seven, but I'm gonna be eight next month."

"Yeah, maybe," Kody said with doubt.

The wind gusted hard then, a strong punch fueled by rain so thick you couldn't see across the street. The building shook violently, the cement floor moved, the staircase behind them creaked loudly, and three floors above, the roof cracked with such a thunderous boom you would think God Himself was coming.

The kid looked up at the ceiling. "Hope the building lasts."

"Me too." Kody stepped away from the wall, trying to think through his blazing headache. He had some of the story on the kid, but not much, and where was Apollo? Knife blades of fear tore through his stomach as he searched the warehouse floor for his cat, or the cat's remains.

He yelled out "Apollo" a few times, and he thought of Jackie, looking down at his arm. His wrist ached from razor burn and he remembered what happened: one of the creature's tentacles had torn his comm-device from his wrist, flinging it away; after that, he remembered nothing until now.

Kody searched the factory floor, his eyes crawling across the debris field of broken red bricks. "Did you see a fancy looking watch around?"

"It went flying," the kid replied. "That's all I know."

"I can't call Jackie," he complained with a sigh. "And I don't know where my cat is." He looked at the kid. "But I do I have you for company. That's good."

"Who's Jackie?"

"My guardian angel wheelman." He motioned at the debris littering the factory floor. "If I had my fancy watch I could call her. Get us out of here. It's too gloomy in here to see well, and my eyesight is far better than a human."

"You're right about it being gloomy mister," the kid said, looking around. "It's like night time, and it's nine in the morning."

Kody went to reply, but held up when a small shower of bricks falling over managed to be heard over the heavy rain. And that's when the cat came back.

Apollo climbed atop a pile of broken red bricks and sat there, his bushy tail wrapped around his front paws. He was mostly gray with a white belly and face, and he weighed in at thirty-five pounds easy, maybe a bit more. The vet had scolded Kody about Apollo's girth, and Kody had replied, "I like him fat, he's easier to catch."

The cat licked his paw. Kody smiled with relief, a smile which touched his cat's heart. Then the cat said, "I'm glad to see you're still alive."

The kid gasped. "Oh wow—a talking cat."

"Who is the kid?" Apollo asked, jumping to the floor.

"We haven't got to that part of the conversation yet," Kody replied, staring down hard at his cat. "Thanks for running out on me."

"Oh yeah right. Like I'm gonna take on Mr. Tentacles. If I hadn't run, you'd be picking up what's left of me in a thimble." The cat stopped before him, looking up. "Are you okay? Cuz you don't look okay."

"I'm fine."

"You don't look fine and, uh, why are you still alive? That thing should have torn you apart."

Kody looked at the kid. "We haven't got to that part of the conversation yet."

"Wow, mister. That's cool, an outer space talking cat."

"You told him we are 'out of towners'."

Kody held up the green blood soaked towel.

The cat nodded. "You could have lied you know?" He turned to the kid, "No offense kid, but we don't normally work with the inhabitants."

"We are today," Kody said, and looked at the kid. "What's your name?"

"Jacob Washington."

"Jacob is a cool name," Kody said. "Now what happened? What did you see?"

The kid came forward a few steps so he could be heard above the pounding rain. "I climbed up the stairs out of the water and came inside, and that's when I saw the monster. It was black and hairy and had red eyes and all kinds of arms."

"Tentacles," Apollo threw in. "With nine inch hooked claws on each one." He looked at Kody. "I can't believe you're alive."

"For now," Kody returned smartly and was back looking at the kid. "Go on."

"It came at you." The kid looked Kody in the eye. "I saw your fancy watch fly away, and the creature hit you square in the face. You hit the floor hard mister. Right on your head. You were out cold."

Kody looked down at Apollo. "I noticed he never mentioned seeing my outer space cat. I guess you had run off by then."

"I can't believe you're harping on this."

"You could have given me a 'heads up'."

"Yeah right, I was too busy running. And did you know we were coming to a hurricane when you asked me to 'tag' along?"

Kody smiled through the pain in his head and turned to the kid. "Okay kid, what happened after that?"

"The tentacle monster was coming to get you—and that's when the man arrived."

"Excuse me?" Apollo yelped and walked over to the kid, looking up at him. "A man?" He looked back at Kody. "What the hell is going on? We've got a kid and a man and you still haven't answered my question. Did you and Jackie know we were heading into a hurricane?"

Kody ignored his cat and stared the kid in the eye. "Tell me about this man."

"He came outta know where. He just appeared. And he was tall, almost as tall as you, yet thin, real thin—not football player big like you—and he was old, and he wore an overcoat. It was gray, and he had a hat."

"An old man wearing a hat saved your life?" Apollo questioned hotly, disbelief weaved in his tone. "What is going on? It's like we're all of a sudden in crazy land."

"What did this guy do?" Kody asked.

"He did something with his hands," the kid went on. "It was weird, and then the black hairy tentacle thing turned, and it ran away up the stairs. Then the man looked at me, and said, 'have a nice life'. And then he vanished. I ain't fibbing mister. He just disappeared."

"This is not good," Apollo rang out.

"Yeah, no kidding. And you're right about it being crazy land."

Apollo rubbed up against Kody' leg and sat in front of him. "What do you figure Kody? A deity?"

"That's my guess."

"Son of a bitch," the cat cursed, sitting up on his hind legs and gesturing with both paws. "What are we in the middle of?"

"Nothing good."

"We have to get out of here—now!" the cat snapped, and scratched his torso with his back paw. "Right now Kody."

Kody held up his empty wrist. "Remember?"

Apollo turned to the kid. "Point in the direction you saw the watch fly."

The kid thought about it for a moment. "It's dark you know."

"I don't need the commentary kid," Apollo said. "Just point." The kid pointed and shrugged after he did. The cat's face twitched into a raised brow. "Thank you for being specific."

"It couldn't have gone far," Kody pointed out. "It doesn't have much mass."

"Stop pretending to be smart," the cat grumbled and took off in the direction the kid pointed. The floor was littered with bricks and wood planks. The cat climbed atop a rusted out cement mixer attached to the wall to get an aerial view, remaining on his perch for only a few seconds before jumping down. He disappeared from their view, and reemerged a moment later with the watch in his mouth. He dropped it at Kody's feet.

"Thanks big guy."

"Don't 'big guy' me," Apollo said with attitude. "You and Jackie know I don't like the rain."

"I'm more worried about the wind," Kody returned, "and what's blowing in the wind—like this building." He picked up the watch, shook off the cat's saliva from the strap without bitching, and looked at the black face. The screen was shattered. He gently tapped it with his index finger. The screen lit up white and a hiss of hard static blotted out the thunderous rain for a moment.

"Jackie?" Kody said with force. "Are you around?"

They listened to static, and the cat said, "She probably went back to Redemption to be with her husband and kid."

Kody strapped the Velcro band around his wrist. "She won't leave us hanging."

And to prove him right, the speakers hidden around the watch face squealed horribly, and then a sweet voice took over, "Kody? Are you there?"

Apollo answered for him. "Barely."

"Hi beautiful girl," Kody sang out. "What's shaking?"

"The whole ship, and I'm a fifty miles above this thing. Did you ever pick a bad storm to go into."

"I knew it," the cat said with an implied, 'ha-ha'. "You knew we were headed into bad conditions from the start."

"Is she in a flying saucer?" the kid asked.

Kody started to reply but Jackie beat him to it, "Who's speaking?"

"It's our new friend," Apollo answered. "You wanna hear the story? And what did I ever do to you?—you sent me into a hurricane. You know I don't like to be wet."

"I liked those pink shoes," Jackie replied hotly. "And who is your friend?"

"Oh, it's the shoes. I knew it."

"Will you shut up," Kody barked at the cat. "Jackie, come get us."

"Have you been drinking spaceman? Katrina is a category five hurricane, at least that's what the Weather Bureau says. To be honest, it looks worse from up here. This thing is a ten plus."

"Yeah, it's a bit overcast, but you're the best wheelman in the business."

"Thanks for the bullshit compliment, and 'best' or not, I'd never make it. Rainfall is coming down two inches an hour. And wind gusts 'spiked' my chart. If I get too close, I'll go down."

"Come get us," Apollo yelped.

"I can't," she shot back.

"We're in a lot of trouble Jackie," the cat continued with a plaintive whine. "You won't crash. You won't even break a fingernail."

Kody told the cat to 'shut up' and to Jackie said, "Are you sure?"

A long pause of static ensued, and then, "I would never get to you."

"I understand."

"Listen spaceman," Jackie went on, "where you're standing, the Ninth Ward, well, it's gonna be twenty feet underwater soon. The levees have broken."

"Thanks for the good news."

"I said I was sorry about the shoes," Apollo spoke up suddenly.

"I put my foot in it," Jackie replied with a stab of malicious intent.

"My shit isn't radioactive. I didn't even pee."

Kody stared down at the cat. "If you live—and if I was in Vegas I wouldn't bet on it—you and Jackie can have this out some other time."

The cat backed away, and Jackie's voice came out of the static. "Listen spaceman I don't know what is going on down there, but I need the story. And who is your friend? We don't work with the inhabitants."

"We do today," Kody said, and turned to the kid. "I need a bit of privacy. Apollo will stay with you." He looked at the cat. "Try not to run off."

"You just won't let it go, huh?" the cat shot back. "Oh, and Jackie, I said I was sorry."

"I put my foot in that shoe."

The kid caught Kody' attention with a raised hand. "Hey mister, can I pet your cat?"

"Don't be asking him," Apollo returned angrily. "You ask me, and, well, I don't know."

"Let him pet you," Kody snapped. "Oh, and kid, my name is Kody. And I'm honored to know you."

*   *   *

Making his scorching headache even worse were the questions running amuck through his head. Apollo was right, it was crazy land. The deity worried him, as did the kid, and the sizzling pain running hot through his cheek kept the monster forefront in his head as well, bubbling on the front burner like an unattended pot. What worried him most was the storm. The building wouldn't last. He was surprised it had lasted this long. Sure, it was sturdy, constructed of thick cement and cinderblock, but this was Katrina, and Katrina was a bitch.

He walked to the doorway. The doors had blown off long before Jackie dropped them off, and the seven cement stairs leading up to where he stood were currently underwater. The wind driven rain came down horizontal, so thick it was a blur. The sky was an angry mess of black and gray. *This is bad*, he thought through his headache, *real bad*. Stepping back a few feet, away from the rain's spray, he sat down on the floor, leaning his back against the wall.

"Kody what is going on? Who is this kid?"

He told her the story as quickly as he could. She stopped him midway, right about the time the man showed up to save his life.

"I don't know, Jackie. He's gotta be a deity."

"Why would a deity save your life?"

"He must want me to do something for him, and I believe I'm doing it now," he said, barely able to believe his own words. "Listen beautiful girl, we'll have this conversation face to face. For now, I want you to find out everything you can on Jacob Washington. I wanna know everything."

"I'm looking now." She paused. "How bad are you hurt?"

"I'm fine. I'm no longer a pretty face, but I'm fine and breathing—well, for now. You have to come get us."

"I can't—in this ship. It's too small. I need Mother."

Jackie was right, the ship she currently bounced around in was small; not even recommended for interplanetary use, (sort of like a scooter on the highway). But Mother was different. Mother was the size of a football field and reinforced for interplanetary use. If Mother can take on outer space and everything its got, she can take on Katrina. Problem was…

"Mother is currently in a million pieces back in Redemption Iowa."

"Not a million pieces," she replied, and continued with, "Hang on a sec. I'll patch you through to Charles."

Like Jackie, Charles, the saxophone playing mechanic, was born and raised in Redemption. Aside from a brief interlude in New York back in 2001, he had gone no where else. He was good with his hands, ask his saxophone and wrenches, but could he put Mother back together in time to rescue them?

"I've got him," Jackie said, and they listened to saxophone music.

"Will you stop playing that damn thing?" Kody belted out.

A sax note died out with a sighing whimper. "Oh, hi Kody," Charles replied, his voice strained from playing his sax. "What's going on?"

"Apollo and I are in a lot of trouble, and we don't wanna die in New Orleans."

"Yeah, I've got the TV on. You are in the middle of the worst hurricane ever."

"I know," he shot back. "I've cancelled the picnic. Now listen to me, I need Mother."

Static bit the line. Finally he said, "Okay, when?"

"Now!"

"It's gonna take awhile."

"It better not, or you're gonna be going to be my funeral. And if you do, don't bring that damn saxophone."

"I thought you liked my playing."

"It's your instrument."

"It's not cursed," he defended hotly, his voice breaking up.

"Right now I don't care. Put my ship together. Jackie will be home soon."

She spoke up then, "I'm home in ten, Charles." A loud click sounded, and then Jackie said, "Just you and me, spaceman. What's your plan?"

"To stay alive," he replied. "What's your plan?"

"I'm plotting a course back to Redemption, ten minutes at the most, and less time coming back if I'm in Mother, but that all depends on Charles."

"He does not instill much confidence in me."

"He'll get the job done," she said. "Oh, I've got something on your friend, Jacob Washington. I've got his school photo on my screen. Good looking kid, though he does need a haircut."

"It's a bit flattened down now thanks to the rain," Kody said. "What do you have on him?"

"Court documents," she reported back briskly. "And court documents are never good, and…" She hesitated, still reading. "That runs true in this case. His mother just got him back from youth protection. Her boyfriend was abusing him, and she was letting it go on."

"How nice of her."

"Does he know where his mother is?" Jackie asked.

"No. He's on his own." Kody paused. "I think he's been abandoned. At least he was. Now he's with us."

A paused ensued, and then Jackie asked, "Are you thinking of keeping one of the inhabitants?"

"Do you have a problem with that?"

Another pause lingered. "No," Jackie said. "We can use a bigger a family." Before he could talk, she rushed on with, "I'm leaving now. What are you gonna do?"

"Survive." He stood and tossed away the towel. "And, since I've got a few minutes, I'm gonna go kill a monster."

*   *   *

Kody walked back into the heart of the building and found Apollo lying on his back, his four feet in the air while the kid crouched beside him, rubbing his belly.

"Oh yeah, right there kid, oh, a little lower. Oh you have great hands." The cat looked up. "Oh hey Kody." He turned over and climbed to his feet, stretching as he circled the kid. "Are we getting outta here?"

"Looks like we're staying for awhile. Jackie has gone home to get Mother."

"What's Mother?"

"Hang on a second kid," the cat interrupted, looking up at Kody. "Mother is in a million pieces. If you recall, she took a lot of abuse our last time out."

"As did Jackie's shoes," Kody threw in with a grin.

"I said I was sorry." The cat looked up at the kid to argue the point. "The only reason I went in her shoes was cuz I was nervous. We were a hundred billion miles from here getting shot at. And the guy we were after—Pirate Pierre—well, it turned out he had a lot more buddies than we thought. A dozen ships were firing on us. So I had to go."

"I have to go sometimes too when I get nervous," the kid confessed.

Apollo rubbed up against the kid's leg. "I'm really starting to like you kid. And you give way better belly rubs than spaceman Kody and his cohort, pink shoes Jackie."

"The litter box was right there," Kody reminded him.

The wind gusted hard then, and they all froze, looking upward, waiting for the cracking roof to give way. The moment passed after a few seconds, and the cat said, "To be honest kid, I hated those shoes. The pink bothered my eyes."

"You should have given her a heads up," Kody said, a small smile touching the corners of his lips. "You should have heard her scream. She was less bothered about Pirate Pierre and his friends than putting her foot in a shoe full of shit."

"My shit is not radioactive," the cat reminded everyone and went to speak, when Katrina took another strong punch. The building moved, and a section of wall to their left gave away. For a few seconds Kody thought the building might start to collapse, but it held and the cat asked, "Do we have a plan when this place crumbles?"

"Not really."

The kid came up to Kody, reached out and took his hand. "I don't know how to swim mister."

"That's okay, Apollo and I do know how to swim, and you're with us now." Kody climbed down to one knee so he could look the kid in the eye. "I want you as a member of my family. I want you to be with us. If you don't want to, that's okay. When Mother comes, we'll drop you at the Superdome." He paused, and placed his hand on the kid's cheek. "New Orleans is sinking, you don't know how to swim, and you're suppose to be a casualty." He shook his head. "But not anymore. I would be honored if you were part of my family—and we will never abandon you. So? Are you in or out?"

Tears flooded the kid's eyes. "Okay, mister, I like you and your talking cat, and I don't like being alone. So yeah, I'm in. I'm with you."

Kody leaned over, kissed the kid on the forehead and stood, looking down at Apollo. "Do you have a comment?"

"Actually I do," the cat said with a measure of smugness. "I commend you, even with a bump on your head the size of a pumpkin, you're thinking smart." He rubbed up against the kid's leg, looking at Kody. "Good work bringing the kid on board. He's the only bright spot in this whole hurricane madness." Then Apollo sat in front of Kody and looked up at him. "It's too bad we're not gonna survive to bring him home."

"We'll be fine," Kody said, putting his arm around the kid.

"Mother is in a million pieces," Apollo said, "and please don't tell me that saxophone playing mechanic is going to put her back together again in time to rescue us. We're on our own, and we need to leave, go to higher ground before this place comes down on our heads."

"You wanna go outside?"

"The place is falling apart. We have to go."

"Where? This is it." Kody leaned over and rubbed Apollo's head. "Don't worry. I've got a sneaky feeling the place will hold until Jackie gets here."

"I wish I shared your confidence."

"Just a hunch," Kody said. "Now listen, while we wait for Jackie"—he drew a shotgun holstered on his thigh. "I'm gonna go get that monster."

"Are you outta your mind?" the cat yelped. "Screw the monster. Let the storm kill the monster. This Katrina bitch will do it."

"We're responsible."

"Not really." The cat looked at the kid. "While we were getting our asses kicked by Pirate Pierre and his band of Nair-do-wells, something let the hairy tentacle thing out of its cage."

Kody looked at the kid. "By the time we got back, the creature you saw attack me had eaten a thousand people between here and Redemption." Kody curtly nodded. "I'm gonna take it out right now." He looked at Apollo. "Stay with Jacob. I'll be back."

"My new brother doesn't know how to swim," Apollo spoke up abruptly. "And even though I do, I'd never survive. Not in the middle of Katrina. We go where you go."

"Fine. I can use the company."

*   *   *

The bitch revved up her ferocity, smacking the Ninth Ward hard. The building shook, and all around them things fell. Kody leaned over, covering up the kid in case something large and heavy fell. The cat snuck in between their legs.

"The roof is gonna give way," the cat sang out, and he repeated the sentence half a dozen times.

Kody stayed quiet, looking upwards, waiting for the ceiling to come down, but it held, and after a long sigh, he motioned them forward, expecting to hear a comment or two from Apollo. But his cat remained silent and walked beside Jacob.

They got to the end of the wall, and Kody looked around the corner into the staircase, his shotgun pointed ahead. The gloom cast by Katrina's evil soul swallowed up most of the stairs. He crept forward, looking up into the darkness. The kid came up beside him, and Apollo jumped up a few stairs to be on eye level with Kody.

"What's the plan spaceman?" the cat asked. "And please tell me you have come to your senses and want to wait by the door for Jackie cuz…"

"Cuz what?"

"Cuz your record as of late has been, well, and I'm not bitching."

"You always bitch."

"I'm a cat, I'm suppose to bitch, and well, uh, you're in a slump. Pirate Pierre almost killed us. Even Jackie is scared."

Kody looked hard at the cat and slapped the double barrel shotgun into his left palm. "The slump is over."

The kid reached up and touched Kody' arm. "I'm scared mister."

"My name is Kody. And there is nothing to be scared about. You're with us now, and we're in a safe spot."

"Safe spot?" The cat laughed and looked at the kid. "I'm gonna blame that one on the bump on his head. He's normally not this stupid" He looked at Kody and blurted out the obvious. "There are no safe spots. If the monster doesn't kill us, Katrina will."

Kody looked down at the kid. "This is an emergency exit. Concrete reinforced."

"Just more shit to come down on our heads," Apollo went on briskly. "And uh"—the cat motioned up the stairs with a paw—"the iron staircase has buckled. It's twisted like a corkscrew." He cocked a brow at Kody. "So much for reinforcement."

"We'll be fine." Kody hugged the kid and looked at Apollo, motioning upwards with his head. "Go locate it for me."

"You're gonna send me? You're gonna send the cat?"

"The cat can see, hear, and smell better than me. So yeah, I'm sending the cat. What do you care, you've got nine lives."

"I lost eight of them getting shot at by Pirate Pierre and his buddies." Apollo looked at the kid. "I'm gonna need a belly rub after this is all over."

Kody reached out and stroked Apollo's head. "Jackie and I looked over the floor plans before we got here. Offices occupy the top floors."

As Apollo went to reply, somewhere upstairs a section of wall gave way and Katrina's fury grew louder. The cat chuckled. "Sounds like someone's office just got a new window." He jumped up a stair and turned back. "If I don't come back, please say you'll mourn my demise."

Kody smiled. "Your death would kill me."

"Be safe, okay Apollo."

"Thanks kid," the cat said. "You're the best."

Apollo ran upwards into the darkness and the kid looked up at Kody. "Think he'll be okay?"

"He'll be fine. He didn't lose as many lives as he thought during our Pirate Pierre adventure. Besides"—Kody hugged the kid with one arm—"This time out, we have a bit of 'magic' on our side."

Katrina punched hard again—the building moved. And fine bits of cinderblock dust showered them. More bricks fell somewhere upstairs. Kody held the kid, thinking of Apollo. The cat was fast, and could dodge the debris, still, Kody worried about him.

The building moved again, and a dusty grit showered them.

"Awe geez, that's not good."

"To say the least," the cat said, and stepped out of the darkness, sitting on a stair so he could look Kody in the eye. "It's at the end of the hall, in an office, looking pissed."

"What is that thing Kody?" the kid asked. "How did it get here?"

"It's a creature from another planet," the spaceman informed. "We captured it for a zoo."

"In case you're wondering kid, the zoo isn't on this planet," the cat said, and looked at Kody. "Hey, why don't you tell the kid how much you got paid for the job?"

"Don't listen to the cat. He drinks."

"I wish I had a beer going right now," Apollo admitted, adding, "We got zippo for the job kid cuz something let Mr. Tentacles out of its cage." Apollo climbed a stair and looked back at Kody. "That saxophone had something to do with it."

"We don't know that. Video showed nothing." Kody took hold of Jacob's hand and led him up the stairs.

Apollo climbed up a few stairs and turned back. "Can you walk softer? The whole staircase is gonna give way under your tonnage."

Kody stared the cat in the eye. "I'm normal size for my species. So is Jacob. Too bad you can't say the same."

"Oh, insult the cat in front of our new family member. I'm sensitive you know. You shouldn't say anything cuz I'm carrying a couple of extra pounds."

"A couple?"

"Awe shut up," the cat shot back, and jumped up a stair, looking back. "The Devil's Breath let out the monster, we all know it. That saxophone is cursed. It was on the Enola Gay."

"What's that?" the kid asked.

"Don't they teach history in school?" Apollo asked.

"It's the name of the plane that dropped the first atomic bomb," Kody explained. He looked at the cat. "It was never documented that the sax was actually on the plane." In his heart, however, he believed the cat was right.

"And it was at the airport when Buddy Holly took off forever," the cat continued.

"That's an old wives tale."

"Here's something that's not an old wives tale," Apollo returned. "It was at 9-11, that much we know."

"I know about 9-11," the kid threw in. "We always have an assembly."

Apollo went to reply, but Kody shushed him, motioning for him to keep moving. As they climbed upwards, it brightened, for despite Katrina's darkness, it was daylight and the upper floor was, well, more roomy now thanks to the storm.

They reached the next floor, and stood by the stairs, the hallway before them. Rain poured in steady through the ceiling tiles. A few had fallen and lay shattered on the wet green carpet. Through the rain, Kody spotted the monster—right where Apollo said it was: end of the hall in an office—its tentacles wiggled like drunken braids out into the hallway.

Kody cocked the shotgun. "Okay, you two stay here. I'll go take it out."

"Hey spaceman, as much as I love you, and I do, my brother and I will have a problem if that thing gets by you."

"It's not gonna get by me."

The cat cocked a brow at him. "Have I bitched enough about your slump?"

Kody thought about it for a moment. The cat was right. He looked down at the kid. "Have you ever held a gun?"

"Hold it a second!" the cat yelped, and swiped a paw at Kody' leg. "Are you planning on giving a child a weapon?"

"Do you have a problem with that?" Kody shot back, "cuz, even though I have a bump on my head, it looks to me like you have paws."

"Oh, insult the cat." Apollo threw up his paws. "This is how I was made."

"You need protection," Kody said, and drew a pistol from one of the holsters strapped across his chest. He stuck the pistol in the kid's hand and told him to "Grip it hard." He showed the kid how to work the safety, and ended the quick lecture with, "Just keep shooting at it until you run out of ammo. And don't worry, the crazy thing about this creature is, it's really easy to kill. One shot will do it."

"I've played video games, so I know how to shoot."

"As long as you don't shoot me or the spaceman," the cat threw in, keeping a few feet away.

"I'll be back," Kody said, and he crept down the hall.

*   *   *

With the grassy field in sight and less than fifty feet below the ship, Jackie sprang from her chair and ran to the door, waiting to feel the four landing pads sink into the ground. A sick urgency pumped through her. A crimson emotion hued her cheeks and her blue eyes, the color of Caribbean waters, were stained red from crying. Why had she let Apollo go? For that matter, why had she let Kody go? Okay sure, the monster was his responsibility, but Katrina would snuff it out. And then a terrible thought, evil and cold crossed her mind—*just like she would snuff out the boys.*

The tears came again, and in her head she screamed, *will this damn thing land!*

The engines revved hard then, and over the roar she heard the thuds of the landing pads strike the ground. The engines shut down with a whining whirr, and she slammed the big red button on the wall with the palm of her hand. "C'mon, c'mon," she yelled at the gangplank as it slowly descended. When she judged she had enough 'clearance' she charged down the gangplank like running from a fire, jumped off the end, and ran out into the field.

The Iowa sun was warm on her face, and she ran full out now toward the huge corrugated steel hanger, lowering the zipper on her navy blue jump suit a few inches to vent the building heat. Her pony tail bounced up and down as she raced inside the hanger, running toward Mother.

The ship took up most of the hanger: a silver dollar shaped vessel, a hundred yards in diameter, raised in the middle like a top. Mother was a reinforced interplanetary beast. Right now, however, she was in desperate need of repairs. Her gray hull, sooted black with car size dents from Pirate Pierre and his friends' bombs, looked weak and fragile to Jackie, and in her mind she thought of the swirling angry bitch parked over New Orleans, pounding the boys. Could Mother survive going into that storm?

All of Mother's running lights ringing the ship were shattered and a few still sparked adding to Jackie's troubled thoughts. She knew Mother's electrical wiring all needed to be replaced. It would take Charles a week to do that. Yet he promised he could get Mother up and running, and Jackie believed him, deep in her heart she knew he could get the job done.

She ran up the gangplank, and down a short hallway to the winding staircase that led up to the bridge. The emergency lights still shone, masking everything in a gloomy pallor. She reached the bridge, panting hard and walked into the semi-circular control room, dropping into the black leather captain's chair, spinning about, sighing as she looked over the blank screens and dark control panels.

"Mother!" Jackie yelled, and stared at a small light on the panel. It stayed dark, and then…it began to flash red.

"Jackie?" The voice rang metallic, yet feminine. "I'm powered down."

"Can you power up?" she asked, urgency dripping from her words as tears spilled down her cheeks.

"Jackie, what is wrong?" Mother asked. "I can tell by the inflection in your tone that you are upset."

"The boys are in trouble," she cried, "and they are gonna die unless you can help." She ached inside with regret. "I let Apollo go."

The engines revved up at once, and Mother said, "Though I am artificial intelligence, I have learned to love. And I love Apollo and Kody. However, Jackie, I'm running on only fifteen percent power."

"Can you fly?"

The control panel lit up like a Christmas tree. Buttons, red, green, and yellow began to flash and every gauge and dial came alive. Hatches slammed shut around the ship in preparation for take off. Then Mother plaintively said, "Charles, please collect your tools. We are leaving in one minute."

Jackie heard footfalls clang on the stairs and then Charles was in the bridge. Sweat dripped from his pimply forehead, and he came forward and pulled down his blue polo shirt over his chubby midsection. He wished he had shaved, and he wished he was thinner, for he had a crush on Jackie. He loved her blue eyes shimmering in pure white; and he loved the sharpness of her face, especially with her brown hair tied up in a short pony tail.

Before he could say 'hi', she looked him in the eye. "Can Mother handle Katrina?"

"Oh sure," he replied as though it was a stupid question. "All the ships stabilizers are working. You won't even feel turbulence. She'll be able to corkscrew, go sideways down streets. Whatever you want." Then he sadly added, "But you haven't got full power, and you have no weapons. So you can't shoot anything."

"We don't plan on shooting Katrina—we just want the boys."

"We leave in thirty seconds Charles," Mother said in a 'move your ass' tone.

Jackie stood and hugged him. He towered over her as he hugged her and smelt her sweat and fear. He knew all about fear, he knew 'fear's' stench, he knew it well.

"Listen Charles." Jackie looked up at him. "The guest room is no longer the guest room. We have a new family member. So please change the bedclothes."

"A new family member?"

"His name is Jacob Washington. I think he's the reason Kody is still alive." She jerked her thumb at the exit. "Hustle."

Charles nodded, whipped about and charged down the stairs; Jackie turned to the control panel. "We're headed to New Orleans. The Ninth Ward. Do you need the map?"

"It's 1016 miles southeast from here," Mother said. "I'll have you there in under three minutes."

"Do you have enough power for driving music?"

"Would you like something to get your heart pumping? Something you can dance too?"

"As long as it's loud."

Piano music blared through the speakers, hot and heavy with a fast beat. "Here is an oldie from the 1970s—best driving song ever—a little number entitled 'Over Me' by a duo named Segarini and Bishop. Get boogying Jackie, cuz were going to do some 'rocking' 'rolling' 'reeling' and 'feeling' all the way to the Ninth Ward."

"Good choice," Jackie said, and she jumped to her feet and started hitting buttons on the control panel. "Let's go get the boys."

*   *   *

As Mother rose into the Iowa sky, a thousand miles to the south, Kody moved through the water pouring down into the hallway, his feet squishing on the green wet carpet as Katrina blew her evil stench. The building kept moving as though in an earthquake, and he suspected most of the roof and a good portion of the walls on the top floor were gone; so, in a way, this was now the top floor.

A wet bloated ceiling tile gave way and crashed onto the floor with a damp explosion, shattering a chalky whitish gray that bled away onto the wet green carpet. The falling tile made the creature stir, and it came out into the hallway and stood in a couch, like an orangutan, its arms flaying about, its hardened yellow claws digging grooves into the carpet and walls. Its blood red eyes zeroed in on Kody. Its reptilian face, coated in thick black hair matted down now with moisture, snarled angrily and its razor sharp fangs gnashed together.

Kody leveled the double barreled shotgun and fired. Even wet and hungry, the creature dodged the round—yet Kody's bullet struck a thrashing tentacle. A foot of wiggling thick black haired muscle and gouging claw flew away in an orange blast glistening with rain water. It spattered like an egg against the back wall and dropped to the floor like a piece of dead meat.

Squealing hideously enough to mask Katrina's evil bark, the monster retreated inside the office, a yellowish white blood spurting from its severed tentacle, dribbling a trail.

Kody cocked the weapon, and charged forward. At the doorway, he threw himself across the opening and fired a blast inside the office. He crashed heavily onto the wet carpet, water spraying upwards, and scrambled to his feet, throwing away the smoking shotgun. He drew two pistols from the holsters on his chest and advanced.

It cowered in the corner, wounded, and Kody took aim. Before he could squeeze the triggers, its tentacles slithered forward, picked up a cheap wooden desk and flung it at him.

He saw the desk coming, and ducked, his feet slipped, and he ended up on his back. The desk shot over his head and crashed into the doorframe with earsplitting force, shattering. Wood dust floated in the air, and the pistols in his hands jumped—the blasts sounded loud and flat. The office lit up with red 'pops'.

He emptied both pistols at it, but he was on his back, and the ceiling and walls took most of the abuse—but not all of it. The creature spun from a bullet wound high near its neck. It squealed with pain, and tumbled into the wall. The soggy drywall gave way, and it crashed through and ended up in the hallway.

Runaway fear shot through Kody as he thought of Jacob and Apollo. He tossed away his smoking pistols and drew two others. A determined snarl chewed pain through his injured cheek and he was on his feet in a flash. Soggy drywall dust swirled in the room and he jumped over the shattered desk and stormed into the hall as gunfire erupted.

As instructed, the kid emptied the weapon—all six shots. Kody saw the creature drop to its knees, its tentacles going soft like overcooked pasta, yellowish white blood spurting out, spraying the walls and the remains of the ceiling. As the last shot echoed flatly down the hall, it dropped face first onto the carpet with a wet thud, and twitched.

Kody holstered his pistols, vaulted over the twitching creature, and ran up to Jacob, waving away gun smoke. The kid held the gun at his side, a calm look of satisfaction on his face.

"Nice shot kid."

Apollo came out of the shadows. "He's been part of the family for five minutes and he's already bagged an alien. Way to go kid. You're the best."

Kody took the weapon from the kid's hand and holstered it. As he went to speak, the building moved again, and part of the wall ahead of them gave way.

"Okay, everybody—we have overstayed our welcome."

"No kidding," the cat bitched.

"We are leaving." He picked up the kid and started down the rickety stairs. It clanged and shivered with each of his footfalls, yet held to the wall. At the bottom, on the last step, he stopped. He never expected this, not this much water.

"It wasn't like that two minutes ago," the cat said with attitude, sitting on the stair beside him. "We're in a lot of trouble Kody. And where the hell is Jackie?"

Ignoring the cat, he jumped down into knee-high water and opened his coat. "Jump in. And don't be clawing me too much."

The cat didn't need a second invitation. He jumped in, sinking his claws into one of Kody' holsters, and then he stuck his back paws down Kody' waistband, his belly flat up against him. "Be gentle."

Closing his coat around the cat, he moved Jacob's arms further up around his shoulders. "Hold on tight," he told the kid, and splashed ahead.

The water rose steadily, and was waist high when Kody reached the doorway. A hundred mile an hour screaming wind greeted them at the door, and Kody paused. Into his comm-device he yelled out, "Jackie! I don't know where you are, but the water is up to my waist. The building is gonna be all over the Ninth Ward soon." He opened his coat, leaned down and kissed his cat on the forehead. "I'll make it right." He kissed the kid on the forehead too, yelled out, "Jackie!—we are in the water!", and he waded out into Katrina.

* * *

Even running on only fifteen percent power, Mother could drive herself, and as soon as the ship rose into the sky, Jackie was out of the chair, boogying to Over me as she raced down the stairs into the medical ward. She quickly ran over in her head what she might need, and immediately went to the oxygen tanks. The tanks were fastened to a small dolly, and after blowing the dust off the masks hooked on the tanks, she rolled the dolly down the short hallway into the darkened loading bay, lit now by one small emergency light.

I'm gonna need more light, Jackie thought, hurrying back to the medical ward for the gurney. She rolled it down the hall, stopped at the laundry for fresh white towels, and after tossing a handful on the gurney, she rolled it into the loading bay, parking it beside the oxygen tanks.

"Can you give me more lights here?" Jackie questioned loudly above the music.

The fluorescent light above her head came alive, as did another above the gangplank. It was an improvement, but not much of one.

Then Jackie thought of something. "Do we have life preservers?"

The song stopped, and Mother said, "Kody deemed 'life preservers' unnecessary. Everyone on board knows how to swim."

Not Jacob, Jackie thought darkly, *I may have to go swimming for him.* Then she asked, "What about flares?"

"We have 501 different types of flares at our disposal. 102 are suited for the conditions. They shimmer a brilliant white, stick to water, and will not blow out in hundred mile an hour winds."

"Good," Jackie returned. "I want the Ninth Ward lit up so brightly you'll be able to see it from space. So when we get there, drop them all."

Mother chuckled, "Bring sunglasses." And then she quietly added, "Uh-oh."

Jackie had heard 'uh-oh' out of Mother before, as recently as two days ago when Pirate Pierre's friends showed up, so she knew the 'uh-oh' meant something bad. Sure enough "I have just thrown seven satellites out of their orbit."

Oh no, Jackie thought, knowing what that meant: **attention**. And then she thought, *fuck it.* "The boys are in trouble, Mother," she said bluntly. "It doesn't matter. Anything goes today."

"Does that mean you want full decent into the Ninth Ward?"

Jackie thought about it.

"Full decent will get us there fifty seconds faster. I will, however, destroy every building in my wake. New Orleans will be flattened."

"Mach two, Mother," Jackie replied. "You'll blow out windows and blow off doors, but we'll blame it all on Katrina."

"A wise decision," Mother said, and the song started up again from the start.

Jackie raced into the laundry, kicked off her shoes and socks, and stripped out of her jump suit, thinking of the boys, a sick knot of worry bloating her stomach; for an intense, almost pounding intuition like nothing she had ever felt before now screamed through her: she would need to go into the water to rescue them. She felt certain of it.

As the song hit the chorus, Jackie danced about in her undies and slipped off her bra, tossing it in the dirty laundry pile near the washers. Still tapping her bare feet on the floor, she picked through the hamper for a clean shirt, something with short sleeves, something she could swim in. A white polo shirt caught her eye; it was over her head in a flash. Wearing only undies wouldn't do, and she picked through the dirty laundry pile for her yellow gym pants. They reeked and needed a good wash. She figured Katrina would handle that.

The song paused. "I have received a message from Kody," Mother said, and played the message.

Kody' parting remark, 'We are in the water', made Jackie's blood run cold. "How long?"

"Approaching New Orleans now." Jackie felt Mother decelerate. "Dropping to mach two." And then: "Jackie!" Mother rang out, a note of urgency in her metallic voice. "I can not find Kody' heat signature, and I should by now."

"What does that mean?" In her head her worst visions came true: Katrina's evil force had washed them away.

"The storm is blocking my heat sensors, and I can not divert sufficient power to compensate. I will need visual to find them.

"Open the channel," Jackie returned, and when Mother said it was open, she yelled out, "Kody—light yourself up!"

* * *

Pounding cold rain and savage wind chewed at Kody' cheeks like tiny teeth, turning them raw as he struggled to stay afloat in the choppy, gravy-colored water. Bits and pieces of seaweed spun wildly in the merciless wind and rain. The levees had broken. The ocean was coming, and where was Jackie?

Jacob nestled his face into Kody' neck, trying to keep his mouth above the water. Apollo clawed his way upwards, turning his face into Kody' chin.

"I'm gonna die over a pair of pink shoes," the cat screamed.

Kody had no reply. Just as well, for the brick factory, or rather what was left of it, blew apart in Katrina's vicious madness. Shattered cinderblocks spun wildly in all directions as the structure spiraled into the water. Kody covered up Jacob's head with his arm, bracing for the pelting blasts, but every piece missed, digging into the swirling water around them like meteorite impacts.

Kody raised his arm above the water to pull Jacob closer to him, and as he did, he heard his comm-device. "...light yourself..."

"Mother can't find us," he said, pulling at the wet scruff on Apollo's neck. "Get on my shoulders. I have to get into my pocket."

He thought the cat might bitch. Katrina's cruelty kept any comments from being voiced, and Apollo scrambled over Kody's neck and sunk his claws deep into his coat, laying flat around his shoulders.

Kody fished through his pockets and seized a palm sized canister. He stuck his hand straight up out of the water, and with his thumb, popped the canister's top. A huge blast of red smoke poured out for twenty seconds. The smoke engulfed them, but quickly blew apart in the rain and the wind. *Was it enough time for Mother to spot us?* Kody wondered, gripping Jacob tighter.

With the comm-device out of the water, and the channel open, the best driving song ever 'Over Me' blared into the Ninth Ward. And then the song paused. "Mother has your location," Jackie said, her voiced strained. "Listen for the boom."

They didn't have to wait long. A huge, mach-two boom peeled over Katrina's bark and Kody spotted a gray blur in the distance, coming hard, coming in sideways like a rolling penny, steaming hot.

"I hope she can stop!" the cat blasted in Kody's ear.

In an instant, Mother turned horizontal, and came to a dead stop, hovering fifty feet above them. As she descended, capping them like a pot lid, the rain stopped. Flares spun out from her belly like a whip, splashing around them with a loud plunk before exploding with a sizzling bright white. Smoke billowed around them, and through the pallor they saw the gangplank open.

With the rain stopped, and with only the wind to contend with, the cat jumped into the water, swimming hard toward the lowering gangplank. He saw Jackie and tears came to his eyes. Could he make it to her? His strength ebbed, but he struggled on.

The gangplank hit the water with a huge splash, too large for Apollo to swim through, and the cat went under. He kicked his feet as hard as he could but his strength ran out and he went limp, dropping into Katrina's darkness.

And then, he felt a hard a tug on the back of his neck— suddenly he was out of the water. Jackie stood at the edge of the gangplank, holding Apollo at arm's length. Water poured off his drenched hide.

The determination look creased on her face melted away, and tears came to her eyes. "I love you," she told the cat, and gripped him tightly against her chest. They were up the gangplank in a second, and Jackie set the cat down on the gurney, wrapping him up in a towel.

"I'm so sorry Jackie," the cat cried out. "I love you."

"You're forgiven." She kissed the cat on the forehead, and motioned with her head. "Gonna go save the spaceman and our new family member."

She was gone in a flash; Apollo yelled out after her, "He gives great belly rubs."

Jackie's bare feet hit the gangplank and thanks to a dripping cat, she lost her balance and slid to the end, her feet sliding off into the Louisiana stir.

Flares continued to pop from Mother's belly, blanketing the water in a reflecting white mist, and Jackie spotted Kody at once. He bobbed twenty feet from the gangplank, struggling to stay afloat, struggling to keep Jacob's head above the water.

Awe fuck, she thought, *I'm going in.* She slid off the gangplank, the water cold and unforgiving, and swam towards them. A competitive swimmer, strong and lean, Jackie thought she could make it to them easily. But she was no match for Katrina's savage wind whistling between Mother and the vicious swirling water. She drifted wildly away from them, and then fought hard, the strongest 'front crawl' stroke she had ever mustered—and she seized Jacob's schoolbag, and pulled herself into them.

She threw her arms around Kody' shoulders. "Hey spaceman," she yelled, panting heavy as she kicked her legs hard to stay a float.

With a smile, he shook his long wet hair out of his face. "Hi beautiful girl, you picked a crazy place to go for a swim."

"I wanted to meet Jacob." She looked the child in the eye. He looked so scared her heart broke. She placed her hand on his wet cheek. "I'm Jackie."

"Thanks for coming," the kid managed weakly.

"Anything for you." Then Jackie brought her face next to the Kody' ear. "I don't have the strength to get Jacob to the gangplank."

Kody stuck his hand out of the water. "Mother," he screamed into the dripping comm-device. "Move twenty feet forward."

The whine of the engines dampening Katrina's bark, increased in volume a few octaves, and the gangplank came toward them, gouging up dirty Louisiana ocean water. Mother stopped abruptly—the gangplank still ten feet away.

Kody put his face against Jackie's cheek, and in her ear asked, "How's your back stroke today?"

"Real good," she said with determination. She wrapped her arms around Jacob, flipped over on her back, Jacob now on top of her, and kicked hard. Every few seconds, she glanced behind her, trying to keep in line with the gangplank. She was getting close, she knew it, and then, 'bang' her head struck the end of the gangplank with jarring force. Katrina's fury blew away Jackie's swear words.

She hissed at the pain, and then reached around with one hand and hauled Jacob up onto the gangplank. She crawled up after him, got to her feet, ignoring the blistering pain chewing on the back of her head, and picked him up. He was light, and she easily carried him into the loading bay. She set him down next to Apollo and wrapped him in a towel. His lips quivered with fear as he softly managed, "Thank you."

Holding him tight for a second, she looked down at Apollo. "Take care of Jacob. I'm gonna go save the spaceman."

"Oh please do," Apollo called out after her. "I'm not finished bitching at him." He crawled up into Jacob's lap and nestled his head on his chin. "It's okay. There's nothing to be worried about. You're with us now."

I hope the 'us' includes me and the spaceman, Jackie thought darkly as she slid down the gangplank. Kody was close, kicking hard, trying to move his hands above the water. She reached out and screamed, "Do I have to go in and get you?"

He grabbed her hand. His weight and the force of the swirling water jerked her hard, and she slipped off into the water. She thrashed her free hand backwards, and seized the gangplank with the tips of her fingers. She inched her fingers forward, and soon clung desperately to the plank with one hand. Her heart thundered, and she knew she would never be able to pull them up. She would have to let him go.

And then, before she could work up the courage to shake loose her friend, Katrina gusted with pounding, merciless force, pushing Mother forward three feet, scooping her up. On her ass now at the end of the gangplank, Jackie pulled on Kody' arm, and he crawled up on top of her.

Looking up into the spaceman's eyes, Jackie brushed aside a thick mass of his blonde hair clinging to her cheek and asked, "How many times have I saved your ass?"

"I've lost count beautiful girl." He inched forward until he could stand, pulling her up to her feet. They walked together into the loading bay.

"Mother," Kody yelled out. "Raise the gangplank—and get us out of here." And then he added, "Hey Mother, do you have enough power to circle the moon a few times? I want Jacob to see it up close."

"Plotting a course to the moon," Mother said, "and Kody, welcome aboard."

*   *   *

They all took showers, washing off Katrina's stench; even the cat, though he bitched about it, and kept bitching about it until Mother diverted the heat from the cooling system out a vent; he was warm and fluffy in no time; and his purr was back. He also liked what Jackie had set out for him on the rim of the control panel: a full bowl of cold Bud.

He jumped up onto the control panel, a sneaky smile on his face. The beer meant Jackie felt bad for sending him into a hurricane. It also meant he would use that to his advantage, well, for as long as he could. He was a cat, after all.

The beer felt like cold, refreshing spring water on his tongue, and as he lapped it up, he had to admit: he certainly enjoyed what Mother had on the screen. He liked seeing the moon, especially up close. If only he had company.

His wish was soon granted, for Jacob walked into the control room with a white towel wrapped around his head like a turban. No doubt Jackie was behind that, and no doubt Jackie had dressed the kid. He wore a navy blue jumpsuit two sizes too large for him and thick white socks that slid on the tile floor. Steam from the cup of hot chocolate in his hand swirled up into his face as he sat down in the captain's chair.

"I see Jackie has you cleaned up."

"She made me hot chocolate too," he said, and stared at the screen. "Wow, the moon is so cool looking."

"It sure is Jacob," Kody said, strolling into the control room. He wore gray sweat pants and a blue t-shirt that clung to his muscles. His hair was brushed back across his shoulders and still moist. His cheeked throbbed, but the cold Bud in his hand was beginning to work its magic. His eye caught a dial on the control panel which alerted his interest. "Mother, we are fifty meters off the surface. Do you have enough juice to get us outta this orbit?"

"Yes Kody," she replied with a hint of attitude. "The moon has $1/6^{th}$ the gravity of earth. Would you feel more comfortable if I shared my calculations with you?"

"Oh, for the love of God, don't do that Mother," Apollo spoke out. "Don't make him any smarter. He was talking about 'mass' when we were trying to find the comm-device."

"It was a valid point," Kody returned.

"Valid or not, Jacob and I did not need to hear the comment," the cat said. "By the way, I almost died you know?"

"I see you didn't. As a matter of fact, I see you lapping up beer." He raised his Bud can at the cat and added, "Besides, would you have wanted to 'sit' this one out?"

The cat turned out his lips in an aloof pout. "It was a good thing I was along to take care of the kid." Then the cat turned serious. "It's a good thing Jackie loves us."

Before Kody could respond, footfalls on the stairs made him turn. His face lit up when he saw Jackie.

She wore a white a t-shirt beneath a navy blue jumpsuit, zipped partway up. Her hair hung loose across her shoulders. Kody waited until she lowered the beer in her hand to wrap his arms around her. Her head came up to the top of his chest, and he squeezed her hard. "Thanks for the pick up beautiful girl."

She hugged him back. "Lean down."

"Am I getting a smooch?"

She examined the cut on his cheek instead, scabbed over now with a yellow-green crust. "I'm gonna have to stitch your face."

"Can we do it after I have a few more beers?" he asked. "And how's your head? Even with Katrina screaming in my ears I heard the bang." He didn't wait for her to reply, eyeing the six inch mountainous ridge of raised red flesh on her scalp. "Looks nasty." He kissed her bump better. "That's about all I can do for it."

She smiled up at him, said "Thank you", and after a long pull on her can of beer continued with, "Okay spaceman, we're face to face, and we have beers going. Let's talk about this deity."

"I've been thinking about him," Kody said. "Something let that monster out of its cage. And why did it track south? Even you said it should have gone west toward the setting sun."

He took a sip of beer. "We were led down here." He raised his chin at Jacob, still fascinated by the moon. "The kid is special."

Jackie stared up into his eyes. "Which way?"

"What do you mean?"

"You said he was special, and I believe you. My God, I believe you, cuz when we were coming down here, something told me I'd have to go in the water for him. So I believe you, but the question is still there. Which way? Good or evil?"

Kody thought about it for a moment. "It doesn't matter. He's part of our family now. His destiny will play out…as will ours."

Jackie put her arm around his waist, and stared up at him. "Why us?"

"I'm not sure. Yet, there is something you need to know. I worked with a deity once before, an angel named Nathanial."

"The old man wearing the coat and hat?"

"No, I've never met him, but from the description, I think I know who it was." He paused for a moment and said, "The Angel of Death."

Jackie sipped on her beer and said nothing.

"Maybe he was one soul over on Katrina. So he called us in." He went back to his beer for a sip, hugged Jackie again, and yelled out, "Mother, take us home. Take us to Redemption."

The End

The Last Cubicle

America the Beautiful played in his head; the music driven by sweet sax notes resonating with perfected timber—and his eyes opened to morning sun slanting through the window, and then a voice, dripping with urgency spoke out in his head: *come see me.*

Charles didn't need to be told twice. He showered at once, and then dressed in his gray suit, all the while thinking of her, thinking of his 'crush', worried because of the dire tone in her words, worried because he knew now with certainty she was 'special'. What sort of 'special'? What sort of 'different'? He had no idea, and that worried him even more.

Soon he was outside into warm September air, headed for the subway, his thoughts in turmoil. What did he know about her? *Not much*, he confessed silently. He'd only known her for a week, a short time filled with conversations lacking substance; fluff conversations for the most part.

He wanted to talk to his best friend, Kody, about her, about the difference in their ages, and the fact that he suspected she was special in someway (a fact he knew for certain now); but Kody was away in outer space battling aliens, so, alone in the city, he kept it to himself and stewed about it.

He smelt her on the subway, even in a car surrounded by hundreds of people he smelt her intoxicating perfume. And he smelt her on the elevator, no matter where he stood, he smelt her, all the way to the 97th floor.

The silver-face clock with the lightening bolt hands behind the reception desk read 8:23. He was seven minutes early, and the tension in his stomach slackened. He'd get to her before nine. He waved at the young blond receptionist with the phone to her ear and kept going, fishing in his pocket for the key, headed to the small closet, remembering now with regret that he had forgotten his tools, for one wheel on his mail cart was loose.

Come now!

The words sunk in with bitter necessity. The key disappeared into his pocket, and he turned, walking ahead through the maze of cubicles. Before he had gone ten steps, he noticed something odd: nearly everyone was at work, and before nine. Something big must be brewing at D. E. Mood Insurance Brokerage House. Not that it mattered to him. He delivered the mail, photocopied, ran errands, and took abuse. The job was easy and, for the most part, uneventful. Then Kim arrived, and things got complicated.

Twenty different fragrances of cologne and perfume assaulted his senses, and with phones ringing and conversations buzzing in his ears, he turned at the end of the aisle and marched ahead to the last cubicle, looking in.

Her warm, chocolate brown eyes twinkled with a mystic beauty too heavenly to describe. His heart sped up. Her thick red lips rose upwards into smooth cheeks dusted lightly with makeup. Her smile took away his breath.

As he collected himself, his cheeks glowing with a thin hue of red excitement, she adjusted her wire gold-frame glasses up on her nose, and pleasantly said, "Good morning, Charles."

Every thought in his head emptied out, and a second later the void filled in with these words, "I heard your voice in my head." The sound of those words, his words, words he never dreamt he'd speak, started a swirling nervous storm in the pit of his stomach.

She rose from behind her desk, a woman of short stature in comparison to Charles, for he stood six-foot three, a full nine inches taller than her. He watched her straighten out her black dress, and her smile—if it was possible—grew even more. Her black hair hung loose today, spilling over her shoulders, shimmering under the lights. "I needed to see you Charles."

He forgot about everything and got lost in her, in her eyes, and in her face, captivated in a moment of beautiful time. It got even better a second later when she wrapped her arms around his chubby midsection, and hugged him tightly. Her bewitching essence ensnared him into stunned silence.

The moment of time stretched out for a good five seconds, and then, as she guided him to the chair in front of her desk, the gnawing love he felt for her disintegrated, and he felt empty inside, alone, and for a short, odd moment he had no idea what was going on.

She retook her seat and crossed her legs. "Did you enjoy America the Beautiful?"

"You...you were responsible?" he managed, and his memory quickly filled in on what was going on. "I thought it was a dream."

"I didn't want you to oversleep," she confessed, her eyes twinkling with delight behind the lenses of her glasses. "So I woke you gently with music from your favorite instrument." She raised a brow at him. "Have you ever played that song on a sax?"

"A long time ago in Redemption, Iowa."

A tight grin creased her cheeks. "You've spoken of your hometown before, the town with the talking cat." As he went to reply, her eyes zeroed in on the clock on the wall behind him, and she lifted her chin a bit and asked, "How long does it normally take you to get to the street? The fastest I have ever done it in was 8 minutes, but that was 5 p.m. and that's rush hour around here."

"I've done it faster," he said, feeling more comfortable now that the conversation was rolling. "At this time in the morning you could be on the street in seven minutes."

"Wonderful," she said. "It's 8:25, so we have a few minutes."

His official starting time was 8:30, so yes, she was correct, he had five minutes; however…he suddenly wanted out of this office—real bad. Something (and for the love of God he didn't know what) was wrong, terribly wrong, and a thin sheen of terror shivered through him. "Uh, I'm really sorry Kim, but I have to start delivering the mail." He glanced behind him at the opening. "It's weird, it seems like everyone is here this morning, and it's not even nine."

Her eyes narrowed, her long eyelashes scraping against the lenses of her glasses, and her cheeks twisted into a critical look that sent a bolt of fear from his head all the way down to his balls. "Everyone who is suppose to be here got a wake up call this morning."

Holy fuck, he thought, and his terror burned hot. *What is going on?* He stood. "I don't want to get fired."

"Trust me on this Charles, you will not get fired." She waved her hand at the chair. "Please sit" and she repeated the words again with more bite, a lot more bite, tersely adding, "We haven't got much time."

He did as he was told, the chair groaning under his weight, the legs wobbled a bit. "I should fix this," he said, more to himself than Kim.

"You like to fix things?"

"Oh yeah, that's my special knack. I can fix anything. You name it: vacuums, toasters, engines. Everything. Once I figure out how it works, I find it real simple." And he proudly added, "I've even worked on Kody' space ship."

Her lips rolled up slightly. "He's the spaceman who lives in Redemption, right?"

He had told her the story once before, sharing something he knew he shouldn't share, but it was Kim, and he was in love with her then, and last Friday when the office was nearly empty, he ran into her and shared the story, not really knowing why, just knowing he had to tell her.

Did she believe him? She acted like she did. Right now, as he sat in the chair, wanting to run, he didn't care. "Kody and I are buddies."

"And he owns the talking cat, correct?"

"Apollo." Mentioning him made Charles feel good inside. "Apollo is my buddy too." He leaned over a bit, resting his elbows on the red wood grain desktop. "And Kim, can that cat drink. He loves his suds."

She marveled at him, her chocolate brown eyes large and shinning with mystical fascination, and he wondered what she thought of him—and he also wondered, *what the hell are you?*

"Redemption sounds like a magical place."

"No evil there," Charles said with certainty.

"Lots of evil in New York," Kim put in darkly. She reached across the desktop and touched his hands, looking into his blue eyes. "You're not suppose to be here."

I'm suppose to be delivering the mail, he thought, and wished he was anywhere else but where he was—in the last cubicle talking with...well, he didn't know what, but he had his suspicions.

"Why did you come to New York?"

He shrugged with a touch of embarrassment. "The sax," he confessed. "I told you a bit about it."

"You told me you played, and that your instrument was stolen"—she looked around the cubicle—"which is the reason you deliver the mail and listen to everyone call you 'hayseed'."

"Not you."

"I have too much respect for people," she said, and stared at the clock. He cared little for the grave look in her eyes. Time was running down, and he wondered, *Oh dear God, what is going on?*

His terror was back, hard now, and his thoughts, shredded with ice cold fingers drumming on his brain, scrambled for anything pleasant to lock onto. He thought of Kody and Apollo then, and wished he was with them now. The pleasant thought evaporated an instant after it formed and a dark scary thought crawled around like a spider inside his head, *Not human... alien?*

"You came here to be discovered?"

So lost in thought, so lost in the terror of the moment, he jumped out of his chair a bit at her words. A crimson hue of bashfulness shone on his cheeks. "Chasing down a crazy dream," he admitted. "Millions of people play the saxophone as well as me." He perked up a bit. "It was fun playing to a live audience, you know, other than the odd wedding or birthday party I played back in Redemption." He grinned, suddenly wanting to make light of the whole dark incident that had landed him on the 97th floor in the last cubicle talking with God knows what. "Kim, whatever you do, never play a gig in Rockaway Queens." And he chuckled.

"Is that where it happened?"

"Outside of a restaurant named Giovanni's." Thinking of the incident made him frown. "There was an odd vibration to the place. I felt it the moment I got there." He wanted to add, *'I felt a similar vibration meeting you'* but kept that to himself and added, "I told Kody about it. He figures the Devil drinks there."

"Yes," she said, nodding, her matter-of-fact look frightening him. "I hear he takes his Cognac on the terrace." Charles went to speak, but the sentence brewing in his head got swept away in what she had said. Luckily, she prompted him. "What happened?"

"When I was heading to the subway after the gig, two guys attacked me." He shook his head at the vivid, terrifying images playing in his head. "They had knives, and if not for this guy, I'd be dead."

"Oh?" Concern shone in her eyes; yet, there was something else stirring in her eyes, and that something else came out in a question, "Someone saved you?"

"A guy named McCluskie," he answered. "When the robbers were gonna knife me, he came outta nowhere and yelled out at them. Then he ran toward us. That scared them off"—he frowned with discouragement—"scared them off with my sax." He looked her in the eye, nodding with admiration. "This McCluskie was under six foot and slim, and theses muggers were big dudes with knives." He thought about the man who saved him. "I gotta say, there is something different about McCluskie. Can't say what it is, but he's different."

"McCluskie?" she thinly breathed, suddenly lost in thought.

"Funny thing is, I know a family of McCluskies back in Redemption."

"Jacob McCluskie?" Her brows rose with haunting suspicion.

"Yeah, have you heard of him? He's a writer."

Her eyes shone at him, and dark, cold words spilled from her mouth, "He's a lot more than that." Her eyes twitched to the clock for a second and she added, "So that's how you ended up here."

"With no sax, I needed work," he explained. "I heard they needed a mail gopher, and the pretty girl in Human Resources, Betty, hired me. She's really nice."

"She's out sick today."

"That's too bad."

"She won't think so."

His blood ran cold at her comment. And a question gouged at his thoughts: *what's gonna happen?*

"I have to ask," she continued, leaning over a bit, her hair falling over her shoulders. "Why did you stay in New York after your sax was stolen? Why didn't you go back to Redemption?"

"I wanted to, but I'd only been in town for seven days. I couldn't quit on my dream so fast. So I planned to do odd jobs until I could afford another sax." The image of Kody popped into his head; it made him feel good for a moment, and fresh words tinted with building fear spilled from his mouth, "Kody wanted me to come home after I got mugged, he wanted to come get me in Mother."

"Mother?" She held up her hand, a smile touching the corners of her lips. "Hang on a second, let me guess, his space ship? Right?"

"Good going Kim," he said, and forced himself to smile as the thought, *get outta this office,* rang repeatedly through his head. He paused, yet his building fright made him talk. "Mother is really cool. I like her sense of humor."

"The space ship has a sense of humor?"

"Artificial Intelligence is a funny thing, especially this degree of intelligence. Remember, Mother was made"—he looked up at the ceiling—"well, not here. So she has developed emotions. She loves the boys and Jackie."

"Who's Jackie?"

"She's Kody' wheelman. She's from Redemption like me." Speaking of Jackie, seeing her in his mind's eye, warmed his heart. "She used to babysit me. She's ten years older." Then he admitted, "I love her."

"I'm sure she loves you too," Kim said, and quietly added, "You belong in Redemption, Iowa with the people who love you."

Right now I belong outta this office, he thought, and with terror clawing at him, he decided to come right to the point, "What are you anyway?"

She raised a brow at him above the rims of her glasses. "What do you mean?"

Her question made him smirk; the fear brewing in his gut made the smirk vanish quickly. "You said Jacob McCluskie is more than a writer, and oh yeah, I believe you." His tone remained even as he added, "You're a whole lot more than an office clerk."

A tight grin touched her cheeks. "I have to ask, and please be honest, because at this point it really doesn't matter: what does the staff say about me?"

Would she detect a lie? he thought, and the creepy feeling scratching at the back of his head made him speak the truth. "I haven't heard much. Most people think you're a witch."

"A witch?" she barked, and shook her head with regret at the outburst. "I'm sorry. I can't believe they'd say that."

"Well, not everyone."

"What do you think of me?"

"I have a crush on you," he admitted. "Well, I did. After your hug, it at all went away. Funny, huh?" He looked sadly at her. "You know, I knew from the start the crush was wrong. You're twenty years older than me, still, it was there, gnawing like teeth, and for a guy like me, a guy who fixes things, I figured out real quick that beauty or not, you had to have put a spell on me." He shrugged with a destitute frown. "I wanted to talk to Kody about it, but he's out of town."

"Sorry about the spell." She looked down in shame. "I felt it was necessary. I needed you in the last cubicle with me at this moment in time."

Holy fuck, what is going on? What is going to happen? His heart sped up, his cheeks felt hot. "All you had to do was ask," he said, amazed he could speak. "I would have come." He paused for a brief moment. "Kim, with or without your spell, my guess is I would have fallen in love with you one way or another anyway. Who cares about age?"

"I love you too Charles."

"Good to know," he said, hot bile now lashing up his throat. He placed his elbows on the desktop and looked her in the eye. "Kim, you never answered my question. What are you?"

"My real name is Envy," she revealed, "and I'm an angel."

"No shit," came out of his mouth as every thought in his head bottlenecked like a Tokyo traffic jam. After a few "uh's", the only thing he could think of to say was, "An angel wearing glasses? Cool."

She adjusted her spectacles, saying, "I like the look."

"You look beautiful either way." A long pause ensued as he stared into her eyes, and then he quietly asked, "Why am I sitting in the last cubicle with an angel?"

A sheet of paper appeared in her hand and she pointed at the letterhead. "Spell D. E. Mood backwards."

It took him a second to do it. "Oh dear God." He got to his feet on shaky legs.

She stood, and a key magically appeared in her hand. She reached over and gave it to him. The top half of the brass key was coated in blue plastic; a red number 7 was embossed in the center. "I need you to do a few things for me."

Anything to get outta here, he thought, nodding.

Her eyes were on the clock for a scant second. "The key is from the Grand Street Bus Terminal. It's a ten minute walk north of here up Broadway."

"I know where it is," he managed, his hand shaking as he dropped the key in his pant pocket.

"I want you to go there now. Understand? Go to the bus locker now and get what's in the locker." After a pause, she added, "There is a note."

He looked her in the eye. "I'm not coming back, right?"

She walked from behind her desk. "The people in this office are suppose to be here. Not you." She went over, threw her arms around him and, stretching up, kissed him on the cheek. "You are a beautiful human being." Holding his hands, she stepped back a bit. "Now listen to me. Time can not be tampered with. You go to the elevator and down to the street. You are to say nothing to no one—you can not change the Timeline. Go. And don't look back."

"What's gonna happen?"

"Something bad"—she gestured at the wall—"and that 'something bad' is going to come right out of this cubicle." She pointed out the opening. "Seven minutes to the street. Don't be late. Go!"

He had no trouble taking orders from an angel, and he shot out of the last cubicle and ran down the aisle. Someone yelled "Hayseed" at him, but he kept going through the maze of cubicles, moving as quickly as he dared. He ran past the blonde receptionist and his heart broke. His compassion screamed at him to stop, to drag her along with him no matter what, to save a beautiful human being: innocent, and too young to die. But the angel's orders were specific.

Someone had already pushed the elevator 'down' button, and he stood back against the far wall, taking deep breaths, trying to control his fear as he waited. It felt like hands were twisting his stomach, and his heart pounded so heavily he feared it would explode. *C'mon, c'mon*, he kept thinking, and how much time did he have? *Not much.* The thought made him want to puke. *Seven minutes to the street.* He needed at least that much time. Maybe more.

The elevator arrived with a ping. Passengers streamed off, and two words drifted like cemetery ghosts through Charles's head: *the doomed.* He slipped inside the car. Three or four people joined him. A man in a blue suit and a young woman with dark brown hair tied up in a bun stood next to him, the man chatting, "Thanks for coming with me. I didn't want to go alone. It's a beautiful day for a walk, and a voice in my head told me to go for one right now."

More Divine intervention? Charles wondered, and as he went to press on the 'close' door button, he spotted a young woman approaching pushing a baby carriage. Her name was Jessie, and Charles had chatted with her a few times on the elevator and knew she was a babysitter from the daycare at the end of the hall. *And oh fuck…the kids…* The thought nearly made him black out. His heart shredded apart, and he wanted to scream out, tell everyone what was going on—pull the fire bell. But he couldn't.

Jessie hesitated by the open door, looking down into the carriage. The angel's words, *say nothing to no one*, rang in

Charles's head. So, he did the only thing he could do: once he had her attention, he stared her in the eyes, begging her with unspoken words bleeding with desperation. *Get in!*

"I forgot his blanket." She looked down at the baby. "He might get cold." Her eyes were back on Charles. The pained look staining his blue eyes sent a knife jab of fear through her. Tears welled up in his eyes, and an electric moment of time passed between them, a scant second, but to Jessie that scant second seem to last a lifetime. An urgency needled her soul.

She rolled the stroller into the elevator. "It's a beautiful day. He won't be cold."

A wave of relief crashed over Charles so strong his knees went weak, and the man going for a walk with his secretary said, "Wise decision."

Charles pushed the 'down' button. The doors closed, the car descended, time ticked on, and the doomed remained unaware.

He faced the buttons, his thoughts shattered, and bits and pieces of his time in the last cubicle with the angel played out in his head like on a TV with a bad connection. One thought kept bleeding through: *what's gonna happen?* Something bad, the angel had said, and it would come from the last cubicle. *What did that mean?*

As the thought gnawed at him, the car hiccupped, and then stopped. The baby stirred. Jessie leaned over. "It's okay little man."

Charles could see Jessie's wristwatch above her sleeve. The white face reflected the elevator lights, and the black hands pointed at 8:44. *Seven minutes* rang in his head, and when did he leave the last cubicle?

The time 8:39 floated above the sewage of frightening thoughts. What is going to happen would happen in two minutes, give or take a few seconds, and *Please God, get this elevator moving.*

The baby cried out. The elevator car hiccupped again, and then descended smoothly. Charles thanked God, and the baby cried.

A minute later, the elevator doors opened to the ground floor. He smiled at Jessie. She looked upset that the baby had cried for 77 floors. "You made the right decision in coming," he told her. "Have a nice life" and he ran off the elevator.

He was outside ten seconds later, and walked down the street, looking up. He counted down from the top, and saw the windows that belonged to D. E. Mood Insurance Brokerage House. All looked well, and he wondered if the angel was looking out the window at him.

And then someone said, "It's strange to see a plane over Manhattan."

Charles heard the roar of engines, and his eyes went right to it. The plane flew low, and he easily saw the two big A's on the tailfin. The word 'American' stretched across the silver and gray fuselage. The wings moved up and down, the speed intense, the engines screaming, and the plane ran right into the 97th floor, right where he thought the last cubicle would be. The plane disappeared inside the building with an orange fireball so intense the burning image echoed in his eyes. Black smoke poured out the rupture, twirling upwards into the blue sky, and Charles knew with certainty that everyone at D. E. Mood was dead.

Icy fingers of shock gripped him, and he shivered, surrounded on the sidewalk now by countless on-lookers. Sirens filled the street: police cars, fire engines, and ambulances. Red lights flashed everywhere.

And then people trapped in the North Tower started to jump.

In horrific fascination, he watched, and saw them come down one after the other. Two people jumped together, holding hands, a man and a woman. They held hands to the end, and Charles cried. And then, with tears flowing down his cheeks, his vision blurred, his shock broke. The angel's words rang in his ears, and he reached into his pocket and touched the key. Time to leave, and he wandered away from the nightmare... and wandered into another one.

As he approached the corner, he spotted it ahead—a plane. The sun shimmered white off its top; its blue belly almost black in the shadows. The plane came in low, making a dark evil cloud on the choppy bluish-green water of the Hudson, headed for the South Tower. A woman screamed, someone yelled out "Holy shit", and the plane, coming in on a swooping angle struck the tower. The impact was deafening. A firestorm of red and orange exploded outward from the impact zone—a fiery, hellish belch, spewing forth a wave of smoking hot destruction littered with glass and metal. A set of melted airplane tires, spiraling thick black smoke rocketed to the street with a 'whizzing' sound that ate up the screams around him and punched a walloping hole in the street twenty yards away from him.

A few people jumped backwards, but no one around him on the sidewalk moved, all gazed upwards at the horror. The angel's words "Go now to the bus locker" floated through his shocked reality, and he stepped out onto the gutter and started walking.

Leaving the madness screaming behind him, he wandered north. His thoughts slowed, and without even knowing it, he soon spotted the sign for the bus terminal.

He picked a good day to come, for the terminal was near empty. Everyone was outside watching the horror unfold ten blocks away. An elderly man with snow white hair wearing a blue security suit and smoking a cigarette at the door regarded him with a raised brow, but Charles kept going, oblivious to everything, and the security guard was too caught up in Time's memorable moment to challenge him.

To the right of the door were seven rows of gray lockers. Charles headed for the back row, looking for number 7. The toilets had overflowed. The smell of urine clung to the air and his feet splashed in large puddles all the way to locker number 7.

As he drew the key from his pocket, a shadow fell over him, and a hand fell on his shoulder. He whipped his head about and looked up into Kody's blue eyes.

The spaceman's blonde hair was tied back in a pony tail and two days worth of beard stubble dusted his cheeks. The skin around his eyes strained rigid, and his mouth was a straight bitter line, grave and judge-like serious.

"We came for you."

The spaceman stood four inches taller than Charles, and he threw his arms around him and hugged him tightly, picking him up off his feet for a moment.

"Thank God we found you," he whispered into Charles's ear.

"I love you man," Charles cried. "I'm so glad to see you. I can't believe you're here." He stepped back, trying to reign in his emotions, wiping away tears.

"Good work, spaceman, you made him cry."

Charles jumped at the sound of Apollo's voice. "Oh my God, Apollo, you're here too."

"Anything for you sax man," the cat said, flicking water of his paw. "Even walking through pissy water." Charles knelt down and wrapped his arms around the gray cat's fat midsection.

"I missed you so much."

"Not so tight," the cat bitched, and then broke free and circled Charles's legs a few times before settling down next to Kody. "Great to see you sax man. When we heard you were in trouble, we came."

"Thanks Apollo," Charles said, nodding. "You're the best cat in the world."

Apollo glanced up at the spaceman with a smug smile. "His mind is obviously intact." The cat was back looking at Charles. "By the way, what tower do"—the cat hesitated—"did, you work in?"

"We've got a bit of a bet going," Kody admitted with confidence.

"Breakfast in bed for a week," the cat threw in. "So? Which tower?"

"The north."

"Really?" Kody questioned.

"I told you," the cat shot back, embellishing wildly with a paw. "Here's the story sax man, we just get back to Redemption, I mean, we hadn't even opened our first beer yet, and Mother alerted us that the North Tower had been"—he raised a brow at Kody—"What word did she use?"

"Compromised."

"Yeah, that's it, compromised, kinda of a nice way of saying that a bomb with wings and passengers hit the building you worked in."

"I'm sure you said the South Tower," Kody pleaded in defense.

"You drink too much," the cat said with a laugh.

"No wonder, I'm hooked up with you."

"I like my eggs over easy," the cat snickered, and looked up at Charles. "Anyway sax man, Mother throws the TV feeds onto the control panel screens and revs up the engines cuz we're all going to the Big Apple to save you."

"I thought you worked in the South Tower," Kody went on. "Sorry man, we would have been here sooner if not for me. As soon as we saw what was happening, everyone wanted to come get you except me. I thought you worked in the South Tower. I didn't think you were in any danger."

"He sat there with his legs crossed watching the North Tower burn," Apollo went on, his lips turned up peevishly at the spaceman. "He was willing to bet everyone that you worked in the South Tower."

Kody put his hand on Charles's shoulder. "Mother is a bit upset with me."

"A bit!" the cat yelped. "There's a gross understatement."

Kody swung his attention downward. "I'll make it up to her."

"Good luck with that," the cat said with a smirk, and then looked at Charles, pointing with a paw at the spaceman. "You should have seen him jump when the second plane hit. Holy shit, sax man, that sure got his attention. He yelled so loudly at Mother to get in the air, the ship isn't talking to him anymore."

"I'll make it up to her," he told the cat, and turned to Charles. "Jackie is a bit upset with me too."

"Jackie," Charles cried, and fresh tears gushed over the rims of his eyes.

"Awe, here we go again," the cat blurted out, gesturing with a paw. "Good work spaceman, you made him cry again." The cat rolled his eyes. "I need a beer."

"You always need a beer."

Charles gripped Kody's arm. "Is Jackie here?"

Kody glanced at the ceiling. "Her and Mother are hovering fifty miles up."

"Talking about you no doubt," Apollo threw in with a chuckle.

"They're not talking about me," Kody shot back. "They're talking about the plane attacks."

"And you." Apollo leered up at the spaceman. "You're lucky it took only three minutes to get here." The cat regarded Charles with a satisfied smile. "Jackie bitched at him the whole way."

"Not the whole way."

The cat smiled so brightly the overhead lights reflected off his teeth. "Maybe you're right spaceman, she did pause for twenty or thirty seconds to curse." His eyes were on Charles. "Her words nearly blistered the paint."

"I had no idea she could swear like that," Kody muttered, thinking of the incident.

"You know spaceman, come to think of it, most of her swear words were directed at you."

Charles smiled and laughed, and that made Kody smile.

"On a bright note," the cat continued, "since Mother isn't talking to you at least you didn't have to hear it from her."

"Mother is talking to me," Kody returned with annoyance. "She told me when she found Charles's heat signature."

"She was talking to Jackie and me," Apollo shot back, and looked at Charles. "Oh, by the way, sax man, why aren't you in the North Tower? Don't get me wrong, thank God you aren't, but why aren't you there?"

"I should have been," Charles replied, thinking of the angel.

"We would have saved you either way," Kody cut in with assurance, smiling now that he had found his friend alive and well in Manhattan's nightmare. "While Jackie bitched at me, we planned a roof decent to come get you." He tapped him on the shoulder, a grin working its way onto his cheeks. "Sure glad we didn't have to. Mother hovering above the towers would not look good on TV."

"You guys were gonna do that for me?" he asked, and started to cry again.

"Good work spaceman, you got him crying again."

Kody threw his arm around his friend, gave him a gentle squeeze, and asked the obvious question, "Why are you in the Grand Street Bus Terminal?"

"It smells like the Grand Street Bus Urinal," Apollo intoned. "I had to tippytoe through urine puddles to get here."

"Don't complain, it gave you a chance to bitch." He looked at Charles. "So? Why are you here?"

Charles pulled out a key. "An angel gave me this."

"Holy shit," the cat yelped, and stared up at Kody. "This is not good. We don't deal with deities."

"Looks like we're dealing with them today," he said, and shushed the cat before asking Charles for the story. He told it quickly, and once it was told, Kody motioned at the locker. "Open it."

Charles inserted the key and turned. The door swung open, and tired air spilled out. In the gloom, nestled in a corner was a dented saxophone. A large white envelope sat in the dented bowl.

"She got me a sax." Charles removed the saxophone and inspected the instrument.

"By the look of it, she didn't spend much," the cat threw in with a chuckle.

Something caught Charles's eye. "Look at the engraving Kody."

Engraved on the bowl's outer rim: *1900 Redemption Iowa. The Devil's Breath.*

"I've heard of this sax," Charles said. "It was made by this crazy scientist named Rodger who used to live in Redemption."

"Looks like Rodger's sax has taken quite a beating over the last 101 years." Kody motioned at the note sitting in the bowl. "What's the note say?"

Charles tore open the envelope, pulled out the sheet of paper and began to read. Kody leaned over Charles's shoulder and read the letter aloud for Apollo.

> *Hi Charles,*
>
> *If you you're reading this, it means you made it out of the tower. I would have liked to have given you more time, but my instructions were to hold you in the last cubicle until the final moments. You were a wild card in the event, an influence, and so, the deity Fate (the bitch) needed to be appeased. All you were allowed was a fighting chance, and little to no time to warn people. My guess is, even with the short amount of time you had, you made a large impact in the Timeline.*
>
> *As you can see, I got you a saxophone. I felt terrible when I heard your sax had been stolen. You need an instrument to express your passion; and this instrument belongs in Redemption, for outside your hometown its notes ring evil, and bad things happen. I found it in a garbage*

> *dump in Kentucky. If you're wondering, and I*
> *suppose you are, I have no idea how it got there.*
> *You belong in Redemption Iowa with your*
> *friends. Live a long and happy life.*

> *Envy xoxo*

Kody tapped the letter with an index finger. "Way to go man, you got x's and o's from an angel."

"And a cursed saxophone," Apollo added. "Don't forget that." He looked up at the spaceman. "Let's go for a pleasant ride south and drop the damn thing in the Artic Ocean."

"It belongs in Redemption," Kody said, and looked at Charles. "As do you."

Before anyone could speak, Jackie's voice blared from Kody's comm-device attached to his wrist. "Kody! Do you have Charles?"

"Yes we do beautiful girl."

"Don't 'beautiful girl' me," she snapped, and then with a stern mother-like tone, added, "Charles? Are you okay?"

"Yeah I am Jackie," he managed, his chin quivering as fresh tears ran down his cheeks.

Kody looked at the cat. "You can't blame me for making him cry this time."

"I can't wait to hug you," she told Charles.

"What about the spaceman?" Apollo threw in with a laugh. "Are you gonna hug him?"

"I can't believe your stupidity."

"Awe c'mon Jackie, we found him," Kody said in defense.

"Listen space man, I'm pissed at you right now and that's the way it is." She paused, and then cryptically added, "Mother tells me the South Tower is about to collapse. Fuck. More dead…I can't believe what I'm seeing."

"Yeah, I know Jackie, bad times," the spaceman whispered. "Can you get us?"

A long moment of silence ensued, and then they heard the rumble of the South Tower collapsing.

"Spaceman," Jackie said quietly. "Head to the roof, we'll hide in the smoke and come get you."

"Okay, see you soon." He turned to Charles. "C'mon, grab your sax, we're going home. We're going back to Redemption."

The End

Dead Flowers

A thin ghostly breath of wind rustled through the forest, shaking the leaf canopy enough to allow slants of early morning light to reach me on the forest floor. The air was warm and moist with humidity and sweat dripped down the back of my neck.

I scanned the semi-darkness, saw nothing moving, and proceeded with caution, protecting the bouquet of flowers in my right hand as I used my left arm to push my way through the undergrowth of dripping green vegetation. The fern leaves dwarfed me and the vines were as thick as my arm. I kept looking for anything crawling or slithering; and I kept wondering, *Where's the path?*

It was suppose to be around here someplace, and just when I thought I'd never find it, I stumbled upon it, and as soon as I did, I found the first sign of trouble. Souls blazed on either side of the path. I had an escort.

The path ran relatively straight, and after reaching a slight incline, I saw a wide opening through the forest and a lawn of grass. Now more souls blazed on either side of me, and a knot of worry ate away at my gut. I was promised all potential threats would be eliminated. So far that hadn't happened.

I reached the lawn. Thirty yards ahead, a three story stone house stood draped in vegetation. A red flag with a black swastika inside a white disk fluttered in the light breeze from a steel pole beside the patio. I had found the right place.

A man sat at the table on the patio, the sun glinting off the medals pinned to his blue uniform blazer with the fancy white lace shoulders pads. He quickly rose to his feet when he saw me approach, stepped off the patio onto the grass and pointed a revolver at me. "Halt!"

I came to a dead stop and raised my arms. "I'm unarmed."

He was a tall man, (taller than me anyway) yet slumped with age, and he was thin, almost gaunt, wearing a baggy blue uniform with lots of medals. His hair, what was left of it, was silver and swept over his age-spotted dome. His face was hound-dog long, and huge pools of skin hung off his jaw line.

"Can I put my arms down?" And I glibly threw in the "The flowers are heavy." A deep weariness of mistrust glistened in his brown eyes and I soon added, "You don't have to worry about me. I'm unarmed."

He cleared his throat of phlegm, his cheeks quivering with tension, and in a thick German accent, gulped out the words, "You are Der Teufel's dog."

"It sounds better in German don't you think? And regardless of who I am, right now, I'm the messenger, and as I said before, I'm unarmed."

He thought about it, his eyes twitching from side to side, and then, with a reluctant wave of his hand, he told me to lower my arms.

"Are you sure?" I stepped forward a few feet, my hands still in the air. "Cuz, I'll let you in on a secret, I can see and hear souls. So I know you have five men positioned on either side of the yard. I suspect they have rifles. I also know there are over a dozen souls inside the house behind you." I cocked a brow at him. "How's my math?"

His eyes widened with a deep unsettled fear, and after a short pause he managed, "Beyond reproach." With a huff, he turned his back on me and walked up onto the patio. With a flick of his hand, he tossed the revolver onto the table as though it was no longer needed. He was smarter than I thought.

He stood behind a chair at the table and motioned for me to join him, telling me once again to lower my arms. Deciding to trust him this time, I did as he said, and placed my arms behind my back in as non-threatening a gesture as possible.

"So what are you anyway?" I asked, standing behind a chair at the table. "You're wearing so many medals I'm surprised you can stand. Are you a general?"

With pride glinting in his eyes, he straightened the lapels on his coat and introduced himself. "I am Field Marshall Barron Otto Von Hidendorft, the third."

"No shit," I said, my smile growing. "That's quite a title you have there Otto. I'm Jake."

"Is that what Der Teufel calls you?"

"He calls me all kinds of names." I tried to contain my laughter but failed, and came out of a chuckle with, "None of them are polite. In any event, Der Teufel's dog is named Jacob McCluskie. You can call me anything you want."

The patio door opened behind Otto then and a voice sang out, "Herr McCluskie." I turned and saw the evilest man in the world walk toward us.

Before I left home, I had 'googled' him, and knew he was sixty-three. He looked it. He was short, puny actually, and his face was round and heavily lined. His hair was long and gray and draped over his forehead like a wave. His trademark moustache remained under nose, hiding the hair sprouting from his nostrils. A conceitedness stirred in his light brown eyes.

It was cooler out here in the open, and Hitler wore a long-sleeve, dark brown shirt buttoned up to his neck. A swastika was embroidered on the arm. His black pants were jacked up well above his waist and tied off tightly with a leather belt. The cuffs were stuffed into his black leather boots. He walked with a limp, and the field marshal hurried over and held his arm until he reached his chair at the table. After guiding him to his seat, the field marshal motioned at me to sit.

I sat, crossed my legs and stared across the table at Hitler. At that moment, I didn't know what to say. Luckily, he had no trouble speaking.

"So you are the Devil's dog?"

"Oh please, say it in German, it sounds better, and yes, I am the Devil's dog." I motioned at myself. "What do you think? More than just a pretty face, right?" He stared at me in semi-bewilderment, and I continued with, "By the way, I had no idea you could speak English. I thought for sure Otto was gonna have to translate."

A proud smile made his moustache broaden out. "I learned English from watching American movies."

"I learned to swear from watching American movies," I returned with a cordial hedge of my brows, and then flatly added, "Thanks for not wanting to do the handshake 'thing', cuz no shit, that would have bothered me, and I've shaken hands with the Angel of Death."

If he was insulted (and he should have been), he sure didn't show it. He looked amused. "Herr McCluskie, you are a most unusual man." He brayed with laughter, showing me his yellow teeth. "What does the Devil think of you?"

"Not much right now," I informed with a bashful laugh. "The boss is pissed at me for breaking into Heaven." I shook my head in dismay, thinking of the event. "Of course, making matters worse, not only did I break in, I shot the place up too. Good thing his brothers were around to stop him from hitting me."

Hitler stared blankly, and leaned forward, his elbow on the tabletop. "His brothers?"

"Gabriel and Michael," I replied. "Two of the best archangels around."

The field marshal and Hitler spoke in German for a long moment, and Otto motioned at the white tea pot adorned with a gold swastika sitting on the corner of the table. "Would you care for tea Herr McCluskie?"

"No thank you. I usually drink beer, and I'm really glad we're not cuz I'm normally not picky about who I drink with but this time I am. No offense. Well, you can take offense if you want. I really don't care."

I casually glanced to either side and noticed the Fuhrer's sentries were vanishing. As promised, all potential threats were being eliminated.

Otto poured up tea in white china cups, and placed one down in front of Hitler. He blew on the tea, took a tentative sip and looked at me with suspicion. "You are an American, correct?"

"Queens, New York," I said with an honored grin. "It's the year 2016 for me."

That sure got their attention and they were back speaking German.

"Are you guys calculating that? Cuz don't bother. I already did the math on the train ride here—sixty four years. That's how many years I traveled back in time for this crazy meeting."

Hitler squinted at me. "What is it like to be a traveler in time?"

"It's a bitch," I said at once. "When I awoke this morning I never imagined I'd be sitting across a table from you today."

My thoughts returned to this morning, six hours ago. My plans were pretty much up in the air. Maybe I'd watch some TV, maybe I'd write a bit, maybe (well, no maybe about this) I'd have a few beers. In other words: a typical day. Then I stepped out of the shower and my plans changed dramatically. The Devil had written on the steamed up bathroom mirror, and the message read: *Giovanni's—right away.*

I threw on a t-shirt, a gray hoodie, and my blue jeans in record time and was still tying up my sneakers on the elevator ride to the lobby. Last year, the Angel of War blew up my T-bird in Manhattan so I had no ride, and I ran the seven blocks to Giovanni's.

I scooted around back and stepped over the yellow cord onto the patio. It was April, and still too cold to sit outside, and I walked up the aisle of empty tables and chairs toward the Devil's empty table. As soon as I reached it, he appeared.

He wore a black suit highlighted with gold flecks. His shirt was a crisp white, his tie a brilliant red. His legs were crossed, a snifter of Cognac in his hand, and he regarded me from beneath the brim of his hat with disquieted suspicion. "Why are you here?"

"You messaged my bathroom mirror. You told me to come right away."

"No I didn't."

It took a second for those words to truly take hold in my head, and when they did, a bolt of fear shot through me. "Oh fuck." The demon gun was in my hand in a flash and the Devil was on his feet, calling for his goons, but none of them came.

Then a voice rang out, "Lucifer, we need to speak about your dog."

"Herr McCluskie...Herr McCluskie," Hitler said with a measure of force, bringing me out of my thoughts. "You have come with flowers."

I tossed the bouquet on the tabletop in front of him. "Thirteen red roses for you."

He leaned over and inspected the bouquet without removing the cellophane wrap. His eyes turned to me. "They are pristine."

"I won't argue the point," I went on. "I'm glad I didn't have to deliver them to your bunker in 1945. Oh, by the way, I went to a poker game in Berlin on the 27th of April of that year. I was told I was only three miles from your bunker."

"I was not at home," he said, a coy grin touching his thin lips. "I left Berlin on the 21st, a day after my birthday."

"Didn't want to hang around to face the music, huh?"

"The Fuhrer needed to be protected," the field marshal spoke out.

"Up till now, it looks like you've done a good job at that," I said, staring now at Hitler. "When I heard you were alive, I almost shit myself. Good thing I had a beer going at the time cuz I sure needed a drink after hearing that news." I shook my head in wonder. "I thought you had gone down with the ship. Silly me. But you know something? Now that I've given it a bit of thought, it would stand to reason that someone of your moral character would blow town, leaving your mess for others to deal with."

The Fuhrer raised his fist at me. "Like Napoleon, I have only retreated."

"Retreated?" I questioned with a laugh. "Oh please, you didn't cross the street. You're in fucking Argentina."

"Napoleon rose again, and so will I," he thundered, and pointed at the roses. "All the flowers are red." And he screamed, "Red!" His face was flush with passion and he smartly added, "The message you have brought is favorable. The Devil's dog brings good news. It means our time is coming. It means the Third Reich will rise again."

I shrugged. "Think what you want. Anyway, the flowers are from Bellick. I gotta say, you guys sure crawled into bed with a nasty deity. He's a fallen angel, and he's as wicked and as powerful as they come. He hates me, and he sure hates the boss."

My thoughts rolled back to this morning at Giovanni's. I stood beside the Devil, the demon gun in my hand, and watched Bellick cross the patio. I had run into him in California in 1941. Our meeting did not go well.

He was a huge deity standing six-foot-five. His hair was short and black and a thin beard trimmed his jaw line. His eyes shone a cold empty black, just like his heart I suspect, and his mouth was set in a bitter pucker.

Dressed in a double-breasted corduroy overcoat, black slacks and boots, he came to a stop a few yards away from us and buried his hands in his coat pockets. "Lucifer, we need to speak about your dog."

The Devil's eyes twitched to me. "What have you done now?"

"Nothing. Honest."

Bellick stepped forward, his hands still in his pockets. "Can we discuss the matter with civil discord?"

"I'm not sure," the Devil returned flatly, and took a step toward Bellick. "I'm in a bad mood. McCluskie is here—and so are you! And I can't decide which of you I want to kill more."

Bellick jerked his thumb at me. "Take it out on your dog." His eyes zeroed in on the demon gun in my hand. "Are you going to shoot me with that thing?"

"Maybe. I haven't decided yet."

"As you already know, it has no effect on me."

"Yeah, but it makes a big bang, and shooting your ass would make me feel good."

He turned to the Devil. "Do you know your dog threatened to kill W. C. Fields in 1941? McCluskie pointed his gun right at his head." Bellick turned to me. "And this was right after he made you laugh."

Thinking of the moment made me smile. "Damn he was funny. When he said, 'I always cook with wine, and sometimes I even add it to the food,' I nearly keeled over."

"Shut up McCluskie," the Devil hissed between his teeth.

"You know Bellick," I went on, "I didn't want to shoot W. C. Fields. He was the funniest guy in the room, but as I said, I couldn't shoot you with what I brought, but I could sure shoot him."

"Shut up," the Devil spat, and cursed at me with such venom I wondered if I should start being nice to Bellick incase I needed him for protection.

"Can we sit and discuss the matter?" Bellick asked, motioning at the table. "Perhaps we can have a drink and a conversation without hostilities."

"Maybe you and I can," he told Bellick, "but you have to remember we have McCluskie to consider, and we both know what he's like. The last time the Angel of Death dropped in to see me, McCluskie threatened to kill him."

"There is a back story to that incident," I put in quickly.

The Devil told me to "shut up", and turned to the patio door. "Giovanni!" he yelled, and the door opened at once.

The restaurant owner peered out, "Yes Master?"

"The usual for me, a Bud for McCluskie and your lowest grade Cognac for my guest." He gestured at Bellick. "Please, sit."

"I don't normally drink this early in the morning," I commented with a laugh.

"As if," the Devil shot back, snickering darkly. "I'm surprised you arrived sober. Now sit down."

I sat to the right of the Devil, Bellick across the table from us. The Devil drained the last of his Cognac. "Okay Bellick, why are you here? What's my dog done now?"

I cleared my throat for attention. "You know, you shouldn't say it like you're expecting the worst."

"It's always the worst with you." He swung his attention to Bellick. "Did he tell you he broke into Heaven? In fact, he didn't just break in, he brought his gun with him, and he shot three angels."

"I didn't kill them," I protested in defense. "I only stunned them."

With a fist, Lucifer gestured with malice intent at me. "It was like I attacked Heaven."

Bellick shook his head. "Why haven't you killed him?"

"I've thought about it. Trust me on this Bellick, I've thought about it a lot. Problem is, if I did, I could not handle the 'wrath'—no one could."

With a tray of drinks, Giovanni waddled out from the doorway. His saggy jowls turned into a grin when he placed the can of Bud in front of me. "It's a pleasure to see you Mr. McCluskie."

"Thanks Giovanni, no one else feels that way."

The Devil snarled at me. "McCluskie, I suggest you drink your Bud and shut up. My brothers are not here to protect you."

"I said I was sorry about the Heaven thing."

"You shot Envy in the face!"

"I didn't know you liked her," I said, and swung my attention to Bellick. "I can't be blamed if the shot went high." I was back looking at the Devil. "I put her glasses back on and said I was sorry."

"I'm sure that helped," he hissed, and turned to Bellick. "Why are you here?"

Bellick sipped at his cheap Cognac. "Your dog is out of control."

"Tell me something I don't know. What's he done now?"

"Do you know your dog brought a woman and two children with him to our meeting in 1941?"

The Devil's eyes narrowed. "I heard."

"The woman was delightful. But your dog brought snot-nosed children." He looked at me. "As W. C. Fields said, never work with children."

"I noticed you haven't mentioned that the eleven year old boy I brought with me kicked your ass in 8-ball."

Bellick hardened his stare. "Which brings me to the point of our meeting." His eyes were on the Devil. "I only agreed to play 8-ball if your dog would do me a favor in the future." He looked me in the eye. "You owe me a favor, and I'm cashing in now."

The thoughts that went through my mind were laced with plenty of swear words and I sipped at my Bud, my eyes on the Devil. "Do you mind if I speak frankly at your table?"

"Why ask McCluskie?" he flung back. "You always do what you want anyway. What's your threat this time? A trip back to the 1940s so you can kill W. C. Fields?"

"I liked him," I said, and looked at Bellick. "At the time, you had leverage on me, you don't now—so fuck you and your favor."

My words had no impact on him, and he continued with, "You have delivered messages for the Angel of Death, you can deliver a message for me."

I glanced at the Devil. "We're gonna have to get this guy a hearing aide." My eyes turned to Bellick. "Deliver your own message."

"You owe me," Bellick stated harshly, and suddenly a bouquet of red roses wrapped in cellophane appeared in his hand. He dropped the bouquet on the table. "There are thirteen red roses and you will deliver them for me."

"Thanks for the magic," I said, and as I went to continue, Bellick cut me off with a wave of his hand and turned to the Devil.

"He will need the Chinaman's train. The year is 1952, the date in July 23rd," and he spat out a series of numbers—coordinates.

"Argentina," the Devil whispered, his eyes wide with surprise. He knew the answer to the question I was about to ask.

"Who am I delivering the flowers to?"

Bellick ignored my question and proudly told Lucifer, "I captured one of his associates last week and branded a message on his back. I informed him Der Teufel's dog would deliver the message." He chuckled heartedly. "That will give him something to think about."

"Who am I delivering the flowers to?"

I came out of the thought looking at the flowers. Hitler had said they were pristine, and he was right—at the time. A few of the petals had turned ash gray since our meeting began. From where he sat, he couldn't see them.

"As the flowers indicate, dog," Hitler said with rising self-confidence, "the Third Reich will rise again, and the deal Bellick promised me will be realized."

Calling me dog, huh? I thought, and now I was unable to contain my smug smile. "Bellick has a few issues with the deal, but before we get to that, first I have to tell you something. Even though I won't be born until 1977, I'm actually involved in a bit of the drama around you. I am the main reason for you downfall."

He laughed. "You haven't been born."

"Wilhelmina Wolf," I said flatly. "You had your Gestapo arrest my prophet. Do you remember her?"

Hitler shrugged at the field marshal.

"You gave her a Nazi swastika pin," I helped out.

He scoffed, waving his hand at me. "I handed out thousands."

"I'm glad you gave one to Wilhelmina, cuz she gave it to me on 43rd Street in Manhattan and it saved my life. It's stopped a bullet. How's that for being lucky, huh?"

The interest in Hitler's eyes intensified and he soon said, "Wilhelmina Wolf, yes, I remember her now."

"Do you remember having the Gestapo arrest her? Cuz that was a mistake. Cuz it angered her friend, do you remember General Luther?"

Hitler's eyes nearly popped out of his head. His attention was on the field marshal and he hotly rambled away in German.

"I see I've touched a nerve."

Hitler swung his attention to me. "Luther was a traitor."

"He was also the demon sent by Bellick to make sure you wouldn't do anything stupid. With him beside you, you'd be running the world now. Arresting Wilhelmina Wolf was the lynch pin in your downfall. You angered a demon. Do you remember what happened?"

Hitler turned to the field marshal and more German was exchanged.

"I hope you guys aren't talking about me."

"It's been a long time," the field marshal admitted. "But yes, we remember Gestapo headquarters in Potsdam being brutally attacked. We blamed the Jews."

"Nothing Jewish about Luther. He's seven foot tall of evil and your Gestapo learned that the hard way. From what I understand they're still washing the blood off the walls at Gestapo headquarters."

In the German they spoke, Luther's name arose a few times, and now Hitler was back looking at me. "Luther acted on his own. He could have come to me and asked to have the woman released. I would have agreed."

"Too late now," I said. "To be honest, I think Luther would have jumped ship on you anyway. He wanted me, and most likely he wanted away from Bellick. So, looking at it like that, Der Teufel's dog did you in."

"A temporary set back," Hitler told me smartly, and flicked his hand at the bouquet. "As you see, the flowers are pristine. The message is favorable." He lifted his chin at me. "What did the great deity Bellick say?"

"Nothing good," I replied, and grinned brightly, wanting to wipe the arrogant look from his face. "He mentioned you started the war too early. You were still three years away from being ready."

"I had bad advice," Hitler flung back as though it was a stupid issue to mention. "Ribbentrop was to blame."

"Who is Ribbentrop?" I asked, really puzzled. "I only know the top gangsters. I'm gonna have to 'google' Ribbentrop when I get home."

The field marshal sadly broke in with, "He was hanged at Nuremburg."

"Okay, good for my side, one less cockroach to worry about." I threw my attention to Hitler. "Anyway, you started the proceedings too early."

"The people needed war—they thirsted for it." With both hands he gestured wildly at himself. "I provided it."

I leaned over the table. "Do you know what 'bullshit' means? Cuz that's what you're speaking. You controlled the people."

"People need to be controlled. Why do you think religion was invented?"

"And your brand of bullshit is any better?"

"Much better," he thundered back, his fist clenched. "Religion is weak. Christians are weak."

I pointed at myself. "Not this one."

His eyes opened with surprise. "Der Teufel's dog is a Christian?"

"As I said before, I'm more than just a pretty face."

A deep mystification brewed in his eyes, and his moustache twitched as he leaned over the table. "A Catholic dog?"

"Just like you," I told him with vast satisfaction, thankful now that I had taken the short time I had before leaving to 'google' him.

He digested my words with a bitter frown. "I denounced my religion."

"It's a good thing," I returned. "If you stepped inside a church now you'd set it on fire. And any confessional you'd give would turn the poor priest into a raving alcoholic."

Hitler countered with, "Does the Devil approve of your religion?"

"He doesn't care." I rested my elbows on the table and stared him in the eye. "If it makes you feel any better, last Christmas I wasn't a Christian. I gave up my faith and went on a rampage." Thinking about that time made me shake my head. "Fuck did I ever go nuts. I killed an angel and a Horseman. It was quite an eventful week."

He stared at me, not knowing what to say, so I moved the conversation along—after all, I had a train to catch.

"Now, back to the matter at hand, you were in a fight with the French and the British, oh, even the Canadians were after you. Man, you've got to be evil when the Canadians get involved. Hockey, beer, sex, keeping warm, that's what drives these people." I laughed at him. "You even pissed them off. No wonder you lost."

"We destroyed the French and British," Hitler shot back. "And the Canadians."

"Don't be patting yourself on the back too soon. Because what you did next proves without a doubt that you have your head shoved up your ass."

The field marshal looked at the revolver on the table, and then at me. "You will treat the Fuhrer with respect, and you will address him as the Fuhrer."

"I don't think so." I looked Hitler in the eye. "See, everything has a shelf life, even leverage, and yours has expired." With narrowing eyes, I glanced at the field marshal. "I swear to God, if you reach for that weapon, I will shove it up your ass before you can blink. Trust me, I can do it. See, when I went on my rampage last Christmas, I rescued the Archangel Michael, the Devil's brother, and as a reward, he jazzed up my neurological system—I'm a lot faster than you."

"Please Herr McCluskie, treat the Fuhrer with respect."

His words stirred up a memory from this morning. Bellick had left, and the Devil and I sat together. He nursed his Cognac, looking off at the ocean, thinking about…who knows what? Me, probably. I sipped at warm beer waiting for him to speak, and I didn't have to wait long.

"You listen to me and you listen good McCluskie," he began, "you will treat him with respect."

"Why do you think I won't?"

He chuckled snidely. "I know you McCluskie, real well. You have a 'smart' mouth, even when you don't have the upper hand you have a smart mouth, and once Bellick eliminates all potentials threats, I'd bet Giovanni the price of the bill you will start in on him."

"I'm not like that."

"Bullshit," he barked. "I know what you did to Oscar Zero."

"Okay, agreed, I was a bit grumpy when I met with Zero, but you have to remember, he stole my car."

"You put a gun to his head," the Devil reminded me. "You threatened to splatter him all over the wall." I struggled to fight off my grin, and he continued with, "I know how you conduct business. But this time, you will have respect. That is an order." And he added, "You're doing this for yourself. Trust me McCluskie, in the morning you will be glad you did."

I came out of the thought and turned to Hitler. "Okay, moving along, and please remember, I'm getting this from Bellick, because I didn't know this, and when he told me, he kept shaking his head like he couldn't believe the stupidity. While fighting the allies, you open up another war front, as if you haven't got enough pots on the stove. I believe it was June of 1941, do you remember that?"

They spoke in German again.

"Oh good, I've got you guys gabbing."

"We needed the Russians resources."

"Be that as it may, Otto," I said, raising both brows at him, "with your hands already full, you went after the biggest guy on the block." I looked Hitler in the eye. "Bellick couldn't believe it."

"They would have soon attacked us," Hitler defended himself with a snarl, and pounded the tabletop with his fist. "We needed to hit them first."

"We gained great victories," Otto piped in. "We took over nearly half the country."

"And then things went 'bad'," I pointed out, "real bad. Now again, I'm getting this from Bellick, he tells me you lost the 6th Army in Russia. Is that true?" I blinked in amazement. "How do you lose an army?"

"They were weak," Hitler said at once. "The campaign needed to be wrapped up before winter, and they failed."

"Bellick says otherwise," I pressed on. "Leadership failed them." I looked Hitler in the eye. "Why mince words, it was your stupidity that doomed them. And you let them freeze." I thought about the South Pole. On my rampage last Christmas, I had led the Horseman Pestilence there, and the temperature had dipped to 130 below zero. Even now, thinking of that moment made me shiver inside. "I know what it's like to be cold, what it's like to be frozen, when you can't move your arms and legs. It's an extremely painful way to die."

Neither of them spoke, and an eerie silence ensued. The wind whistled through the jungle canopy, the Nazi flag flapped, and my thoughts drifted to the Chinaman. He was my ride home, and now I was thinking, *how long until departure?* I had an hour, and I wondered, *how long have I been looking at Hitler's ugly face?* At least twenty minutes I figured, and with a ten minute walk ahead of me, I had less than thirty minutes to wrap this up.

"Now, again, I'm getting this from Bellick: he tells me that against strong advice from your generals, you diverted your panzer divisions to help in the siege of Leningrad when you were within striking distance of Moscow." I shook my head. "Cut off the head of the dragon, no?" He went to speak but I stopped him. "You don't have an argument on this one. It was ego, plain and simple. Leningrad was the first city you couldn't easily take, and that rubbed you the wrong way. Lesson from the Devil, something he taught me in a Manhattan alley: he told me to shove my ego in my back pocket." I flicked my hand at him with disgust. "You should have done that."

"Please Herr McCluskie," Otto protested. "Treat the Fuhrer with respect."

"I am simply stating the truth."

Hitler shook his fist and barked fiercely in German at me.

"Hey man, did you just swear at me? Cuz I gotta say, it sure sounded nasty. Good for you. If you're gonna swear at me, at least do it so I can understand, though I must admit, German is a beautiful language."

Saying those words made me think of Smitty, for he had said pretty much the same thing when he picked me up in front of my apartment building this morning in his black Chrysler 300 with the hemi.

He was a large deity with a shaved head, a good natured face and a red rim of beard stubble running along his chin. His smile was as bright as the noon day sun, and as soon as I settled into the passenger seat, he raised a friendly brow at me. "What have you gotten yourself into this time?"

I quickly told him the story and ended with, "I wish I spoke German."

"It's a beautiful language," he said, and chuckled under his breath. "How do you get yourself into so much trouble?"

"I have that special knack."

He laughed, threw the car into gear and stomped on the accelerator. Every horse in the engine woke up and we blasted off down the street. He was quiet for a moment, and I knew he was thinking about something. Sure enough, "I understand the Devil is pissed at you."

"He's always pissed at me."

"More so this time."

"It's because of my attack on Heaven, and who I shot."

"The Devil wanted Envy to come with him when he was banished from Heaven," Smitty told me. "She refused." His eyes shifted to the road and he added, "You shot someone he loves."

"I figured that," I grumbled. "Happy times Smitty, happy times. Another typical day for me." I glanced out the window and, wanting to change topics, asked, "Where is the Chinaman's train stopping today?"

"Redemption Iowa."

His reply caught me by surprise, and I dug my phone from my pocket. "I have a cousin that lives in Redemption." I scrolled through my contacts. "Yup, her name is Jackie. I have her on Facebook, and she lives in Redemption, Iowa."

He motioned at me with two fingers. "Gimmie your phone."

I handed it to him, and he cupped it in his huge hand. A second later, the phone buzzed and he tossed it back in my lap.

"What did you do?"

"I sent her a message. I told her to come pick you up. Remember, I can only get you so close to the Chinaman's train. You don't want to walk."

"You're the best Smitty."

I came out of the pleasant thought of being with Smitty and was back looking at Hitler. His eyes narrowed, and with a snarl, he snapped, "Don't preach to me dog. You know nothing about war; you know nothing about battle."

I almost lost it then, and for a good second, I actually considered leaning over the table and punching him in the face. I thought of the Devil, thought of his order to treat Hitler with respect, and then I thought, *could I adequately explain to the Devil why I punched Hitler into a pulp?* I figured I couldn't do it, not without him hitting me first, and I took a deep breath and restrained myself.

"I have been to battle," Hitler boasted. "I have seen the horror of war."

"Me too, Herr Fuhrer," I said evenly. "I know all about war. I participated in it. I have been at the bloodiest day in U. S. history. I have been at Antietam."

The field marshal blinked in amazement. "The Civil War battle?"

I was impressed a European knew about the battle, and I curtly threw in, "It was a bad day in Maryland," and struggled to stop the tears building in my eyes. "If the politicians witnessed what I witnessed that day, there would be no more war. They'd be deciding issues with coin tosses."

A tear rolled down my cheek, and I quickly wiped it away. Hitler laughed. "The Devil's dog is weak," he noted, his thin lips poised upwards. "The dog has emotions." He cocked a brow at me. "Does the Devil approve of your emotions? Does he scold you for having them?"

"The Devil is gonna scold me when he hears how I treated you," I returned with such baneful distaste my cheeks hurt. "Cuz up until now, I have tried to remain polite. But not anymore." I leaned over slightly. "Fuck you—evil man. If not for the Devil's order, your head would be down around your asshole by now."

"Herr McCluskie, please," Otto broke in, his hands raised in defense. "Please remain civil."

"You know something Otto, for an evil fucking Nazi, I like you. I don't know how much blood you have on your hands—probably a lake full—still, you have been pleasant. So I'm gonna give you a strong suggestion: leave now."

He gasped, his eyes wide and troubled. "I would never abandon the Fuhrer."

"It's time you do," I said. "It's only the three of us left. All your sentries on either side of the yard are dead. So is everyone in the house. I only detect three souls—ours. It's time for you to leave."

Hitler rose to his feet with such force he knocked over his chair. He barked at the field marshal in panicked German, his arms waving wildly. Otto shot to his feet, looking around in desperation, yelling loudly in German. No one came to their aid. And soon they turned to me.

"I told you."

"The flowers are pristine," Hitler screamed at me. "The message is favorable."

"We're not finished yet." I motioned at his chair. "Sit down."

The field marshal righted Hitler's chair, and after guiding the Fuhrer to his seat, he sat as well.

"You should leave Otto," I urged.

"I will not abandon the Fuhrer." His brown eyes glinted with a sad desperation. "Besides Herr McCluskie, I have no where to go."

"I sure do," I said, a tinge of urgency ran through me. "I've got a train to catch."

Thinking of the Chinaman and his train brought me back to Smitty. He always knew where the train would arrive. Today was no exception.

He pushed a small orb attached to his dashboard. Suddenly, we weren't in New York anymore. Time bent, and a few seconds later we barreled down a two lane country road. The sky was a cloudless blue with an early morning sun.

"Welcome to Iowa," Smitty announced.

"It looks green and flat."

He pulled over to the shoulder and pointed ahead at the road sign. "As you can see, we have reached the town line of Redemption. This is as far as I can bring you."

"According to the sign, the population is 777." I smiled at him. "7 is my lucky number."

"I hope it is today."

I brightened up. "Okay Smitty, the flowers and I will work it out."

"Since 7 is your lucky number maybe your cousin Jackie will get the message and meet you." He shrugged like he had no idea. "If not, you're walking to the train."

I gave him a hug; he told me he'd be back for me; and I walked up the road with a bouquet of flowers. A short time later, I spotted a blue Honda Civic in the distance, rumbling toward me. The car slowed, pulled over to the side, and a woman climbed out. Her smile lit up my heart, and I blinked into 'soul' mode. Her soul hummed pleasantly and was awash in blues and greens and yellows.

"Are you Jackie?"

Her blue eyes shone like newly minted pennies, and her smile widened. "You must be Jacob McCluskie. My Facebook buddy and cousin."

She was my height at least, maybe an inch taller in her boots. She wore blue jeans and a gray poncho, kind of like what you'd see Clint Eastwood wearing in a western. Her brown hair was tied up in a bun, and a few strains hung down around her ears.

She opened her arms and hugged me. She had some meat on her bones, and was strong, and I got a good strong hug.

"Oh, thanks for the hug," I said, my grin wide. "I'm near positive now you're gonna be the highlight of my day."

"The hug is for saving Charles," she said, her expression thoughtful. "I considered telling you this on Facebook, but I knew in my heart that one day we'd meet so I could tell you in person."

"Tell me what? And who is Charles?"

"In case you've forgotten, in 2001, you saved my friend from two muggers outside a restaurant in Queens, New York."

"Holy shit, I remember that." I nodded to myself as I recalled the incident. "He's the sax player?"

"And you saved him," she reminded me. "My cousin from the big city saved him." She shook her head in wonder. "It's a small world."

Not that small, I thought and asked, "So Jackie, how are we cousins?"

"We have the same great-grandfather," she informed, brushing strains of brown hair from in front of her eyes. "Ian McCluskie came here in 1900, and soon had two boys. His first son was named David, that's your grandfather. His second son was named Sean, he's my grandfather."

"That is so cool," I admitted, "thanks for filling me in."

She glanced at the flowers in my hand. "For me?"

"I wish," I said with a laugh. "I wouldn't wanna give you these flowers anyway. These flowers are for the evilest man that has ever walked the earth."

Her eyes widened slightly at the news. "Can you be more specific? Because I could rattle off about ten men right now that fit that description."

"I doubt this guy would be on your list."

The memory sadly faded away then and I was back looking at Hitler.

"The flowers," he shouted in a vain attempt to reinforce his argument that the Third Reich would rise again. "They are—" He came to a sudden halt. Nearly every rose was now ash gray.

"Your flowers are dead."

His face whitened, and the field marshal put his hand on Hitler's shoulder and spoke to him softly in German. Hitler shook the man's hand from his shoulder, reached into his pocket with a jittery hand, and drew out a revolver, pointing it at my head.

"Gee, I never expected you to have gun," I managed dryly.

"The Devil's dog will not return home," Hitler said, "he dies here." And for a second I thought I was dead. Yet he hesitated, and in that moment of indecision, his eyes shifted to the field marshal. It was all the time I needed.

The Archangel Michael's gift paid off handsomely, for I was out of my chair and around the table before he knew what had happened. I tore the revolver from his hand and, in spite of the Devil's order, and because of the fear he had put me through, I punched him square in the face with every ounce of strength I could muster. The punch sounded like it did in the movies, with a solid smack, and a blistering wave of pain shot up my arm. My hand throbbed. Still, it was worth it.

A gasp of pain blew hollow from Hitler's mouth and he tumbled backwards, his arms spinning wildly in an attempt to stay erect. His effort failed, and he ended up flat on his back on the patio, blood streaming from his nose and mouth.

Thinking about it now, I was shocked I didn't break his nose. It looked intact, blood ran from his nostrils, however, but his nose was okay and so were his yellow teeth. Only his lip was cut, and though I hated to admit it, I thought I got the worst of the exchange, because my hand ached like a rotten tooth.

The field marshal screamed in horror, his face contorting in a shocked wave that rustled the loose skin pooling off his jaw line. He flew from his chair like a rocket, knelt beside the Fuhrer, took his arm and helped him to his feet, gently encouraging him along in German.

I retook my chair, shaking my stinging hand and cursing inside. I held the revolver in my lap, now considering the worse possible scenario: what if I had to shoot Hitler? *How the hell could I explain that to the Devil?*

The field marshal wiped blood from the Fuhrer face with a napkin, guiding him to his chair. And as Hitler's drama unfolded before me, my thoughts leafed back to my time with Jackie. Thank God I had something good to think about. In her blue Honda Civic, we motored through Redemption's business district, a trip that lasted twenty seconds at most, and was back driving between fields.

"You know, there is no train that stops around here." She had more to say but the sight of the Chinaman's train parked in a dead cornfield, mud buried halfway up its wheels, stopped her.

The engine looked like it had been built in the mid 1800s. A cowcatcher was mounted on the front and a smokestack rose from its black, ironclad bullet shaped body like a tall building, spewing out clouds of white smoke. Six passenger cars trailed behind the engine.

"I gather that's your ride."

"Well don't say it like that Jackie," I said, chuckling, my eyes now on the Chinaman. He sat on the top step of the black metal stairs extending down from the engine's control room. A cigarette smoldered between his lips and he motioned at me.

"Are you going to tell me what's going on?" she asked sharply. "We don't normally get too many antique trains stopping in the middle of cornfields around here."

"I already told you," I said, laughing. "I'm time traveling back to 1952 to give these flowers to Adolph Hitler. What part of that were you unclear of?"

She stared blankly for a second, but soon her lips turned up in an aloof pucker "I thought you were bullshitting."

"I wish."

The Chinaman stood, and sucked on the last of his smoke, straightening his conductor hat. He was short and squat, and his skin was Chinese yellow. He wore jean overalls, smooth with wear, and a dirty grimy t-shirt. He tossed his burning smoke away into the field, and motioned at me, yelling, "C'mon, we haven't got all day."

"I gotta go Jackie."

I got another hug, and a smooch on the cheek. "Please be careful."

"I'll be fine Jackie, my luck is better than the Devil's."

I was laughing when I said that, but all my humor was gone now as I watched Otto and Hitler retake their seats. My hand throbbed, yet I was happy about one thing. "Thanks for bringing a gun to the party. I now have a good story to tell the Devil, and a good explanation."

"Herr McCluskie," Hitler began slowly, sniffling back blood. "I have vast wealth."

"Oh for the love of God, are you trying to bribe me?" I asked with a widening grin, and though I tried to contain my laughter, I just couldn't. I came out of a chuckle with, "You know something? I should have expected it from you."

"I could make you rich beyond your wildest dreams."

"I'm richer than I look," I told him. "I'm a good poker player; the Archangel Michael is not." I pointed the revolver at Hitler's head, just because I was still pissed and my hand throbbed. "I sure hope you don't have any more weapons on you, because if you pull anything else outta your pants, you're gonna get more than a punch."

"Herr McCluskie," Otto spoke out.

"Otto, are you still fucking here?" I barked at him, and after a long hard stare, turned to Hitler. "Now I've got a train to catch, so listen good. Even so Bellick mentioned this right off, I kept this to the end. I wanted this to be the explanation point to this meeting. It's time to talk about your 'final solution'." I paused then, allowing those words to sink in. Then I added, "And please don't pretend not to know what I'm talking about because if you do, my hand to God, I will punch the fuck outta you." I paused again, and then coldly added, "It's time to talk about the Holocaust."

Hitler's eyes bulged slightly and he spoke in German to me.

I disregarded what he said and pushed on with, "I want you to know this is coming from a fallen angel, the evilest prick I have ever met: he told me he was stunned at how evil mankind could get, for even he would not have done what you did."

Hitler fired back with, "It needed to be done."

"Unnecessary is the word Bellick used," I returned evenly. "Concentration camps, extermination camps, is a waste of resources. Keep a work force and send everyone else to your enemy to feed."

Hitler laughed, and went to speak, but I pointed the gun at his face.

"I should blow you away for what you did, for hurting people. Children, women, and the elderly." I grimaced at him. "How can you do that to people, people just like you, and sleep at night?" For a moment, I considered shooting him, right in the face, right in his moustache. Sure, killing Hitler would be hard to explain to the Devil, still, I felt I could put up a fairly decent defense.

With a sigh, I lowered the gun. "You are the most repugnant thing I have ever encountered."

Hitler hand combed aside his wave of hair, a determined evil stirring in his eyes, and said, "The deity Bellick is not as smart as I thought. The Holocaust was necessary to control my people." He raised his chin at me. "Herr dog, people need an enemy they can easily blame, that they can easily crush. It's human nature to pick on the weak. And as I said before, religion is weak, finding a scapegoat was easy."

"Holy fuck, that's so evil, I may need a minute to think."

Hitler didn't allow me the time, and shot back with, "I was the perfect leader for mankind, I would have run the world with precision."

"Oh please," I said with a scoff, rolling my eyes. "You're a well-dressed corporal with delusions of grandeur. You are gonna go down as the stupidest leader in history, and the evilest."

"Herr McCluskie," Otto interpreted.

"Are you still here?" I asked him sharply. "I told you to get your ass outta here. Now go. You still have a chance."

He leaned over and whispered in Hitler's ear. Hitler nodded glumly and they stood. Otto raised his arm in salute to Hitler, and then he hugged him and turned to me.

"Herr McCluskie, I will need the revolver on the table."

"Are you planning to go out honorably?"

He nodded.

"Why don't you make a run for it?" I told him. "I've been to Hell twice, and each time, I've run for my life. As you can see, I'm still here. Why die now?"

"Why prolong the inevitable?" He slowly reached for the weapon. I watched him closely, my gun trained on him. He cocked the revolver, placed the barrel in his mouth and, without hesitation, pulled the trigger. The back of his head exploded and his brains sprayed out in a violent splatter of blood, hitting the patio stones with a wet splat.

A billow of gun smoke swayed in the sunlight around Hitler and the smell of cordite stung my nose. Hitler glared down in stunned silence at the body of his last solider, watching the man's hands twitch.

He soon looked at me, and my smile was bright. "I guess it's your turn now."

A look of indifference stirred in his evil eyes. "Bellick and I will make another deal," he said with confidence. "Like the last time." He lifted his chin at me. "Did he tell you how we met?"

"No. Maybe he wanted to but he ran outta cheap Cognac before he could."

"It was in World War One," Hitler continued, his cadence slow and deliberate. "One night I awoke and saw him standing at the rim of my foxhole. He motioned at me to join him, and the moment I left the foxhole, a mortar struck, killing all my comrades. He had saved my life. And then he promised me the world."

I grinned at him with smug appreciation. "It's too bad you fucked it all up."

"We will make another deal. The Third Reich will rise again."

"You have dead flowers," I reminded him, and now I couldn't think of another reason to stay. I stood. "Thank God our meeting has come to an end. Cuz I have to tell you, I have walked through history, I've seen good and bad, I've been to Hell twice, yet sir, being with you was the worst—simply a repugnant time for me. If I had known the favor Bellick would want of me, I would have declined at once."

"The Third Reich will rise again," he said strongly.

"I'm from the future, remember, and believe me on this, the Third Reich does not rise again." I stepped back from the table. "One more thing, Bellick said, and I'll quote him on this, he said, I'm going to take it out on him. I don't know what that means, but I suspect nothing good."

"Herr McCluskie," Hitler said, rising to his feet. "Will you kill me?" He gestured at the revolver in my hand. "Please."

"No disrespect intended," I said, "but, fuck you!"

With that said, I turned and ran across the lawn for the path. I never looked behind me. I hit the path, and before long, I heard a scream so loud it made my blood run cold. A few minutes later, I broke through the jungle and found the Chinaman sitting on the top stair of his engine, a smoldering cigarette in his hand. "You're early," he said. "Seven minutes to spare." He grinned. "How did it go?"

"Message delivered."

The End

Printed in the United States
By Bookmasters